Love,
LIES and
Lemon Cake

Sue Watson

bookouture

Published by Bookouture

An imprint of StoryFire Ltd.
23 Sussex Road, Ickenham, UB10 8PN
United Kingdom

www.bookouture.com

ISBN: 978-1-909490-45-1

eBook ISBN: 978-1-909490-43-7

Acknowledgements

This story is about a woman's journey and, as with all my heroines, I have travelled with her. Along the way, some very special people joined us, bringing their own brand of help, humour, love and lemon cake...

A huge thank you to Oliver Rhodes at Bookouture for his wisdom, guidance and belief in this book from the very beginning when all I had was a handful of thoughts and cake crumbs. Thank you to Emily Ruston, my fantastic editor who put zest in the lemon cake, cream in the frosting and transformed my ingredients into a delicious read.

A very big thank you to my friend Louise Bagley for her hilarious and fascinating insights into hair and beauty salon life, to Emma Richardson for the dating dramas, and Lesley Mc Loughlin, Sarah Robinson and Liz Cox for advice, inspiration and everything in between.

Lots of love and very large glasses of wine to Jan Holman, Jackie Swift, Sheila Webb, Diane Tilley and Sarah Douglas, who have all contributed thoughts, malapropisms and brilliant anecdotes. Love and hugs to friend and 'Book Whisperer' Kim N and my girls and cheerleaders Alison Birch, Sharon Beswick, Sue Johnson and the legendary 'Literary Ladies Wot Lunch'.

Thanks as always to my mum Patricia Engert, who started me on my own journey by always telling me anything is possible. And last, but never least, my love to Nick Watson—what would I do without you?

For Eve Watson, wherever you go and whatever you do, know I'll always be there... with cake.

Chapter One
Film Star Fingers and Fake Bake

'I want you,' he breathed, sliding his warm hand under my gown, then slowly, sensuously along my thigh. I lay back on the white sunlounger, the infinity pool lapping at my toes, him lapping at my neck, all hot breath and sensual friction. Dressed only in diamonds and Fake Bake, I smiled provocatively, playing hard to get and stirring on the lounger so he could enjoy me in the best possible light. In his free hand he held a dirty martini to my lips and I swallowed gratefully, framed perfectly by the Hollywood sign nestling in those star-studded hills.

'Ryan... I shouldn't be here,' I said, admiring the way he held his glass and moved his hand around my body at the same time. It can't have been easy, like rubbing your head and patting your stomach in sync.

'I have washing to do,' I panted. 'Then I have to.... ah... clean the windows, and then I'm... oh... making the tea.'

He didn't care; he was too wrapped up in lust, his twinkly eyes and film star fingers caressing my whole body, and aching for the moment I would be his. I wasn't the first and wouldn't be the last he made passionate love to by an aqua infinity pool in LA. With total disregard for my washing pile and in complete denial of my filthy windows and uncooked tea, he gently pushed his knee between mine, panting in my ear about just what we would be doing next. The stars were out and I lay back in his arms, waiting for the passion to explode, when the sound of Craig's voice bore through the air like a bloody bullet.

'Are you going to spend all day in that bath?'

I looked up. Ryan Gosling's twinkly eyes faded through the mists of steam and foamy bubbles, along with the dirty martinis, white leather sunloungers... and hope.

Unlike Ryan, the last time Craig had touched my thigh was about two years before when his hand had slipped as he turned over in bed... asleep. We'd been married for about a hundred years so romance was a distant memory and sex something I only saw fleetingly on TV. After the usual passion and wanting of the early days, we'd settled down to married life. The chaste good-night kiss, the 'did you have a good day?' for a while, which then petered out into nothing and, like siblings sharing a house, we carried out our rituals and roles independently, while pretending to ourselves everything was fine.

While my daughter was growing up and I was juggling work and childcare, I was happy to live like this, with no distractions, but recently I'd begun to question where my life was going. Was this it? A life lived on film star fantasies and vague memories of a marriage that once was? Craig lived for his work and had long ago given up on romantic evenings fuelled with wine and sweet nothings; he was always too busy. For my part, I'd given up competing with his plumbing business and the sheer excitement that leaking stopcocks and faulty faucets brought him. Faced with the glittering prospect of a flange crisis at seven a.m. the next morning, Craig found it hard to contain his excitement and had little left for a night of marital sex with his middle-aged wife. Ryan Gosling, Brad Pitt and the boys, however, had plenty of time for me, even if it was only in the Hollywood of my head.

I climbed out of the bath and dried myself, trying to remember how it felt to have someone else's hands on my back, round my undressed waist. I craved the warmth, the body of another human—a real man as opposed to the film stars I could only dream about.

It wasn't just the lack of sex; I missed the physical affection and closeness we'd once had, and with each day merging into another, before I knew it another loveless year had gone by. It wasn't like I hadn't tried; a few months before, I'd taken the bull by the horns and suggested we have 'an early night'. He'd looked at me like I was mad.

'But... *Top Gear*'s on...' he'd gasped, incredulous, and as always missing the point.

'We could go to bed and you could record *Top Gear*,' I answered trying to keep my voice seductive while wanting to smack him in the face.

'That would be stupid,' he answered incredulously. He didn't look at me, just continued staring at the TV screen while slowly turning the pages of *Plumbing Monthly*. Craig had all he needed right in front of him. Who needed sex with a human when you had a pressure-reducing valve glistening and just begging to be fitted? Tightly.

'Yes, going to bed together would be very stupid,' I'd snapped back, trying to push all thoughts of poison and paying a hitman from my mind. It had been a while and, being generous, I wondered if Craig may be a little shy and needed more encouragement. I put both arms around him awkwardly and, closing my eyes and pretending he was Brad Pitt, I kissed his face. I'd read in a magazine at work that if you behaved in a loving way with your partner, even if you didn't feel the love, it would come... So imagine you're feeling deep resentment, disappointment and nothing towards your part-ner during the dying embers of what was once something like love (just an example, you understand). If you then force yourself to hug and kiss them like you are back in love, all those pesky feelings of deep, dark hatred and unadulterated loathing will be replaced by love and affection. I was ready to give anything a go. My negative feelings towards Craig were causing my skin to flake. It had to be worth a try. My worry was that the very act of hugging him may turn into an act of violence on my part. It was no coincidence that Craig was planning a new patio in the summer, and I was think-ing less about decking and more about where to hide the body.

Kissing Craig was like sucking lemons and, as I pulled away, he looked at me, surprised. Going against my gut feeling, I thought of the shared mortgage, gave him another smouldering look and left the room. I went upstairs and carefully took out the faded nightie I saved for holidays and sprayed 'Angel' all over it. Wafting it around the room, I tried to set the scene so when he came upstairs the 'intoxicating and alluring' fragrance would render him helpless to resist. I'd read this 'love tip' on GetYourManHotNow. com. and, also taking the website's advice, dotted a few lit tea lights around the room so it would be just like a love scene from a film where they fall into a room, dazed by lust and glowing by candlelight. But Craig saw tea lights as a fire hazard, so rather than upset him, I blew them all out. I'd save them for Johnny Depp, who never complained about a little fire in the bedroom.

After about ten minutes he still hadn't appeared, so before I lost all interest and went to bed with *Good Housekeeping* and a slice of cake, I padded back downstairs. I stood in the doorway of the living room, waiting for Craig to look up from his magazine. He didn't.

'Craig. Would you like to go to bed... with me?' I tried. It was my last-ditch attempt to see if there was anything at all left in our marriage. His silence hit me like a slap as he turned from the screen and looked me up and down.

'Not tonight, love. Clarkson's testing the new Audi.'

Even if he genuinely preferred to watch Jeremy Clarkson drive a fucking car than have sex with me, the least he could do was fake it. After all, I was willing to lie back and think of Johnny Depp... surely he could do the same with Jeremy Clarkson? When your own husband rejects you in the bedroom (the living room doorway, to be precise) for a loud, opinionated, middle-aged man driving a fast car, it's a sign that:

a) You need to shave your legs.

Or b) Your marriage is in deep shit.

I gazed sadly at myself in the steamy mirror, recalling this last rejection only months before. When did we stop loving each other? Did it happen in a minute, in an hour? Or had our feelings slowly decayed over the twenty-odd years we'd been married? Like a lifeboat at sea, disillusion and regret had slowly seeped in and we were all but capsized. I was torn between accepting my fate and fighting for something better—and recently I'd been dreaming of the latter. I didn't want to live the rest of my life and never feel another hand on my thigh, the frisson of passion, that first kiss with strange lips... the kiss with someone I loved.

When we were first together, Craig would look into my eyes and tell me he loved me every single day. I was always the crazy one who booked weekends away at the last minute, ran into the sea fully clothed, sang the loudest karaoke and always had a funny story to tell. Once he came home from work and I'd set up the tent in the back garden, with a bottle of cava and a takeaway because we couldn't afford to go on holiday. He'd said one of the things he loved most was my optimism and the way I never let anything get me down; 'You are such a dreamer,' he'd say, his eyes bright with love. Funny how later in our marriage he used the same words to criticise me for forgetting to pay a bill or trying to see something from a positive perspective; 'Oh, you're such a dreamer, Faye. Why don't you see what's in front of you and stop always looking for the happy ending?' he'd yelled in my face. 'Because there isn't one!'

I knew one thing for sure: Craig wasn't my happy ending. My heart would sink at the scrape of his key in the door each evening and it was impossible to imagine how once upon a time I'd been excited about seeing him after work. I'd recently read an article in a glossy mag during my coffee break at work, 'How to Get Your Marriage Groove back,' which suggested it was common for married couples to suffer a dip and, like an infected wound, as long as you got it in time, it wouldn't kill your relationship. But the time had passed for saving the life of our marriage. I was now forty-two and couldn't bear the thought of staying with Craig for another twenty-odd years until it was too late. But what could I do? And where could I go? I had plenty of time to plan my escape as I sat in my chair near the window, silently waiting for bedtime as the TV droned on.

Still in my towel I wandered into Emma's room to breathe in the remnants of her perfume and pretend she was still living at home. Emma's was the only room with a full-length mirror—I didn't want one in ours; after the age of thirty, a full-length mirror is not something one wants to be confronted with on a daily basis. I held my breath, stood to face it and dropped my towel. I tried not to make an agonised noise as the towel fell, but staring at the horrible truth, I couldn't help it. The body that had once skipped along beaches in bikinis, wiggled past boys in tight jeans and carried my beautiful daughter to full term was gone.

What replaced it had lumps and lines and, though I optimistically spotted a bottle of Emma's left-behind scented body lotion and began slapping it on, I knew this was a far bigger job than mere lotion could cope with. Scaffolding would be more appropriate for this task I thought, suddenly spotting wrinkles on my knees. I didn't even know it was physically possible to have furrowed knees.

That face cream I'd bought from Debenhams hadn't worked either, I noticed, trying not to think of the new knee crisis and going in for a facial close-up I knew I'd regret. Apparently there was a scientific formula inside that extremely expensive little pink pot that imitated babies' skin cells. Mandy the Beauty Therapist I worked with had insisted I would be transformed from being an 'old and wrinkly forty-two-year-old' (her words) to looking like a perky eighteen-year-old again in just two weeks! However, it was now exactly two weeks since I'd started this new regime and I still looked like a forty-something me and not the glowing, well-preserved supermodel pictured on the label.

'It's not moisturiser; it's like something from a science-fiction film,' Emma was keen to point out when I'd called to tell her about my new face cream.

'Mum, think about it—if it worked as they say and your own skin absorbed these cells and reversed the ageing process, you'd literally be a time traveller... or a baby!'

We laughed at that. She had a point and she'd always been more sensible and down to earth than me, more like her dad in that respect.

I looked back at myself in the mirror. Faye Dobson forty-something faced with the physical manifestation of gravity, empty nest and married life with an indifferent plumber stared back at me. My head, heart and body were in limbo—we had no place in the world; my leaky lifeboat was cast adrift and I wasn't now needed on anyone's voyage.

I opened my wardrobe and waded through a few old skirts and dresses. I hadn't been anywhere in the past few years to justify a nice dress or a pair of heels. It occurred to me I hadn't worn high heels and an evening dress since before Emma was born, and she was now twenty-one!

Then I spotted the bright pink rucksack on top of the wardrobe. I pulled it down, blowing off the dust, and smiled to myself, recalling how I'd bought this bag as an eighteen-year-old with global travel in mind. I clicked apart the plastic locks on the bag. It was probably old-fashioned now in its garish pink with blue piping, but I'd loved that rucksack, spending all my birthday money on it and convincing myself it was 'an investment' because I would use it all the time travelling to all those places I'd dreamed of. I was going to see the world with that bag. It was small but I'd be able to squeeze in everything I'd need.

I didn't use it once.

I held it to me, imagining the airports, the ferry terminals and mountain treks the bag had never seen. Reaching in, I was reminded of all the other things I'd dreamed about but never done. I tipped the bag up onto the bed, scattering the photos, friendship bracelets, hair toggles, postcards and maps, and like a magpie my eyes went to a scarlet silk dress. I unfurled it gently from the aged tissue paper it had lived in all these years. It was still heavenly soft and strikingly red. I was nineteen again and at the seaside with Alex, the only boy I'd ever kissed apart from Craig. I was deliriously happy as we wandered arm in arm, the seagulls yelling above us—a stolen weekend by the sea. The dress had been in a shop window on a mannequin and when I'd tried it on, Alex had said I had to have it because I looked beautiful, just like Julia Roberts. It cost a fortune but I decided to spend it on the dress instead of eating that month. Like the rucksack, I saw it as another investment in my fabulous future—a future of world travel, scarlet dresses and good-looking college boys like Alex.

I slowly put the red dress back into the now crispy tissue paper. It had never been worn. Too late now. Perhaps Emma would like it? I picked up a purple Filofax, all the rage in the eighties before the Internet and online diaries. My whole life had been in this purple faux-leather book. I opened it, landing on a page with three scrawled words: *My Living List*. 'Oh, God, I'd almost forgotten about this...' I sighed under my breath. It had been my plan for my life, a list of all the hopes and dreams I'd once believed I could achieve. How naive I was.

My Living List

Learn to Ice Skate

Lose 10 lbs

Make a wish at the Trevi Fountain in Rome (then ride a pistachio-green Vespa through the streets.)

Swim naked in the ocean

Drink champagne on a New York roof garden

See a Santorini Sunset

Eat macarons in a Parisian tea shop

Be a bride

Be a mum

I closed the Filofax, my heart squashed somewhere inside the purple covers. These random desires had been jotted down years ago, between A-level revision, putting make-up on, making music tapes and drinking lager and lime in the pub with my friends, all long gone to other lives. Reading through the list again, I could see it wasn't as random as it first appeared; these things had an order to them... ending in marriage and children. I liked things in their place and, subconsciously, even as a slightly chaotic, hormonal teenager, I'd planned my life in a certain way. Going through the list, I was hoping to tick off a few, but it was only when I came to the end I realised I could only tick the last two. I'd achieved only a fraction of the life I'd planned as a young woman. It was like I'd been waiting at the bus stop for my life to turn up but it had been cancelled. And no one had let me know.

I looked through the postcards. Other people's travels from places I'd never been, from half-remembered friends. A girl with a lisp called Melanie I'd known briefly at university had sent me a card from New York. Almost twenty years old, the colours were now washed out, the picture cracked from the many times I'd held it and looked into it. I turned it over and read the few scribbled words:

'Dear Faye, I finally made it to NYC! Mel x'

'Good for you, Mel,' I thought, sitting on the bed and gazing into it again. I was years older and wiser, but the picture still had the same effect on me. A rooftop in New York on a dusty golden evening; the stars were emerging above, the city lights bright and blurry below. Two glasses and a bottle of champagne on a table for two—and if you kept on looking, in the distance a shadowy couple were dancing.

When I'd first received the postcard, I had been both scared and exhilarated by it. Pregnant with Emma and still in a state of confusion that my life had changed radically within a few weeks. I was unsure about the decisions I'd made, worried about the pregnancy, the birth, my future, my baby's future. Yet I found it a comfort to look into this postcard. I'd spent many hours longing for escape to a rooftop in New York at dusk.

Once Emma was born, I'd packed my foolish dreams back into the rucksack, put it on top of the wardrobe and bought a nappy-changing bag instead. Once she'd arrived I couldn't imagine a life without my perfect baby, the safety of my marriage and my neat little home. I was the lucky one I thought, and had no lust for Melanie with the lisp's glamorous, childless existence in New York.

I jammed everything back into the rucksack, a symbol of my failure to achieve anything. I didn't put the postcard back with everything else, though; I kept looking at it, fascinated by the scene, imagining myself there, a saxophone playing in the distance, distant traffic sounds rising like smoke from the streets below. The picture filled me with the same fear and exhilaration it had when I'd first received it all those years ago, but now it gave me a twist of hope. Sitting on my bed wrapped in a towel on a wintery morning in the Midlands, I could hear that saxophone, remembering the life I'd once hoped for and how far from that I had landed.

'Christ, are you out of that bathroom yet?' Craig's voice cut into the mists of time like a bloody sledgehammer. 'I've got a crimp fitting system to put in today and you've made me late waiting for the bathroom... I've got a street load of frozen pipes to do this morning.'

'Sorry, I was out of the bathroom ages ago—meant to tell you,' I said, entering the kitchen and taking a slice of warped pleasure from his fury at the news he'd been waiting for nothing.

His face was flushed with anger and I wanted to throw his mug of tea at him—resisting not because I didn't want to hurt him but because I didn't want to spend the morning in A and E with his scalded face. I ignored him and put some toast on. It was early February and Craig's favourite time of year, when combi boiler problems blossomed everywhere needing his surgeon-like attention. Throughout the season, Craig's skilled hands were paid handsomely to warm frozen pipes lovingly back to life. Shame he couldn't do the same for me.

'I won't be home tonight; I'm spending an evening at my lover's penthouse apartment,' I said, spreading low-fat butter on my toast.

'Oh, so I have to make my own tea?' Craig replied, his mind clearly on other things.

'Yes.'

'What time will you be home?'

'How long's a piece of string? We're doing champagne and caviar on his yacht. Then straight after *Coronation Street,* he wants sex on deck, under the stars...' I took a big bite of toast.

'Take your house keys then,' he grunted, getting up from the kitchen table and abandoning the internal organs of a dying dishwasher to head for the bathroom.

I always tried to attract Craig's attention before I left in the morning, as if I needed proof that after twenty-two years of marriage he wasn't listening anymore. My after-work 'plans' had become more outrageous, expensive, sexually adventurous and generally more unlikely over time but still he didn't hear me—or perhaps he just chose not to? I'd recently told him I was getting a tattoo of David Beckham on my left buttock after work so might be a bit late... and a bit sore. 'Don't make a noise when you come in because I'll be asleep; I've got an early start in the morning,' he'd said.

Had he always been like that? Perhaps I just hadn't noticed, but I was certainly way down the food chain when it came to fancy stopcocks. The way he handled a two-headed faucet was fascinating—I almost envied the inanimate object—and there was no doubting where his passions lay. He'd once told me he never remembered a customer's face; he only knew them by their machines. When he opened up the back of a Hotpoint, he said he knew when he'd laid eyes on that circuit board before. I wondered, was there such a thing as plumber autism?

Still chewing on toast, I took a last slurp of coffee, threw on Emma's old parka, jammed on her woolly panda hat and set off for work as usual. I had decided, for health reasons, to try and walk into town at least three days a week, and though Emma's old clothes did not epitomise worldly sophistication and glamour, they kept me warm.

I had once cared about what I wore—never into high fashion, but always liked decent high street clothes, and wore a little light make-up. In the last few years, though, it had all seemed a bit pointless and it wasn't like anyone looked at me. I was at an age where I was invisible to the naked eye and comfort was winning over appearance—hence the flat shoes and thick tights combo I was working that morning. It wasn't flattering but at least I was warm and the tights covered up the newly discovered wrinkled knees. Good job I didn't really have a lover and wasn't really going for sex on his yacht after work because that day's outfit would have been quite inappropriate. I pulled my hood up, thinking how it would be too cold for sex with anyone on the deck of a yacht this time of year, even a millionaire's.

We were going to be really busy that morning in the salon where I worked. Two weddings and a twenty-first birthday party would keep us on our toes and, with three foil highlights, seven cut and blows and a perm that afternoon, things weren't going to slow down. I knew if I didn't pick up something to eat on the way into work, I would pass out with starvation (well, as much as anyone around ten stone and five foot two can claim 'starvation'). I felt like a change from my usual pasty from Greggs Bakery so popped into the new deli to buy a sandwich. Sue, my boss, was on a diet; Mandy, the beauty therapist, lived off bags of Monster Munch to work off her permanent hangover; and Camilla, our posh junior, lived on organic leaves—so it was just me looking for lunch. I scuttled down the road, head down, pushing myself against the icy blast of wind rushing down the high street, and ran into the deli, almost blown in and having to force the door closed as I landed inside with a loud gasp.

❀ ❀ ❀

The deli had only opened a couple of weeks before; it was my first visit, and once inside I was mesmerised. The shop was groaning with food, every corner utilised, every shelf stuffed—even the ceiling was filled with hanging meats and sausage. I wandered through, taking it all in. A savoury tang sliced through the air making my nostrils twitch, and with so much to look at I almost crashed into the glass counter right in front of me.

Coming face to face with a counter top of plump green ol-ives in terracotta bowls with various sample dips and chunks of nutty, seeded bread was making me hungry. I'd only just had breakfast but was salivating at the sight of rich, garlicky hummus and sun-dried tomatoes, scarlet and glossy in olive oil. I had to stop myself reaching out and plucking one from the bowl while no one was looking. I was imagining the illicit tart sweetness of a sticky stolen tomato when the guy behind the counter asked if he could help me. I looked up from under fur-trimmed parka hood at the source of this lovely voice. It was a happy yellow accent full of laid-back Aussie sunshine, and... oh, yes, it matched the owner. He was a blond, tanned Australian with a killer smile. 'Can I help?' he asked again. Yes, indeed, I thought, *you* can certainly help me—you don't get *this* in Greggs. I smiled shyly, gesturing blindly towards the cabinet—this bronzed god was as exotic to me as every other tasty morsel in the new emporium of continental delights. He looked like he'd just stepped off a surfboard I thought, dragging my eyes away from his boyish tanned face back to the tomatoes, then the olives. I asked for a slice of quiche and, as he wrapped it carefully, my gaze rested on his arms—brown, covered in wiry blonde hairs, slightly muscular and weathered, like they'd been left out in the sun... on a hot, hot beach. Our eyes met and we smiled and the woman in me wanted to rub olive oil into those arms, while the mother in me wanted to wrap a cardigan around him. It was February after all.

I left the deli planning to call Emma that night and tell her all about it. She'd been to Italy with the school so would probably be very interested. Wouldn't she? Or was I just using it as an excuse to call her? I'd always dreamed of going to Italy—it was on my list. But then so were many other things I hadn't done. Trudging to work down the windy high street with its charity shops and sun-faded windows of baby linens and pound emporiums couldn't be further away from a pistachio-green Vespa whizzing through the streets of Rome. The deli was a start though, and opened up a whole new world of continental culinary opportunities for me on a daily basis. It was a shame the guy behind the counter wasn't a dark-haired, brown-eyed Italian to go with all the Italian produce. As eye candy went, the blond Aussie was quite cute, but God only knew what he made of the locals, especially me dressed in a panda hat. I smiled to myself; the one silver lining in the cloud of Emma being miles away in Manchester was that she couldn't see me rocking her old parka and panda hat. As I opened the door to the salon, I realised that, as much as I missed her terribly, in Emma's absence I could wear what I liked—and enjoy a taste of personal freedom as much as she could at uni in Manchester.

'It's cold out there,' I announced, walking into the warm, hair-spray-scented cocoon and taking off my coat. This place of chatter and changing hair was my life, my sanctuary. Here in 'Curl Up and Dye,' everyone knew my name and my story, not that it was a particularly exciting one, but I was accepted for just being me.

That morning, Sue, the owner and my closest friend, was in full flow brandishing a colour chart and telling Mrs Harvey how scarlet hair dye would match her skin tones and yelling over the noise of the dryers. 'It will bring you alive, love.' Spotting Mrs Harvey like a recumbent corpse in front of the mirror, I wasn't convinced.

But Mrs Harvey had been there before with Sue and her Technicolor dye jobs and wanted reassurance it wouldn't turn her hair green as it had last time.

'No. It's opposite green on the Technicolor wheel, love,' Sue said confidently, trying to blind her with science while not actually understanding it herself. 'It's a very hot shade; it'll take years off you. It's... what I'd call a... *Sarcastic Scarlet*,' she added screwing up her eyes like this was a mysterious but good thing. She smiled at me while pressing a hair swatch against Mrs Harvey's greying skin and grimacing; 'Ooh, look, Faye... is Mrs Harvey going to look the spitting image of Cheryl Cole or what?'

I marched over to gaze in the mirror at the marriage of 'Sarcastic Scarlet' and the fat fifty-something face. Cheryl Cole would have sued.

'It's stunning,' I declared (which wasn't a lie), nodding slowly with what I hoped was a look of awe and admiration. 'You go for it, Mrs Harvey! If you're that shade when hubby gets in from work tonight, he'll think Cheryl Cole has broken in and she's cooking his tea.'

Mrs Harvey pursed her lips and Sue caught my eye in the mirror with a grateful look. It seemed I had pitched it just right. It was the push Mrs Harvey needed—but who could blame her for being reluctant, having once endured green hair for several weeks? I went to collect my next client from reception, wondering just how sarcastic that scarlet would be on those greying curls.

Times were hard and, as the hairdressing business had been hit big time by the recession, Sue had been forced to change our usual hair dye brand to a much cheaper one. Keeping the business going was paramount, and despite her accountant telling her to reduce staff costs, Sue had refused to do that, saying we were her family. So in order to save money, she had to economise elsewhere and had purchased a job lot of the cheapest hair dye on earth. The dye was from Lithuania, not the 'go-to' hair dye country for other hairdressing luminaries, but Sue Lloyd was a self-styled hairdressing pioneer. She was also great at PR and told clients it was 'a radical new approach to celebrity hair colour.'

Despite her sharp selling and shameful PR, Sue hadn't considered the fact that none of us spoke Lithuanian. As the colour description and instructions were in that language, we were often as surprised as the client at the 'celebrity' results when the dreaded stuff was rinsed off.

So in the absence of a definitive Lithuanian translation for each colour, Sue was forced to 'invent' descriptive shades, often on the spot. She couldn't use the hair colours of reputable companies because 'They might get me on the Trades Prescriptions.' Who 'they' were and why it was prescriptive I didn't ask—it would only add to the general confusion and chaos. In spite of her inability to understand Lithuanian, Sue's confidence was never an issue and she felt qualified to translate *Perlas* šviesūs into 'Wicked Cinnamon', *Imbieras* into 'Malevolent Blonde', and *Pilka* into 'Strident Peach'. Sue's comprehension of English words was bad enough, but this was hair dye dyslexia.

'Oh... I thought malevolent meant glamorous,' she sighed when someone pointed out it didn't really work as a hair colour.

'Cruel Plum' though was christened instinctively, born of desperation when Jayne from the chemist (two kids both C-section, husband in fitted carpets) emerged after her dye job and threatened to take us to court. I had to give it to Sue—'Cruel Plum' was spot on.

Sue loved the glint of celebrity spotlight and, regardless of the fact we were a small salon on a small high street on the outskirts of Birmingham, she longed for a real celebrity client. In the unlikely event of a visit from Cheryl Cole or Nicole Kidman, two of Sue's personal favourites, she made the best of what we had—and that was Gayle Jones. Gayle's claim to fame was that she'd once had a spit-roast with two premier footballers, and what gave her even more celebrity credit was that this liaison was reported in a national Sunday paper. When Gayle first came in for extensions, Sue had been very excited. She'd wiped down the chairs and wiped down Mandy, our beauty therapist, and told her not to speak or go anywhere near Gayle. Mandy was loud, sometimes drunk, and when she wasn't swearing and shouting was keeping the salon up to date on her latest trip to Kavos, which sounded less like a holiday and more like Dante's Inferno.

That morning, Mandy had apparently turned up late and in a bad mood. She was usually quite an upbeat girl and at only twenty-one had a full (if alcoholic and promiscuous) social life, long shiny hair and a body to die for. However, her looks and her lifestyle were at odds with each other. She looked like European royalty, but behaved like a sailor on leave. I knew we had a problem when I mentioned to her that her first bikini wax was waiting and she rushed into the stockroom in floods of tears.

'All I said was bikini wax!'

Sue shook her head. 'It's not you, Faye. Mandy's a bit upset today,' she sighed, tugging hard on Mrs Harvey's calf lick. I looked at her enquiringly.

'Didn't she tell you? Terrible news... Lady Ga Ga died this morning...' Sue was nodding into the mirror at her client, pulling a sad face. The client let out a gasp and put her hand to her mouth.

At the mention of Lady Ga Ga, Mandy emerged slowly from behind reception, tear stained and looking like a little girl.

'I'm so sorry, Mandy,' I said, dabbing at Mrs Jackson's grey roots with the foul-smelling 'Cruel Plum'.

'I was the one that found her, Faye. They're saying... suicide... I'm literally gutted.'

Not literally, I thought, but left it as Mandy was prone to arguments and, when upset, fights even. To be fair, her fly-kicking skills were only apparent after several vodkas, and I had never been on the receiving end, but in her current state I wasn't taking any chances.

I wasn't sure of the etiquette involved in enquiring about a hamster's suicide, but I wanted to be there for Mandy. Her mother had died from cancer when Mandy was only sixteen, and as they'd had a difficult relationship she seemed to be left with guilt that she should have spent more time with her mum. Consequently Mandy was fragile under all the bravado and I knew even a hamster's death would be traumatic for her and must be taken seriously.

'So why did she... what made her do it?'

'Who knows what was going on inside her little furry heart, Faye. I even made her a pink wig out of Barbie hair... she looked proper cool she did. My dad says she was probably depressed running on her little wheel all day... but it was a pink and glittery wheel, so why?'

I wondered for a moment if wearing a pink wig had affected the hamster's feelings of identity... then remembered she was a hamster.

'Lady Ga Ga will always be with you, burrowing away in your armpit,' Sue called loudly over the hairdryers. Unaware this was the name of Mandy's hamster, some of our newer clients were surprised by this remark, amazed not to have read of the star's death (and apparent penchant for armpits) in their daily newspaper that morning. Sue and I just carried on like the performers we were, used to rolling out clichés for all occasions at 'Curl Up and Dye'. We were at the ready for any occasion, be it celebratory or consolatory; we had a wardrobe of faces, voice pitches and scripts. Salon life was like a small planet where everything happened within four walls and the tiniest things took on major proportions. We lived and counselled through first dates, pregnancy scares, deaths, divorces, betrayal and wild love affairs—all of human life was here between the back washes and the guilt-edged mirrors. We'd actually experienced a live birth when Marie Cooper's waters broke by the roller trolleys to the strains of Wham's *Club Tropicana* and Mandy's guttural screaming. Fortunately one of our clients who happened to be a midwife was in for a cut and blow so brought baby Michael safely into the world with hot water, towels and little fuss. There would have been time to get Marie to the hospital before the head appeared, but Sue never missed an opportunity for salon publicity and called the local paper before she called the ambulance.

We were all over the papers that week: 'Bouncing Baby Born in Local Hair Salon' and a big photo of me and Sue holding the baby between us and beaming, Mandy and Camilla with their arms around us like two proud daughters... Sue was right: we were just like family.

Later, I caught up with Mandy in the coffee room. 'Are you feeling a bit better, love?' I asked, putting my arm around her.

'Yeah... I just get upset... about stuff, you know.'

'I know, love, but you can always talk to me or Sue if you're feeling low, you know that, don't you?'

'I keep thinking it was my fault... that she died.'

I doubted we were still talking about a hamster. 'No. No, Mandy you must never think that. People... hamsters... have their own reasons for saying goodbye to this world. Perhaps she finally realised that, despite its glittery appearance, the wheel she was running on was going nowhere, and if she didn't get off she'd keep running nowhere for the rest of her life,' I heard myself say, knowing just how she'd felt.

Chapter Two

Bulging Muscles and Historical Hams

The sign said 'Sandwiches and rolls made on request,' but I couldn't imagine how one would ever decide what filling to have, there were so many. The following day I was back in the deli watching a swollen pink ham swinging from the ceiling and contemplating lunch. I didn't know if I even wanted anything to eat, but I just loved the smell and the feel of this salty, sawdusty place. I was salivating at the sight of marbled orange chorizo, spicy and oily and begging to be tasted, above huge wheels of deep yellow and blue-veined cheeses. My eyes lingered over those cheeses, perfect tight drums to be hacked open and enjoyed, sour, creamy, nutty or tangy on the tongue. There was no cheddar and pickle on white here... not unless the cheese was buffalo and the pickle made from vintage Italian walnuts nurtured under a baking Tuscan sun.

'Are you looking for anything... particular?' the Australian voice asked, probably wondering why this strange woman was licking her lips and staring blankly and wordlessly at the various cured meats.

'Ham,' I said, nodding my decision, playing safe and point-ing, like a child.

'Yes, I'll have... a ham... sandwich,' I nodded.

'Is Serrano ham okay?' he asked.

'Oh... er, yes...' I muttered, then I decided he had kind eyes so I would be honest... Eyes like that wouldn't judge me: 'I usually have boiled ham... now I feel a little out of my depth.' I pulled an awkward face.

'Oh, I'm sorry. I didn't mean to sound like a ham snob, but all hams are not the same,' he smiled. 'The Serrano is delicious; it's made from white pigs fed on acorns, so the flesh is tender and quite sweet.'

'Oh... good.'

'It's air-dried in the mountains of Serrano...'

I nodded in acknowledgement. What could I say? I wasn't even sure where Serrano was.

'Would you like just a little sun-dried tomato with it?' he asked, moving those golden arms over the bowl of scarlet toma-toes. 'You only need a hint—they are quite intense.' I watched his lips move in an Australian way over tomato... soft Ts and voluptuously rounded Os.

'...Echoes of chilli... it's a taste they call umami, which means yummy in Japanese... It's a new, fifth taste after sweet, sour, bitter and salt...' he continued, engrossed in the ingredients.

He looked up at me. I was salivating. It wasn't the tomatoes.

'I'm sorry; you didn't need to know all that. It's a tomato—get over it Dan,' he laughed, slapping his hand on his forehead.

I smiled. 'Oh, no, it's fascinating.' So he was called Dan? It suited him—one syllable, laid-back, easy-going. Dan.

'I'm one of those annoying people obsessed with food. I have to taste everything and know its story. You know?'

'Yes, I do. I love food too, but I'm not knowledgeable like you... and I doubt my usual boiled ham has a story I'd *want* to hear,' I replied.

He chuckled at that. 'Yeah... I bet you're right. Anyway, where were we...?' He looked straight at me, into my eyes, and I looked away, convinced he had the ability to hypnotise me.

'I think you were suggesting I have tomatoes on my sandwich. Having had the ham history lesson, I guess you were about to tell me the origins of the sun-dried tomatoes... dried on the thighs of young virgins perhaps?' I offered, encouraged by his smile.

He laughed. 'Ah, so you are familiar with that method?'

Smiling, he took down the huge ham from its hook on the ceiling and I tried not to look at his arm muscles bulging. He sliced it and I watched, almost in slow motion, imagining those big strong arms round me, the blond bristly face nuzzling my neck.

'So, is this your lunch?' he asked, placing the tomato pieces with loving care on the ham. He looked up and caught me watching him. I had to turn away pretending to be fascinated by the stuffed peppers.

'Yeah. I love the sandwiches from here. I used to go to Greggs but I like to watch you make them... When I say "watch you",

I don't mean that I like to watch you, like a stalker or something...' I said, sounding like a stalker.

He took my money and opened the till. He was younger than me and my friendliness may have come over all wrong.

'Oh, that sounded really weird didn't it?' I said, not wanting him to think I was some kind of cougar type.

He smiled at this and handed me my change. 'Whatever does it for you. You're welcome to come in any time and watch me make sandwiches... if that's your thing.'

'Oh, God, no... I like coming here to see the food. It's not like I... I'm not looking at you in that way... I wouldn't want you to think...'

He was smiling, his eyes twinkling. 'I'm teasing you.'

'Oh... Then again, there are women who would pay good money to see you in action... not that I'm one of those... you know... women?' I tried to joke, going along with it.

'Yes... now you come to mention it, I've noticed lots of women coming in here to buy stuff. And I thought it was the French goats' cheese they were lusting after.'

I giggled. He was funny. I really had to stop coming in here— I couldn't help flirting with him, he was cute, but so much younger than me it was positively indecent.

❊ ❊ ❊

The following weekend Emma came home from uni. It was an unscheduled trip because she wanted her hair done and I was delighted. I'd changed the duvet in her room, bought her nice bubble bath and made her favourite dinner of sea bass with ginger and spring onion. I loved to cook and Emma was always a pleasure to cook for—if I'm honest, I never felt my dishes were appreciated by Craig so refused to spend hours poring over recipe books for him anymore. That weekend though, even Craig rallied round. He didn't complain about bones in the fish or too much ginger and was slightly more animated and engaged than usual. But despite trying hard to be nice to each other in front of Emma, it was a strain and we bickered. He would say something nasty, or simply not answer when I spoke to him, which would irritate me and I'd build up to boiling point and we'd end up rowing again. Though we never addressed it, we'd both given up trying, yet I didn't want Emma's stay ruined by our troubles—I was worried she'd never come home again if it meant listening to her parents arguing. This made me feel under pressure and consequently even more stressed and prone to snap at Craig.

'Dad's so bloody grumpy all the time,' Emma complained while on a "girls" shopping trip in town for new shoes.

'Oh, I'm sorry, Em. He's no different from usual—you probably just never noticed when you lived at home. I don't see it anymore,' I said, annoyed that we'd spoiled her short homecoming. We had stopped at Costa where Emma always insisted on going for fancy-flavoured coffees with whipped cream and toppings. She ordered vanilla lattes as we chatted about Craig's irritability.

'He's always been a moody sod,' she sighed, leaning against the counter. 'I don't know why you put up with him... he doesn't even talk to you.'

I felt uncomfortable. For Emma to be so critical of her dad, it must be bad, but I didn't want to burden her with my unhappiness. 'He was lovely once, Em; he was kind, considerate, and though he's never been a big talker he is a good dad. I think he found it easier when you were little, but life changes you, Em. Work and worry take over and we all turn into what we said we never would. His own dad was always mean to his mum... your dad hated it.'

'Don't let him be mean to you, Mum. I can't imagine him being anything other than "grumpy Dad". He never really talks to me either... just *at* me.'

'He doesn't find it easy to communicate, and now you're an adult I think he probably finds it hard to think of the right thing to say.'

'He certainly isn't short of words when he's telling me how much my rent is and how he's had to put back retirement for five years because I'm at university...'

'Oh, don't feel guilty about money, love. He'll never retire anyway. Imagine your dad without plumbing?'

'Like Ant without Dec,' she laughed.

I made light of it to Emma but was angry with Craig for implying it was her fault he couldn't take early retirement. We paid her rent but the rest was a student loan she'd one day be crippled with and I felt bad we couldn't do more for her. She lived on nothing as it was and I noticed she'd lost weight, which might have been intentional, but could have been due to the fact she was short of money.

'Are you okay? Can you live on the money we give you?' I asked. 'You are eating well aren't you, love?'

'Oh yeah, great. I eat too much... it's fine, honestly, Mum.'

She'd say that anyway, not wanting to worry me—but I did worry about her all the time. Why did I always feel the guilt for everyone? I felt guilty on mine and Craig's behalf because we couldn't buy our daughter a new laptop or a car or simply give her more to live on. I had some money put away and every now and then I'd send her a cheque, but she would send it back saying she was fine and it was my rainy-day money and I might need it myself someday. Perhaps she was right? It wasn't exactly a secret, but I'd never mentioned to Craig that I had a small savings account. It gave me a feeling of security knowing I had something just for myself.

'Your dad's good at what he does, but I think he's lost custom over the years because of his...'

'Personality?' she asked.

I smiled. 'Not exactly, but he just doesn't do small talk and never smiles. Where others are nudging and winking and flirting and flattering, your dad can come over sometimes as... a bit rude.'

'Yeah, he has no concept of customer care...' she sighed, tapping her fingers on the counter. We both watched steaming foamy coffee land in white mugs to the background noise of a very satisfying frothing sound.

'I think you're a saint for putting up with him.'

She sat down while I placed our drinks on the table.

'My friend Vicky says her mum and dad are loving having the place to themselves now she's at uni. Getting jiggy with it all the time, she says.'

'Thanks for that little glimpse into other people's bedrooms, Emma—I can assure you dad and I are not "getting jiggy" with anything.'

'Oh gross, Mum. Please don't use that expression to describe you and Dad...TMI.'

'People over forty do *have* sex, you know.' I didn't point out I wasn't one of them.

'Don't remind me. Makes me want to barf.'

'And it's not always with the people they're married to...' I smiled, imagining for a brief moment a night of passion with Johnny Depp.

'Mum, that really is enough,' she teased, mock horror on her face.

'If you think I'm bad talking about sex, you should hear about Mandy's daily exploits—or should I say nightly.'

'Oh God, Mandy Johnson. I forget you work with Mandy— how is she? She was always round the bike sheds at school, smoking and snogging the lads...'

'Hmm, well, these days she's out of the bike sheds and in the nightclubs, only now she's "humping and grinding" the lads,' I giggled. 'Whatever that means.'

'Sounds like she's taken the Mandy road show on tour and it's more outrageous than ever,' she smiled, sipping her drink. 'You should see the stuff she puts on Facebook.

'Oh, she's okay, just a bit young and mixed-up.'

'She's the same age as me...'

'Yeah, but you're worlds apart. Remember she doesn't have a mum, and whatever you may think, I believe I have contributed ever so slightly to your success as a perfect human being,' I smiled.

'Yes, I suppose you did something right somewhere along the way. If you hadn't I'd be humping and grinding with Mandy in the West Midland's premier night spots.'

'Instead of humping and grinding in Manchester perhaps?' I asked, my eyebrows raised enquiringly.

'No... You are kidding. I'm not like Mandy Johnson.'

'Before the grace of God, Emma,' I said, feeling a little disloyal to Mandy who at times felt like a second daughter to me, particularly since Emma had gone. I had known Mandy since she was fifteen and had started work at the salon as a Saturday girl. Twelve months later, her mum had lost her fight with cancer and Mandy had been devastated. Sue and I had both felt for her, and Sue had offered to pay for her beauty training. I'd talked her through the bad days, trying to convince her the pain would ease. Over the next four years she'd blossomed, though there were still days she didn't cope well, and she still liked a drink, but it had changed from something she used to kill the pain to something she did on nights out.

I looked around the coffee shop and back at my beautiful, smiling daughter who'd come all the way from Manchester to spend a weekend with us. I felt so lucky. It made me think of

Mandy's mum. She must have known her time with her daughter was limited and she'd never see her grow up into a young woman, never see her wedding, her children. And then there was Mandy, left in a crazy, mixed-up motherless world and trying to make sense of it all.

That night I highlighted Emma's hair in the kitchen as Craig worked on a dishwasher motor on the kitchen table. Emma was sitting on the kitchen chair, her hair covered in foils as we chatted and Craig grunted every now and then. The radio was on and when 'Wannabe', the old Spice Girls' tune came on, Emma and I started singing, and within seconds Craig was banging out the drum bits on the machinery he was working on. It was a song Emma had loved as a kid, especially the 'Zig-a-zig-ah' bit, that catch-phrase of the nineties we both used to sing with her in happier times. She'd been about five when the record came out and we'd bought it on CD, and even Craig would dance around the house with her. I lovingly pasted on more bleach, wrapping each tiny piece of foil gently round her hair, and as we all sang along, I thought of what we'd lost, and tried not to cry.

Chapter Three

Ryan Gosling and a Dirty Martini

The following week was tough without Emma. It always took a little while to settle back again as I missed her so much, and with only Craig for company was forced to go back to spending my evenings having (fantasy) romantic encounters with gorgeous film stars in fabulous locations. .. Constant thoughts of Ryan Gosling and a dirty martini by a pool in LA were the only things keeping me sane. In reality, my evenings were spent with Craig and *Ice Road Truckers*. The sound track to my life was not Vivaldi (as it often was with Ryan or Johnny Depp), but the TV bragging of hairy truckers and petrol heads. Then there was the incessant football... there was always somebody playing a game somewhere in the bloody world, and who needed a soundtrack from Vivaldi when one had the monotonous droning of football commentators? I'd lift my head from my book to see another pitch and ten more men in shorts chasing a ball and think how the precious remainder of my

life was being slowly swallowed up in ninety-minute chunks—
with no extra time.

The following Tuesday morning, I popped into the deli to buy
lunch. Who am I kidding? I went to lust over the gorgeous man
behind the counter *and* buy lunch.

'I do hope those "yummy" tomatoes were harvested from the
Tuscan slopes near a fig tree on the outskirts of Florence?' I asked
with a serious face.

'Ha... the exact same ones: third fig tree from the left. You
know your stuff,' he smiled. 'Now for the bread... what kind
would you like?'

'Focaccia?' I tried to say this with an Italian accent, like I ate
it every day, but focaccia wasn't easy on my English tongue and
emerged sounding vaguely indecent.

His pale blue eyes twinkled with amusement at this forty-
something in her parka and woolly panda hat stammering ob-
scenities. I blushed slightly at my own image of myself, but was
thankfully distracted by a heaving wall of sweet delights. These
were biscuits... but not as I knew them. As he lovingly placed
chorizo and chilli jam onto the bread, I dragged myself away so he
wouldn't think I was getting cheap thrills watching him. Which of
course I was. I took myself to the other side of the shop to cruise
the sugary morsels, reaching out to run my eyes and fingers along
the brightly coloured beribboned packets crinkly to the touch.
Biscotti, Panettone, Florentines and Cantuccini were strange and
wonderful biscuits bursting with nuts and almonds and chocolate. I never bought stuff like this; Craig preferred Rich Tea and as

I was always on a diet I rarely ventured beyond the odd Jaffa Cake at work, but this was a lovely, unexpected new biscuit experience. And the sheer Italian ambience in there was making me feel quite cosmopolitan, so I picked up a pack of Florentines.

'Something sweet,' I smiled, placing it on the counter as he gently placed the tomatoes on my focaccia. As he was busy creating, I kept on talking... I'm good at that. I was used to filling silences all the time when home with Craig.

'These Florentines look delicious; I'm sure I'd love them... but I'm dieting so I won't actually be eating them. These are for my friend.'

'Oh...' He continued to work on his masterpiece.

It would have been nice if he'd looked surprised that I was dieting, even suggested I didn't need to lose any weight, but he probably *wasn't* listening. I'd recently put on a few pounds due to lack of exercise. Emma and I used to run some evenings when she'd lived at home, but I didn't want to run on my own, it wasn't the same. I wondered if I'd ever get used to her not being there. Her absence had made more of an impact than I had expected and my life seemed suddenly empty. She didn't need me to cook or wash for her anymore, and my taxi service wasn't required either... but more than that, I just missed chatting with her, hearing about her day, her friends, her life.

I watched Dan ringing the pack of Florentines into the till. Long, slender fingers, a battered metal pinkie ring on one, his wrists covered in faded braided leather and cotton, reminiscent of the friendship bracelets Emma used to wear.

'These Florentines are imported from Italy... caramelised almonds... crisp, but real sweet on the tongue. A hint of ginger and orange zest gives them a spicy, citrusy... zing. Basically, they're addictive; once you open them you'll have to eat them,' he smiled.

'Oh, I'll try to resist. Like I say, they aren't really for me— these are for my boss, Sue. She owns Curl Up and Dye where I work. She's been a bit down lately because her husband made a fortune in plastic balls then left her for an anorexic stewardess.' I added, unnecessarily, 'He kept the house and all Sue's soft furnishings, and Sue gets upset imagining them making love on her Laura Ashley throw and matching handmade cushions. She calls her 'flight-deck floozy or Aeroflot Annie.' I looked at him and he smiled, not quite sure how to react. I am one of those people who by nature are shy, but this lack of self-confidence is a strange contradiction as it also compels me to fill silent air with my own waffle.

'She has ginger hair and does things with her tongue,' I added. 'Aeroflot Annie, I mean... not Sue.' I doubt blond Aussie Deli Guy wanted the intimate details of the mistress of some man once married to a woman who worked in a hairdressers down the road, but he was getting them. As I progressed on to more pointless minutiae about Sue's tragic marriage and monumental struggle with Internet dating, I guessed it was a matter of time before he switched off. I should stop now, I thought, as I heard myself telling the story of Sue's date with a man who could only have sex dressed as Darth Vader, and a high-court judge who

kept only his judicial wig on throughout. Now why did I feel the
need to tell him that? It wasn't even my story to tell. I was waiting for his eyes to glaze over as Craig's did when I addressed him
for longer than thirty seconds. But, throughout my monologue,
Dan was laughing, genuinely amused at my stories. I decided to
quit while I was ahead, when I still had his attention and asked
how much I owed for the sandwich. He told me and as I rummaged in my purse, a teeny chink of silence dared to open up. It
was, of course, my duty to fill this silence.

'Where are you from? Are you here permanently or on one of
those extended holidays... you get Australians doing those here
don't you? You all live communally... sleep together... sleeping
with each other... I meant sleeping asleep... not anything sexual.
God, no... Europe... yes, are you "doing" Europe. When I say
"doing", I mean...?'

'Yeah... I'm from Sydney.' He folded his arms and leaned
back, watching me, still with an amused twinkle in his eyes. 'I'm
staying with the British side of my family, who happen to own
this shop—and being Australian doesn't mean we all sleep together. I have been to Europe—sadly I haven't "done" it yet. Oh,
and my mother's maiden name is Smith, and my inside leg is...'

'Oh, I'm so sorry. I wasn't being nosy. I just...'

'Don't apologise... I'm joking,' he smiled. His eyes crinkled
and for a stupid nanosecond I allowed a little sparkle to tinkle
through my veins. It was good to feel that again, the indefin-
able frisson of attraction—from me, anyway; I doubted it was
reciprocated, but who needed reciprocation? I'd been getting it

on with half of Hollywood in the past few years and none of my partners were even aware of it.

'I'm having a gap year.' he was still smiling. 'It's kind of delayed, you know... I should have done it when I was in my twenties, but I'm thirty-three... this is my European gap.'

A quick mental calculation told me he was nine years younger than me. Was that a bad thing? And more to the point, why did I feel the instinctive need to work that out? It wasn't like it mattered. There was no way anyone like him would see me in any other way than what I was—a boring, middle-aged, married woman.

'Sweet and tender,' he said quite seductively as he pushed my wrapped focaccia towards me across the counter. 'Kissed by the cool mountain breeze.'

'I take it you're referring to the ham...?'

'Take from it what you choose,' he smiled, getting me straight away, which was lovely.

'I wonder, could you tell me which particular mountain?' I asked.

'Of course, madam. It's the one with the snow on and the hanging hams.'

'Okay... I suppose I'll have to take your word for it,' I nodded in mock seriousness. 'But if, when I taste it, I discover it was dried in the breeze of a different mountain... I shall be back.'

'In that case, I hope I'm wrong, because, madam, you have rather entertained me this morning.' He reached over and popped some of the dribbly green olives into a polystyrene pot. 'And here is a little thank you—an accompaniment to your focaccia, on the house.' He bowed slightly and handed me the pot, our eyes meeting.

I loved the attention, and as he opened the till, his smile was captivating and my mind had gone on ahead. There was no law that said I couldn't pack 'Aussie Boy, the fantasy' into my bag to be savoured later along with Brad Pitt, the focaccia and the Florentines—not all at the same time you understand, that would be greedy. Okay, I wasn't kidding myself; I knew his twinkly smile and flirty nature was all about customer service and flogging fancy hams... and those free olives were a loss leader, not a come on. But a girl could dream.

'Your hat's... cool, by the way,' he said, ringing my money into the till and shuffling for change.

Now, there's mild flirting with a woman to whom you want to sell overpriced Italian meats—and then there's patronising, or worse, making fun. He clearly found me very amusing, regaling my friend's weirdo love life to him in a floor-length fur-trimmed parka with a panda on my head. I felt a rush of humiliation, and as he handed me my change, he saw the look on my face.

'I didn't mean to embarrass you,' he said uncertainly, placing the coins into my open palm. 'It's a cool hat...'

'It's my daughter's... and I didn't put it on because I wanted to "look cool"—I'm aware I look completely ridiculous,' I mumbled, feeling stupid, putting the change in my purse and the pack of Florentines into my bag. I pulled the hat off and jammed it into my pocket. I wasn't just wearing the hat and parka to keep out the cold; it made me feel closer to Emma and I suddenly felt a deep surge of maternal longing. How dare he make fun of the hat my daughter wore when she was thirteen. I remembered buying it for her from a stall at the German Christmas Market in Birmingham and she'd worn it constantly. I even caught her wearing it in bed once, and remembering that made me suddenly, incredibly sad. How quickly she'd grown and gone; how like yesterday it seemed that she held my hand in hers and took her first wobbly steps. I bit my lip, my eyes brimming with tears. Where the hell had all this emotion come from?

'Hey... I'm sorry. I didn't mean to upset you. I *do* like your hat... really, it's... cute.'

I attempted a smile, but my bottom lip was quivering. 'I'm sorry. It's not really what you said... I just... I'm being silly. I just miss my daughter.' I started to cry.

'Ah, don't cry,' he said gently. 'My dad called last night, worried about me being halfway round the world, and I'm a fully grown man. It's perfectly natural to miss your daughter. Why did she leave?'

'She's at university in Manchester. Stupid, but I don't think I'll ever get used to her being away. It's like my heart walked off and left me behind.'

'Hey, does she know you've got her hat? Won't she be cold... without it?' He was trying to lighten the mood. It didn't work.

'Oh, she wouldn't be seen dead with it on now. In fact I doubt anyone over thirteen years of age would.'

I thought about how gauche I must seem to someone worldly like him and how embarrassed Emma would be to see me dressed like this. I started to really blubber then and no one was more surprised than me... except him. He stood there with his arms hanging limply, an awkward look on his face. After about a minute, when he realised I wasn't going to stop sobbing and I might be bad for business, he moved around the counter and continued to stand helplessly by as I dripped salty tears all over his artisanal breads. I hadn't cried about Emma going back this time. I thought I'd crossed a bridge, but I hadn't. I'd just bottled it all up until that moment, because someone was nice to me and actually listened to what I'd said. I felt an emergency napkin being pushed under my nose and without looking up accepted it gratefully.

'Thanks.' I blew my nose and thought about how this guy must be wishing he'd never started the conversation with the crazy lady in the parka.

'You okay?' he asked, and by the look on his face it was clear he thought I needed professional help. Trust me to spoil a beautiful fledgling friendship which had begun with such promise—firm arms, filled focaccia and free olives.

'I'm okay. I'm quite okay. Thank you for the napkin,' I smiled. 'If anyone walked in now to see a woman blowing her nose in a fur-trimmed parka with a panda on her head, it might not be good for custom.'

'Yeah, I'm not sure you're exactly good for business,' he raised his brows with a smile, then the concerned face flickered back. 'Oh, and... I'm joking, so please don't start crying again.'

'I won't.'

I smiled and he seemed to relax but continued to stand awkwardly like he was waiting to catch me if I fell. For a moment the air was quiet, save the sound of cars outside and an ambulance in the distance, but even in deep distress I had to fill the air with my bloody voice.

'I feel really stupid. I don't normally burst into tears when I order a sandwich. I can't remember the last time I cried... it was probably my birthday—I drank too much cava,' I said, throwing the handle of my bag over my shoulder and pulling the fur-trimmed hood around my head. 'Emma... that's my daughter, says I talk too much sometimes. She's right, I do. I talk and talk and... Anyway, I'll get off. Thanks for the tissue.' I wiped my eyes and walked towards the door.

'I never caught your name, by the way,' he called after me.

I turned and smiled awkwardly, trying not to be swept up in those eyes. 'Faye... I'm Faye.' I opened the door and, clutching my focaccia like a protective sword, walked out onto the street. I had to get out of there with what little dignity I had left before making even more of an idiot of myself.

I headed back for the salon and safety. Curl Up and Dye had always been my sanctuary, my second home. I'd worked there since Emma was six and had started school, and what started as a temporary job became more permanent and then it was too late for me to give it all up and go back to studying. I had now reached the dizzy heights of Senior Stylist, and although I had always dreamed of studying again, Craig had always advised against rocking the boat and messing about with college at my age.

But recently I'd thought about going back to college, travelling, and doing some of the things I'd always planned to do. Rediscovering my New York postcard had made me think more about my life and how it had turned out, and though the salon had provided a wonderful, happy environment all through my twenties and thirties, I'd never intended to stay forever. I loved the girls but recently I had yearned for something else: people I could learn from and share new experiences with—and I didn't think Sue or Mandy (or Craig, for that matter) were those people. The Lithuanian situation was causing more daily stress than necessary; I couldn't take another story from a customer about a neighbour dispute or an incident at Aldi, and Sue's obsession with online dating and astrology was driving us all mad. We were all like Lady Ga Ga the hamster on her relentless wheel, going nowhere and coming back for more every day—the same stories, the same faces, the same mistakes. It was a tiny world and I wanted to escape for a while. I had these same feelings at home and I didn't want to stay with Craig either. I didn't have the courage to just walk out, but if I stayed I knew I would die a slow death.

I could almost hear the clock ticking.

'Faye—you need to make a decision, love,' Sue had said. 'You either get on with it and put up with him, or get out before it's too late. I'm a bit older than you and, trust me, it gets harder.' Sue was forty-five and single and spent her evenings with strangers she'd met online—was that the only option for an older, single woman?

'Last night I was the oldest woman in a line of speed daters,' she'd told me only that morning. 'It was like being at school all over again. I was always the last one picked for netball... and last night I went through it all again. So take my advice: get out while you're young enough to enjoy being single.'

The clock wasn't just ticking now; I was on a timer. On one long, lonely evening with Craig I'd even worked out exactly how many hours I had left if I lived to my seventies. Now it scared me to think of each hour being eaten away, swallowed up by unhappiness and my own perceived failure.

But what scared me even more was the thought of spending those hours as a woman like me, with a man like Craig in a life that didn't work.

Perhaps I'd never dance on a twinkly New York rooftop, or sip dirty martinis with Ryan Gosling; and the chances of ending up anywhere near Johnny Depp's place were nada even though he was now officially single. For many middle-aged women who'd been married twenty-odd years, this would come as no surprise and they'd accept their lot, stoically boiling pasta for tea and putting another load in the washer. My tragedy is that I am a dreamer. My mother always told me anything was possible; I just had to believe in myself and do it. I had taken this literally from the age of five, and even as a grown woman I couldn't let go of the idea that I could do anything. Perhaps this is why life had so far disappointed me? I'd never got my degree, achieved little on my Living List, and I'd never even been abroad. Yet being the contradiction that I am, my blind, ridiculous optimism continued to keep me naively hopeful that I would, one day, find what I was looking for.

Since rediscovering it, I'd kept the New York postcard in my handbag and would often take it out, imagining I was dancing on that rooftop, along with the man who belonged on the other empty chair. I had no idea who the man was, but I knew it wasn't Craig.

Is this it? I thought, seeing only a long, straight road ahead with all the signposts in place, no sudden bends, the odd traffic light, but no surprises and no treasure at the end of the journey. Just a greying bra, ageing breasts and sex with the same man until I died? No empty chairs at rooftop tables, no dancing under the stars and no champagne waiting for me on ice.

❄ ❄ ❄

'Dan from the deli has a look of Ryan Gosling, don't you think?' I said to Mandy as we locked up one night.

'The Aussie? Yeah, I know what you mean. He's cute. Are you going for young blokes now, Faye?'

'God, no. I don't fancy him. I was just saying... he looks like a rugged Ryan Gosling.'

'It's okay even at your age to fancy other men, Faye,' she said earnestly as we walked home together. 'My mum had a thing for a bloke she'd gone out with at school, her first love. She'd not seen him since they were sixteen and every year she'd get an invite to the school reunion and I'd say, "Mum, you have to go," and she'd put the invite in the bin and say, "Nah, they'll all have big jobs and fancy cars and I haven't got anything." She always promised she'd lose weight, get a posh frock and a cut and blow and go next year. Then when she got poorly and the invite came, she said she would definitely go that year. She wanted to see him and her old mates one last time and was all excited. She even bought a new dress. I was going to do her hair and make-up... then a couple of days before the party she ended up back in hospital and she never came out. She never got the chance to see him or her old school buddies, and her dress is still in the wardrobe... Man that was tough.'

'Oh, Mandy, how sad she never made it.'

'One of the last things she said to me was, "Go for it. Don't wait to be asked. Don't put anything off—do it now. None of us know how long we've got and you have to live every day." That's what she said.'

Mandy's story about her mum made me think about how I'd been playing around on the edges of life. Just like she'd kept putting off that school reunion through fear of being judged or rejected, I'd been doing the same with my life for years— playing safe, not taking any risks. Like her unworn dress in the wardrobe, my red one lay folded in the rucksack... two unworn dresses and lives unlived. As Mandy's mum said, you have to go for it because you don't know how long you have. I suddenly felt homesick for Emma, so when I got home checked my phone to see if she'd texted. She hadn't and I considered texting her, but reminded myself Emma needed her own space now, her chance to live her life—which was ironic because for the first time in my adult life I had loads of space but nothing to do with it now she wasn't filling it.

That night, I lay in Emma's single bed and gazed at the New York postcard. Who would dance with me in my dreams tonight? I kept thinking about Dan and his big blue eyes. He was younger than me, but seemed older he was so knowledgeable about food and he'd obviously travelled and experienced life. I was sure he would be a very pleasant dinner companion in my dreams; he'd wax lyrical about continental meats and olive trees, and hold my hand in the candlelight while explaining why cheese turned blue. It would make a nice change from Brad Pitt and the boys who, let's face it, had all become a bit of a cliché for middle aged women like me. I was just another well-married woman, grateful to spend an evening with someone who bothered to make eye contact and whose pants I hadn't washed a million times.

The timing of Dan's arrival was perfect. He'd landed here from paradise, just a few doors down from the hairdressers, a post-Christmas gift from the eye-candy fairy for all of us girls to enjoy in the aftermath of tinsel and onslaught of nothingness.

Walking home from work on those wintry dark evenings with the remnants of a rain shower threatening to ice the roads, I'd pass the lighted deli and see Dan in there, chatting with a customer or busy stocking shelves, and had to stop myself from going in. I found the savoury air and the warmth so comforting, along with his lovely sunshine smile. Some evenings I would power-walk past the deli, pushing away intrusive thoughts about cured meats and bronzed biceps. Yet my mind was often dragged back, kicking and screaming, to Dan in underwear (okay, I was thinking fitted, white Calvin Klein boxers if you must know).

Perhaps with Craig at home and a nun-like existence at work, I was being starved of male attention and overcompensating? I'd definitely begun to look at men in a different, more sensual way; for example, I'd watch a film and whereas before I'd admire the leading man's acting, my first thoughts were now, 'I wonder what he looks like naked? Or, 'I wonder what he's like in bed?'

I was shocked at my own thoughts as they came unbidden into my head. It was getting worse and I couldn't count the times I'd come home to discover Kevin Bacon naked and 'oven-ready' on my kitchen worktops.

Sue said it was hormonal and I was probably 'peripausal.' She often mixed her words up, so I googled it and I think what she meant was I was going through the peri-menopause—but whatever it was, I felt hot in the presence of men... and not in a good way.

I had to ask myself, was I having a midlife crisis? Didn't that usually involve a raging affair or a sports car? I was enjoying nei-ther—but if a midlife crisis meant feeling old and insignificant and that life had lost its meaning, that's exactly what was going on. Since Emma had gone, I was beginning to look at myself in a different way. I had more time to think about my life and where it was going, I also had time to consider the past, play old music, remember old friends and remember the old me. I hadn't always been a married mum; I'd been young once—and I'd have given a year's wages and more to feel that way again.

Chapter Four

Metamorphosis for a Marriage

'Oh, we had a wonderful evening...' Sue was saying to Jackie, her client (single mum, double garage) as I returned to the salon the following day. Another day, another revolution of the hamster wheel, I thought.

Having joined a new online dating website for 'wealthy men and gorgeous women', Sue had been on yet another date and this time she felt she might just have cracked it.

'I met him in the restaurant. It was very posh—he ordered for both of us... such a gentleman,' Sue was saying. 'Gestapo soup in a big latrine... but I had to send it back. I took one mouthful and it was bloody freezing!' she screeched. 'You'd expect something better for £100 a head, wouldn't you Jackie? It wasn't just cold, it was icy... I was furious. Keith (six-figure salary, hot tub, wife ran off with the plumber) said, "Oh, no it's just right—you can't send it back." I said, "Watch me!" The wine was nice though; we had a lovely red—cost a fortune. Keith's an expert... Now, what did he say...?' She looked to the ceiling, lifting the hairdryer away from Jackie's head, which apparently aided her memory. 'What was it now...? Oh, yes. He said it was full-bodied with an afterbirth of oak.' She nodded, smiled and carried on blow drying vigorously, delighted with her new boyfriend and his extensive wine knowledge.

I was happy for Sue and glad that after all the dating trauma she may have finally found Mr Right. She'd been abandoned in so many restaurants and night clubs since the divorce, her perspective had become a little skewed. It had reached the point that if a man stayed for dessert, Sue called it an engagement, and if he went back to hers for coffee we were talking bridesmaid colours. Jackie was loving Sue's account of the date, open-mouthed at the luxurious setting and millionaire companion. This must have been the tenth time I'd heard about it as Sue relived every moment, hairdryer in one hand, iPhone in the other, flicking through photos of Keith and close-ups of every plate of food and glass of wine they'd consumed.

As she talked, I tried to remember how it felt to be in that first flush of love: the waiting for him to call, the anticipation of seeing him, and I realised I wanted that again. I wasn't sure I'd survive this brave new world of dating though. Sue said these days it was all mapped out online first, with no opportunity for small talk. She said you already know their profession, marital history and views on Syria from their dating profile on the website. Despite being unhappy with Craig, I wasn't ready for a life of dating partners who selected each other from a list of self-defined attributes on a page. If I had been single, I'd have wanted nothing less than heart-stopping passion, love at first sight and candlelit romance. Perhaps I was old-fashioned, but the dreamer in me wanted a more organic seduction—just eyes across the room and whispered nothings, without Internet access or Android kisses.

Despite potential hook-ups with inappropriate men and the inevitable disappointment when they never called, I envied Sue her dates. I longed to wake up in the morning not knowing what was going to happen that day. The idea of going out with a stranger, hearing a new story, holding a different hand, and a stubbly kiss from strange lips thrilled me. Sometimes the thought of Sue's dates made me feel quite tingly inside, until I remembered it wasn't going to happen for me. I was going home to Craig, with the same lips and the same old story.

❊ ❊ ❊

That night Sue let Mandy and Camilla leave at five p.m. as they all had an exciting weekend ahead. Saturday night was always party night in Mandy-land, Sue was going on a date and Camilla was off to a boat race early the next day. 'Camilla's jumper must have cost a week's wages,' Sue was saying as she wiped scum from the back washes. 'She doesn't mention her mum much and her dad must be rolling in it. I think I'll ask her if they're divorced,' she said, clinging to every lifeline. She was so scared of spending time alone, she was becoming slightly desperate. I wiped down mirrors and swept up hair, contemplating how I would fill the next forty-eight hours at home with Craig without going mad.

'I wonder how many times I've cleaned this mirror?' I said, rubbing hard on the smears. Close up it always looked perfect, but when I stood back, a million more smears would appear in other parts of the glass.

I loved working at the salon but was beginning to think it had imprisoned me as much as my marriage.

'There must be more to life than doing hair and cleaning up and going home,' I sighed. 'I mean, the hair regrows and the salon gets dirty again... it's like being on a never-ending loop and the only time it stops is when you're so old you can't stand up anymore. Then someone else will do our jobs, start all over again, cutting dyeing, sweeping... cleaning... going home.'

'Oh, Faye, you're depressing me. You really need to jizzy yourself up, love. I know how you feel, but I told you, it's your hormones—too much cholesterol. You'll be growing a beard next.'

'How can I jivvy myself up?' I didn't correct her—she used the phrase all the time with customers and though it often took *them* by surprise, we were used to it and spoke 'Sue' well after all these years.

'Mandy's twenty-one and Camilla's only nineteen; they both seem so young and it makes me feel so old, Sue. Bloody hell—my own daughter thinks I'm a dinosaur, but I don't *feel* old. Sometimes I have to remind myself that I'm not nineteen anymore, but inside I *feel* nineteen: skinny with long hair and a lust for life... Don't you feel the same Sue?'

'Yeah. Inside... Oh, to be nineteen again. I'd do things so differently. The trouble is when we were young, we didn't realise how gorgeous we were. We thought we were fat and no one would ever ask us out...'

'Oh, you are so right. I was going through my old rucksack the other day and found a photo of me at sixteen. I'd always thought I was so ugly, and there I was, a beautiful, blossoming teenager... Why didn't anyone tell me?'

'You wouldn't have listened, babe. You were a teenager...'

I nodded and kept scrubbing at the mirror; 'How does it feel, Sue... you know, to kiss someone after Ken?'

'What do you mean?'

'Well, after only kissing your husband all those years, to kiss someone new, on a date... what does that feel like after all this time?'

'I don't know. I don't kiss them. I wouldn't do it to Ken. It would kill him.'

'Christ, Sue—he's been doing it to you with the queen of the skies, not to mention all the others over the years. How on earth do you have sex with someone without kissing them... that's what prostitutes do, don't they?'

'That's how I feel with anyone other than Ken. And one day he'll be back, with my cushions and my throws. Glad I had them Scotchguarded... God only knows what stains would have been on them by now.'

I ignored this comment. This was about more than cushions. 'Sue, until you accept he's gone and isn't coming back, you will never move on. You have to face what's happened and embrace being single.'

'I don't want to be single; I want to be married, with everything as it was. You're lucky—at least you're not spending your weekends going from one disaster to another, always hoping this next one will be it.'

I looked at her. Sue was obviously under the impression that, as I had a husband, all was fine in my world. Here was a sensible, financially independent, attractive woman who was wasting her best years waiting around for Ken who'd betrayed her all their married life. She still believed she needed a man, a husband at any cost.

'Stop looking for another Ken. Just enjoy the ride. If it makes you feel any better, I think *you're* the lucky one, Sue. Husbands strangle your dreams and turn you into mush. I can't even drive with Craig in the passenger seat because I go to pieces waiting for the criticism; I just sit there like an empty vessel waiting for his instructions. It's not his fault—it's mine for becoming that way and it's stupid. I drive perfectly well on my own—but sometimes being married makes you stop believing in yourself.'

She stopped scrubbing the basins and looked up.

'Is that driving story a metamorphosis for your marriage to Craig?'

I smiled. 'I suppose it is a metaphor for our marriage. I've always seen being married as safe, cosy...but these days I just feel trapped. I'd give anything for just one more kiss with someone else before I die. I'm not saying I'm giving up on men or the idea of love—I just want something different... before it's too late.'

'Oh, God. You're not yourself are you, love?'

'That's the thing, Sue: I've never felt more like me than I do now,' I said, realising it was true and wanting everything, before it was too late. 'I want to sit on a white sun lounger by a pool in

LA and be seduced by a handsome stranger. I want to dance on a rooftop in New York and be kissed under the stars. I don't want to die and never have that wonderful rush again.'

She gave it a moment and carried on scrubbing. 'When you put it like that, I can see what you mean. You need to decide what you want before it's too late.' *Before it's too late* was a phrase I'd been thinking a lot recently.

She called me later that night after I'd eaten dinner, drunk two glasses of wine and eaten far too many Maltesers. I was half watching a film and leafing through a brochure for Greece I'd picked up earlier that week for recreational purposes only. Craig had gone to bed and I was languishing by an Olympic-sized pool in Mykonos with Brad Pitt, Johnny Depp and a large Greek salad when the phone rang. I was suddenly thrust into the here and the now by the shrill noise. I leapt on the phone hoping it might be Emma—even though I knew it was Saturday night and she would be out with her friends.

'Faye, my love, I'm worried about you,' was Sue's opening gambit. 'What you were saying about the dating and it being exciting and I should go for it. You're right and... I want that kiss too. I want the earth to move and my heart to flutter and all my insides to turn to jelly, but it never gets that far. And if Mandy makes you feel old, you want to try meeting a stranger on a Friday night in a wine bar full of teenagers. While you're making small talk, he's eyeing up the eighteen-year-old in the mini skirt and looking straight past you. Don't envy me the dates, love. I'm a Gemini; I talk them up... the view's just as bad from here.'

I was aware that, by many people's standards, I was very lucky. I was married with two salaries, our daughter was happy and healthy and I should perhaps have got on with it and stopped longing for something I couldn't have. But the other side of me (the one who slow-danced with Kevin Bacon and slept with Brad while Angelina was away on UN business) said life's too short and you have to grab it while you can. 'Putting up' with your husband is not a marriage and 'getting on with it' is not a life. And to top it all, Ryan Gosling was mixing us a couple of dirty martinis and telling me straight: 'Take what *you* want Faye and stop putting everyone else's happiness before your own,' he urged. Ryan was a listener and always good with advice... then again, he is a Scorpio. And you know what they say about Scorpios...

I held the phone but Sue had gone—no doubt to pour herself another glass and think about Ken and his current mistress. We were both as sad and lonely as each other, I thought. Sue and I were living the same life in different houses. But surely Sue's life wasn't the only other option open to me was it? There must be something better?

Chapter Five

Cakes, Coke and a Cute Australian

It was a Tuesday morning and I told myself we needed cake in the salon, so I went into the deli on the way to work.

'Cake is like coke to me,' I heard myself telling Dan as he placed six cupcakes into a lovely brown cardboard box.

'Yeah?' he sniggered. Those eyes were still smiling at me, making my knees feel empty, just waiting to collapse. I hadn't met a real-life man I'd found this attractive for a long, long time. The last man I actually fancied in the flesh was a teacher at Emma's school when she was about eight, so this was big for me and I had to keep it in perspective. I knew it was a harmless crush. I just loved looking at this guy who had come from halfway around the world, and hearing sunshine and beaches and barbies in his voice, and as I'd walked in that morning he'd seemed pleased to see me. It was all relative—I'd had a whole weekend with Craig and anyone would look gorgeous and pleased to see me after that. Perhaps Dan smiled because he just knew I would say weird things that would make him laugh, and if that was the case it looked like this was his lucky day as I'd only just arrived and was already comparing cupcakes to A Class drugs.

'When I say cake is like my coke... I've never actually had cocaine,' I felt it necessary to point out. 'I mean, I'm not a drug addict or anything... it's just, cake is like a drug to me. Not that I'd snort it... I wouldn't put the cake anywhere other than in my mouth.'

'That's a relief,' he smiled. Oh, how cute he was. Oh, and how I wished I could stop talking. 'So I hope you're going to forget your stupid diet and eat one of these yourself?' he asked.

Oh, he remembered I was on a diet. But he didn't think I *should* diet.

'Yes, I am definitely going to have one of those,' I said, pointing to them. He said to come back and tell him what I thought and I smiled, leaving the deli with a spring in my step and a song in my heart. I walked to work thinking how Dan from the deli was the only man I'd ever met who could possibly match up to my fantasy stable of Hollywood hunks.

I was just walking past the dry cleaners when I felt a hand on my arm. It was Dan. 'You forgot your change,' he said, handing me a twenty pence piece. I thanked him, but wondered why he'd run down the high street just to give me 20p?

'Is that where you work?' he asked, obviously wanting to continue our conversation.

'Yeah. For now. I started on a temporary basis... and it's, er, been a little longer than I anticipated.'

'How long?'

'I don't want to think about it,' I smiled. 'I just sometimes feel like it's swallowing me up and I need to get out, but it's not easy to find work at the moment.'

'I know what you mean. It's good to make changes, throw everything in the air now and then and see where it lands—but it takes guts to do that. Worth it though... if you can.'

'It's scary though; I mean there's loads of things I want to change and loads of things I want to do, but it's not just about having the courage.'

'What is it that's stopping you then?' We were having this weird conversation about life in the middle of the street, outside a pound shop early in the morning and I wasn't ready for his interrogation.

'What's stopping me...? Good question,' I sighed. 'I have a daughter, a job, responsibilities. I'd love to go to Paris for the afternoon and eat macaroons in a beautiful Parisian teashop but a) I have to be at work in five minutes, b) I can't afford the air fare, and c) I don't have a passport... other than that, nothing's stopping me.' I hadn't mentioned the fact I was married and would be going home to cook tea—he didn't have to know everything about me.

'No passport? Well, I reckon that's your first stop,' he said. 'Get passported up and book that flight to France.'

'Yeah... tomorrow,' I smiled, making to walk away. I was late for work but flattered he wanted to chat. 'Today I'm doing a Santorini sunset and making a wish at the Trevi Fountain.'

He smiled and touched my arm. 'Just don't be away too long.'

'Don't worry,' I called behind me, walking now, 'I've got a full head of highlights at three p.m., so I'll have to be back by then.'

It was just beginning to rain but he didn't seem to be aware—just wanted to chat as if we had all day and it was blazing sunshine. He didn't move, just leaned against the dry cleaner's window waving me off until I reached the salon. I walked in, greeted by the familiar rush of heat and hairspray, which filled my head and squashed my heart and made me long to just run outside and find Dan again.

Chapter Six

Slow-Pulled Pork and Ice Road Truckers

I was still missing Emma, and the gap that had re-opened again like a wound was hard to put back together. I'd found the past couple of weeks difficult, readjusting to me and Craig alone again. Without Emma there was no laughter, no fun and the only place I felt at home, ironically, was at work.

I'd gone out with Craig since we were fifteen and we'd stayed together during my first year at university when he was an apprentice plumber. Then, in my second year, I'd met Alex, a fellow English student, and on a visit home had told Craig it was over. He agreed it wasn't working long distance and we slept together for one last time... or so we thought. I went back to uni, started to see Alex more often, and just as I was beginning to fall for him, he slept with someone else. It was then I discovered I was pregnant with Craig's baby, which was devastating. I told Craig and he immediately did the right thing and suggested we get married. It wasn't what I wanted, but I was pregnant and alone and at the time it was the only thing to do. I was grateful to Craig; he'd stood by me and it made me fall back in love with him a little, especially after Alex had treated me so badly. I decided to leave uni and continue my degree once the baby was old enough, and a registry office wedding was hastily arranged by parents on both sides. I didn't know it then, but that day in my pale cream dress and coat I said goodbye to everything I'd planned. It was the end of a university education, world travel, and the start of a life with someone who'd never share my passions or want the same things I did.

We lived a married life of sorts, contributing to the love and upbringing of our daughter, and I'd never really considered an alternative. There had always been problems in our relationship, based on the fact that we were incompatible, but recently I'd become more aware of the differences between us. I wanted spontaneity, romance and adventure, but Craig didn't like change, do small talk, or eat foreign food. I wanted a husband who would take me on the kitchen table and sing to me under the stars, but Craig liked sex in bed, his tea on the table and everything in its place. I enjoyed reading and cooking, but Craig wasn't interested in books and his dodgy digestive system caused him to taste only the essence of 'battery acid' in my delicate, lovingly prepared sauces. But the biggest catastrophe for me was that I'd always longed to see the world and Craig was scared of flying and Weston-super-Mare was as far as he'd go. I dreamed of that trip to the Trevi Fountain, that Vespa ride through Rome, but the nearest I'd get to Italy with Craig was a takeaway pizza.

My mother's death two years earlier had shocked me into the awareness that my horizons were shrinking as each year passed. It's sad at the end of your life to realise that you never saw those faraway places with strange-sounding names. But knowing in early middle age that the man you will share the rest of your life with won't even get on a plane was devastating... even for an optimist like me. If I stayed with Craig, I would never tick anything off my living list, but would just go on adding more futile dreams that would never come to fruition. I had gone over and over in my head what I would say to him when it came time for me to leave, but hadn't really worked out when that would be. Was there ever a right time to end your marriage? Was I just putting this off, like I was everything else? As Dan from the deli had said earlier that day; 'What's stopping you, Faye?'

I think, ultimately, this was what gave me the courage to do what I did on that wet Wednesday night in February—the idea that being married to Craig was holding me back. I was using him and my marriage as an excuse, and it was stopping me from being me. I would tell him tonight.

I arrived home late with the ingredients for a gourmet meal to find Craig birthing the innards of a washing machine on the kitchen table, the overpowering smell of WD-40 permeating the house.

'Craig,' I tried, hearing the nagging in my own voice, 'I've been to the supermarket and bought food for a nice meal... I want us to have a proper talk tonight...' I couldn't concentrate for the overpowering stench. 'That stuff gives me a headache—why don't you open a window?' I plonked the bags with the ingredients on the kitchen worktop.

'I'm not opening a window; it'll let the heat out... it's February in England, not the bloody Caribbean.'

'I wish I *was* in the bloody Caribbean,' I hissed.

'Yeah I wish you were too,' he muttered from somewhere inside a washer drum.

So, what a great start—both wishing the other were on a different continent. Good luck with the difficult conversation, Faye, I thought.

'Will you need the table for long—I want to set it?' I snapped.

'Oh, is someone coming?'

I sighed and put the kettle on. 'Craig... we have to discuss... stuff. *Okay?*' I looked at him and for a second he glanced at me and I detected a faint nod.

'What are you making?'

I sighed again. 'Slow roasted pork with spiced rhubarb.' I picked up the packet of rhubarb and began reading from it; I found it easier to read from a script than talk to him. 'This delightful British rhubarb has been grown in the dark and harvested by candlelight. Forced rhubarb has a superior, delicate flavour and is more tender than the summer version…'

'I don't know why you bought pork. You know I don't like pork; it plays havoc with my guts.'

I wanted to whack him in the face with the bloody pork but remembered I had to keep things on an even keel.

'Forced rhubarb is a seasonal fruit grown in the British Isles and...' I continued reading, 'used to shove up the arses of husbands who won't eat pork.'

He didn't flinch. Then I remembered I had to keep things nice if I wanted it all to go smoothly so slipped into my default voice of cajoling Mum, 'Please, just try the pork—for me?' I asked, hating the pleading in my own voice.

Craig was now texting, leaving the mechanical patient to fight for its life while he smirked into his phone. 'Well, you can put me a bit on a plate,' he sighed, looking away from his phone for a nanosecond, 'and I'll see what I can do.'

'Thanks, that's so *kind* of you,' I said sarcastically. Here I was, presenting this man with the dying embers of my love, smothered with the sweet stickiness of rhubarb harvested by candlelight—and he just didn't get it.

'If you don't want this pork, I'll save it for that millionaire I met online. He likes to rub the sticky sauce all over me before we do it on the dining table. Doggy style,' I added loudly. Nothing. I was chopping and stirring, making this meal for the two of us, knowing it would be the last time. I would soon be free from Craig and his frozen pipes, constant criticism and refusal to leave terra firma. He didn't read books, he didn't make me laugh and he didn't love me—all this and an indifference to the food I cooked had been the recipe for a failed marriage. I never had gastronomic indifference from Kevin Bacon. He would run his tongue lovingly around my culinary delights while groaning with pleasure... and then there was Dan, who would, I was sure, appreciate my rhubarb. He wouldn't reject my delicacies as being too much of a challenge for his digestive system. Dan would welcome my sticky slow-pulled meat, embracing it with enthusiasm, and no whisper of 'havoc' being played with his 'guts'. *There* was a man who appreciated good food—hell, he'd even know the spot where that rhubarb was force-grown... take me to it, then take me *on* it.

Craig was still face-deep in washing machine colons with no sign of moving, and as the minutes went on I just knew it was time. I wasn't wasting any more of my precious life hours on this man who made me feel permanently hurt and angry. I wondered about his reaction; I suspected what was a natural end for me may not be for him. I chopped and marinated and whisked and tasted, and tears dripped from my face onto the pork. Eventually, I composed myself and we ate in silence on trays on our knees. Our marriage was haemorrhaging and I was offering the last rites with a lovingly prepared gourmet dinner, but it was wasted on him.

Later, after he'd eaten the 'tough' pork and pulled his face at the 'sour' rhubarb, I took a deep breath and prepared myself for what was to come. Watching him sip his tea, reading his paper, oblivious to what I was planning, made me feel guilty—but relieved. I had finally made up my mind and there was no going back. It was the right thing for me... for both of us. This had been coming for a long time.

I opened my handbag and took out the picture of the New York rooftop. You could just about see the Empire State Building lit up in the distance—what was stopping me? What *was* stopping me? Only I could get myself to that rooftop, and the first step on that enormous journey would be facing Craig with the truth. I put down my coffee cup. 'Craig... I think we need to talk,' I said quietly, calmly.

Our marriage was a dying dog in the corner of the room. Now, finally, one of us was going to put it out of its misery.

'Craig... I'm not happy.'

He was engrossed in *Ice Road Truckers* but I wasn't going to let that stop me as it had many times before. I just swallowed hard and went for it.

'I've tried to tell you before... but you won't hear it... but I just don't want to do this anymore.'

'But I thought you liked *Ice Road Truckers?*'

'I'm not talking about the fucking TV,' I shouted, losing it slightly. I stood up, marched across to the TV (he of course had the remote) and I turned the sound down, as it was the only way to get his full attention.

'I need you to listen to this because it's important,' I started, almost wishing I could do this by PowerPoint because he'd probably need visuals if he was going to take any of it in. It struck me that a clever woman would have been able to use the insides of a washing machine as an analogy to explain the break-up, but I may have ended up hitting him over the head with it and killing him. Murdering Craig was a little extreme, even for me.

'Craig, we don't sleep together. We don't talk to each other. The only thing we have in common is Emma and she's not here anymore. I'm sorry, but I just don't love you anymore... I want to separate.'

He sat up in his chair with a look of surprise. 'Are you having me on?'

'No.'

'What's got into you, Faye?'

'Nothing and everything... I just can't live with you any longer. You don't even talk to me.'

'That's not true. I told you before about that Miele at number thirty-four but you weren't listening... do you need to see a doctor?'

'No, I don't. Just because I don't care about the fucking Miele at number thirty-four doesn't mean I need medical attention. I don't *care*... and even if we did talk to each other, neither of us would listen because we know exactly what the other one's going to say.'

'You say that like it's a bad thing.'

'It *is* a bad thing, Craig. We don't predict the other's thoughts and words because we're soulmates; we do it because we're so predictable to each other... and bored, so bloody bored. Haven't you noticed? We aren't *together* anymore. I sleep in another room. I stay late just to clean up at work. I try to go out more so I spend as little time as possible around you.'

'It was your idea to sleep in Emma's room... I thought it was because you were missing her. I thought you were coming back to our bed...'

'I'm never coming back, Craig. There's no such thing as 'our' bed. I left it and you a long time ago.'

I was shocked to see big tears suddenly dropping down onto his chin and he began to sob. Huge, great racking sobs, with his head in his hands. I hadn't realised he was capable of such raw, strong emotion—especially when it came to me and our marriage. I began to cry too and went to him and, holding him in my arms, I rocked him like a baby. 'I'm sorry, Craig... I'm so sorry, love. But I can't go on...'

Eventually, when he'd emerged from his tears, he sat shaking his head. I brought him a cup of tea and we sat together on the sofa holding hands, finally coming together at the end.

'I know you get fed up and you've wanted a holiday. We can do that... we can go wherever you want, Faye, do whatever...'

'It's not about a holiday, Craig. It's more than that. I just... don't want to be married anymore.'

We sat together by the light of the TV, as always, but now it was different. I couldn't believe what I'd just done and felt scared, guilty and elated at the same time.

'I think we both want someone we can talk to who will listen, Craig. I want someone who isn't constantly criticising me and making fun of my stupid ideas... I know they're daft, but you shouldn't laugh at people's dreams. I want to see the world, Craig. I want to meet new people and have new experiences... I might even finish my degree one day. You might find this hard to believe—but I don't get an awful lot of fulfilment from washing your pants.'

'You can't just go like that... is there someone else?'

'No, there isn't. We both need some time apart,' I said.

'We can live apart, we can do that... but stay in the same house.'

'No. We've been doing that for years. We need to live in different places, Craig.'

'But... I still care about you Faye,' he added, like an afterthought. I shook my head and smiled sadly at him.

'You could go and live at your mother's?'

'I'm not going there,' he said, suddenly changing his tone from victim to master. I didn't blame him; he didn't want any of this. Not because he loved me and couldn't bear to be without me—he just didn't want the hassle, the upset, the change. He was even more scared than I was.

I was tired of battling, so offered to go and stay at Sue's for a while.

'You do what you like. You'll be back with your tail between your legs,' he snapped, his resentment building now he knew my mind was set. I expected this and it was only right he should feel angry. I almost welcomed his anger. I could deal with it far more easily than his hurt.

I called Sue, who, as always, was there for me.

'Hmm, I knew he wouldn't leave that house... Taureans are very stubborn. Pack your bag. The spare bed's made and there's a bottle of rosé in the fridge,' she said. I wanted to cry with relief.

I took one last look in Emma's room. I tidied her teddy bears, moved a few books around and ran my hands along the blue satin throw I'd bought in the Rackham's sale years before. I remembered bringing our baby home from the hospital and almost understood Sue's strange emotional attachment to her cushions—our lives were woven into the fabrics of our home. Whatever we did and whoever we loved next, mine and Craig's lives were sewn together, with Emma binding us all like the delicate stitching in the blue satin throw.

I packed my stuff in my suitcase, put the bright pink rucksack on my back and, leaving Craig by the flickering light of *Ice Road Truckers*, I closed the front door for the last time.

Chapter Seven

Looking for Mr Waitrose

Sue was waiting outside and, after hugging me and telling me it would all be okay, we put my bags in the boot and headed to hers. I felt a mix of relief it was over, but fear of the future alone. As much as I worried about telling Emma, a part of me welcomed this new life and the cacophony of colour and chaos it would hopefully bring.

'I should feel terrible,' I said to Sue as she poured the wine back at her house. 'I should hate myself—but I don't; I feel delirious and free. But that makes me even worse. I am a bad person, whichever way you look at it.'

'You're not a bad person. Stop blaming yourself and putting yourself down at the first opportunity. Faye, you're always self-defecating.'

I wondered for a split second what I was being accused of but assumed she meant *self-deprecating* and nodded. We talked long into the night and Sue kept filling my glass up, offering her own brand of astrological advice and telling me it would work out.

The following morning before work, I called Emma.

'Oh, Mum, shall I come home?' she said, sounding tearful.

I insisted she stay in Manchester; it was important she didn't miss lectures and I didn't want her work to suffer because of something I'd done.

'It's all for the best,' I said. 'Dad and I haven't been happy together for a long time and I know it's the right thing for both of us, so don't be upset.'

'How will Dad cope?' she asked. 'You know what he's like; he can't even make toast.'

'It won't do him any harm to learn. He can be a domestic goddess for a change. I always washed and cleaned and cooked after a day's work... it's just that I did it for both of us... three of us when you lived at home. Sometimes I'd be in later than Dad and he'd still be waiting for me to make his tea and wash his bloody overalls... Now he can do it himself. I just want more now Em. I need more.'

'Is Dad upset?' she asked. 'Is it just a trial separation?'

My heart ached for her. I felt dreadful for robbing her of the mental security that all was well at home and added it to my rapidly growing '100 things I feel guilty about' list.

'Dad will be okay, Emma. I could have kept the status quo to keep him happy, but I've been doing that for over twenty years. It's not a trial separation; I can't go back to your dad. I felt like I had no future, nothing to look forward to, no one to dress up for—nothing to get excited about. One day Dad will get over this... but if I went back, I would never get over it.'

She was sad and quiet, but seemed to understand, and was measured enough to see it from both sides and take it quite well.

The following few days were difficult. I was happy, ready to make a new life, and had no regrets about what I'd done—but after twenty-four years with someone, it took a little while to readjust.

Sue had been a wonderful support and had said I could stay as long as I liked in her spare room. I would pay rent, but wanted to thank her so suggested we take a lunch break at the Pizza Express across the road. I couldn't afford anything too fancy, but wanted to make Sue feel special and appreciated.

Before we'd even looked at the menu, we ordered a glass of wine each, some breadsticks and a bowl of olives.

'I know it's 796 calories for a whole pizza, but I've had enough of the Cambridge for now. Gayle Jones (spit-roast with a footballer, millionaire hubby) was telling me how this friend of hers had dieted like mad, starved herself to get into her wedding dress. She wouldn't celebrate her sister's twenty-first because she couldn't go near cake, she ate celery for Christmas Dinner and even missed her own hen night...' Sue said from behind the menu.

'Then... guess what happened, Faye? This woman was walking out of the church, size ten wedding dress, confetti everywhere, and a gargoyle landed on her head and killed her!' she slammed down her glass in a mini re-enactment.

'Oh, God, that's awful,' I sighed, suspecting it was yet another apocryphal tale from Gayle Jones's treasury of Z-list celebrity stories. 'And the moral is "don't go on a diet or... you'll be killed by falling gargoyles"?'

'No. The motto is "life is short and we have no control over our destiny..." It's fate, all in the stars.'

'Yeah, you can do all that Mystic Meg stuff, Sue, but I reckon the real message is "life's short—eat cake." When you think of all the Black Forest gateaux that bride could have had?' I sighed. 'Okay, I don't agree, but I like your theory—it's a good excuse to have a pudding.' She smiled, and, as we waited for our 796 calories of pizza to arrive, we dribbled over the dessert menu.

I lifted my head from photos of cheesecake and ice cream and my eyes met with a guy on a nearby table. He had a kind, handsome face and was so attentive to his daughter it made him even more attractive to me. 'I bet he's a lovely dad,' I said to Sue, nodding discreetly whilst watching him and sucking hard on a bread stick, completely oblivious to the body language I was sending out. I found myself imagining whether he was still with the girl's mother and what he was like... naked—and, okay... what sex would be like with him.

Sue gave me a look. 'You've been lusting after men a lot lately, haven't you, Faye?'

'Yes, I have,' I sighed, gazing at him.

'I told you—it's your age. You've only ever been with Craig and you're a Leo, love... you want to roar a little and take a walk on the wild side. You're wondering what sex would be like with another man... and you're worried you'll never find out,' she said, waving her breadstick at me.

'Sometimes I'm convinced you can read my mind. Forget Mystic Meg—meet Psychic Sue,' I said.

'Well, I don't blame you. It's a new beginning, Faye. Sow your oats; a little bit of lust never did anyone any harm.'

'Yeah,' I smiled. 'I'm not ready for any of that yet... I'm only looking.'

'No harm in looking, either,' she said, taking a sip of wine.

'I've been looking a lot lately,' I giggled. 'I play this game at the supermarket where I spot someone quite attractive and try to work out what kind of man he is from the contents of his basket.'

'And have you found the perfect "supermarket man?" Sue asked with a giggle.

'Almost. I'm still working on it, but Waitrose is best; I reckon they are richer and classier and probably more intellectual.' I was probably looking for something that didn't exist—that perfect Waitrose man—a divorced Kevin Bacon lookalike three years older than me with a love of English literature and a second home in Tuscany. Waitrose men bought salmon smoked on whisky-charred chippings, pink salt from the Himalayas and coffee from the Blue Mountains of Jamaica. They cared about the world and what they put in their mouths, their bodies, their lives... their women... and I liked that in a man. But did he really exist? And would he want me if he did?

'I reckon *he's* a Waitrose guy, 'I said, watching the man on the other table. 'An evening with "Waitrose Man" would mean good wine, great food and stratospheric sex. Just a theory based on my own recent supermarket findings,' I added.

Sue raised her brows and I was vaguely aware we were both now gazing at this man, observing every move, every nuance. He leaned towards his daughter... and we stopped nibbling our breadsticks; like two hamsters we waited, alert, our mouths open. His daughter leaned in and he put his arm around her in that lovely protective way dads do. Sue and I looked at each other with an 'aw' face... and then he reached his hand under her chin, lifted it and... gave her a great big French kiss right in the middle of Pizza Express. With tongues. At lunchtime. 'Oh, shit... it's not his daughter,' I hissed, horrified and disillusioned as Sue and I choked on our breadsticks, averted our eyes and tried to stop laughing.

'Well, there goes your Waitrose theory,' she snorted. 'She must be thirty years younger than him. So what do your "supermarket findings" say about that?'

'They say that true Waitrose Man doesn't exist. I'm destined to a loveless, sexless future because I'm too old and past it even for men my own age. Life just isn't fair,' I sighed, watching the very young woman virtually licking the old man's face.

'You can say that again, love,' Sue took a big gulp of her wine. 'She's probably his fourth wife... she's doubtless got the third wife's soft furnishings in the back of her car now.'

I giggled and emptied my wine glass. It tasted so good and so warming inside, I ordered us another.

'A man can be with someone young enough to be his daughter—but if I went out with a younger man I'd be the talk of the salon,' I sighed.

'Talking about anyone in particular?' She was looking at me, breadstick poised, lips pursed.

'No,' I replied, but we both knew she was referring to delicious Dan.

'Well, I wouldn't blame you. It's about time you started to have some fun,' she said. 'You're clever and funny and so attractive, and you deserve someone better than Craig. I mean, he wasn't bad looking, but he always seemed so grumpy.'

'He was.'

We played with our wine glass stems, two women struggling through life in our own ways.

'Oh, love. It's hard being with them and hard being without them, isn't it? You and I married too young. Bloody hell—I hadn't a clue about anything when I first slept with Ken; I thought a clitoris was an exotic fruit!' she laughed.

'Yeah. I should have seen the writing on the wall when Craig packed a copy of *Know Your Lathe*, into his luggage on honeymoon,' I smiled, remembering how he'd folded the top of the page over with more tenderness than he'd shown me in the later years of our marriage.

Our pizzas arrived, along with our second glass of wine, and as Sue had a bit of a cold we decided it was medicinal.

'Young women today get to shop around a bit, don't they? If I had my time again I'd sleep with lots of men,' she said, biting the end of her breadstick.

'Yes, and me... and it scares me a bit to think about what lies ahead, but there's nothing to stop either of us now, Sue,' I said, raising my glass to hers. It wasn't too late anymore and I could do anything I wanted in this new single life. It was so intoxicating, I wanted to laugh out loud with excitement and anticipation... and fear.

'I told you, it's our hormones,' Sue said. 'We're both looking at men like we did when we were teenagers... too much cholesterol.'

She meant testosterone, but she'd be right on both counts in my case, I thought, finishing my cheesy pizza and wishing I'd been good and had the salad. '

We ate dessert, drank coffee and walked back arm in arm with a bounce in our step, feeling so much better. Lettuce never tasted like pizza and cheesecake, and I don't care what they say— cheesecake *does* taste as good as slim feels.

❋ ❋ ❋

Later that afternoon, I popped out for something nice to have with our afternoon coffee. Yes, I could have gone elsewhere, but I thought, as we'd had an Italian lunch, we'd keep the theme going—so I went into the deli.

Dan was standing behind the counter chatting to some guy about the French Brie and fig jam and I stood nearby, looking around the shelves, just listening to his lovely voice. 'There's this really great fig jam?' he said, ending in that high inflection of the Aussie accent. 'When I first tasted it, with the brie, I was so excited.'

The way he said *exoided*... I heard soft, sugary sand, tumbling waves and sunshine. I loved that he got excited about fig jam; it was something I could get excited about too, and I made a mental note to buy some with a slice of brie next time.

I picked up a packet of Florentines—they would be perfect and keep Sue (and me!) on the 'high' we'd had since lunchtime. Sue's company had definitely cheered me up, but just seeing Dan and listening to his lovely voice was even better than the Veneziana Romana pizza. My heart was pounding and a thrill shot through me every time I glanced at him. It occurred to me that next time I wanted a 'sugar high', I should just come and gaze at Dan in the deli. I'd lose twenty pounds in a fortnight, I thought, smiling secretly.

'Hey, you look happier than you did the other day,' Dan said as the customer moved away from the counter and he spotted me.

'Yes—a nice lunch with some good wine and lovely company is better than Prozac,' I said.

Shyness, stupid teenage embarrassment and the two glasses of wine at lunchtime caused me to plonk the packet of biscuits onto the counter with a little too much enthusiasm. This caused my bag to fall off my shoulder, sweeping the bowl of olives, artisanal breads, and several more Florentine packets off the counter and crashing onto the floor. I was mortified.

Within seconds he was on his knees wiping up the mess, no doubt wishing I'd just paid and left. I wanted to die, and with my head bowed over the Florentine shards on the olive-oiled floor, I heard Craig's voice scolding, reminding me how clumsy I was.

'I'm so sorry... I'm so stupid and clumsy. Let me pay for these,' I muttered, wondering just how much this was all going to cost.

'No, it's no problem,' he smiled. 'You're not stupid or clumsy—it's the way I'd stacked them,' he added, scooping up the pack and all its Florentine fragments. I was waiting for him to be angry, or irritated at least, but he was so laid-back, so easy, he just kept smiling. He was kneeling holding one of the packs of smashed biscuits, and he looked up at me as I gathered a fistful of olives.

'These Florentines are made from the best Mediterranean almonds, you know?'

I nodded at him down on the floor.

'They have been finely crafted, delicately covered in Belgium's finest chocolate and hand-packed with love,' he said.

I nodded again, feeling a little awkward, but I liked listening to him; it gave me an excuse to gaze into his laughing eyes.

'They then endured the long journey from Rome, through Milan and Zurich, before flying first class across the Alps...'

He was looking at me. I pulled my mouth down on either side in mock dread.

'And do you know what, Faye? They stayed intact.' My mouth stayed in the same shape as the olives now squidgy in my hand.

'Hey, but two minutes with panda lady and they are totally destroyed,' he finished, smiling at me.

I laughed. 'I'm not "panda lady"—do you see a panda anywhere here?'

'Yes,' he said in mock seriousness, standing up and pointing at me.

'Do you know I've not worn that panda hat since you made fun of me... and it was warm. I liked it.'

'Ah, that's a shame because you did look cute. When you weren't smashing stuff up and bursting into tears.'

'Yes, I'm sorry about... all this.'

He took a fresh pack of Florentines down from the shelf. With his back to me, I noticed how his jeans hung on narrow hips, like they were a little too big—but it looked good.

He turned round and I offered to pay for them again but he wouldn't hear of it. 'I love broken biscuits,' he said, walking behind the counter. 'In fact I have just had an idea—I could bake a cake with those broken-hearted Florentines. If you are around tomorrow, you should come in and try it... take a piece for your broken-hearted friend.'

'Oh, Sue? Yes, it's all gone a bit pear-shaped again for poor Sue,' I smiled, regaling him with more of Sue's dating exploits. He laughed in all the right places, which showed he was listening. I liked Dan, and I liked making him laugh; it made me feel like I existed.

'Oh, God, is that the time? I have to go... I have a "Spiteful Scarlet" at three,' I said, and when he looked confused I promised to tell him all about 'the Lithuanian situation' when we next met.

'Come in tomorrow—tell me all about it and you can try your broken Florentine cake,' he said.

I walked towards the door, but in my rush to leave while attempting to defy facial gravity, I slipped slightly on the olive slick left from my earlier disaster. I shot quickly across the floor, grasping at the basket of artisanal breads to break my fall, which sadly just came with me.

I managed to save myself from landing on the floor but it looked weird that I'd just moved the bread display three feet while doing a strange jerking movement, which had been necessary to get my balance back. I stood back, admiring the bread basket in its new position like I'd just done a little product dressing on my way out. I thought I'd got away with it and hoped to God he hadn't noticed, but as I turned to say goodbye, he was laughing. I rolled my eyes like it was all the fault of the artisanal breads.

The delicious continental titbits that had excited me on my first visit were now a crime scene, and if I didn't get out quickly, weighty hams may crash from their ceiling hammocks, whole trays of freshly baked croissants let loose from their moorings... and I would be on my back in the centre of this epicurean carnage.

'I'll get that cleaned up... could be a disaster,' he chortled.

I apologised again and reached for the door, hot and flushed with embarrassment.

'So... your lunch... was it a romantic lunch by any chance?' he asked.

'Oh, you mean today? No it was Pizza Express with Sue.'

'Oh... I ask because you seem... happy... or is that the wine?'

'That'll be the wine,' I nodded, thinking it was probably hormones, and making my escape before I caused any more damage.

Was it the wine, or was it being near him that made me feel so overwhelmed? He wasn't my usual type, but that smile, his love of food and lovely voice were utterly delicious.

'I've not tried the Pizza Express... is it good?'

'Yeah... I like it.'

'I should try it out while I'm here... we could go together, one lunchtime?'

'Yeah...' I probably sounded reluctant, when what I really meant was, 'Oh, *God, yes*... When?' I wasn't sure how to handle this; it had been many years since anyone of the opposite sex had suggested lunch with me. Was it a date, did he want to spend time with me, or did he genuinely just want to see the inside of Pizza Express? I decided it was too risky to hang around and find out. I was still flushed at having smashed most of his biscuits and hurled olives around his shop. I wasn't going to risk one of my Tourette's-style conversations talking about going out for lunch with him. I wasn't going to say one more word or cause one more disaster in the deli, so decided to leave on a high. 'I must go. See you,' I called, lifting my face up to defy gravity so my wrinkles weren't quite so obvious.

I walked down the high street back to work feeling ten years younger. He'd smiled at my clumsiness and laughed with me as I slid around in olive oil moving bread displays across the floor at high speed. Dan had a calming effect on me and, despite the embarrassment and untold damage I'd just caused in the deli, he didn't make me feel foolish and hate myself.

Chapter Eight
Porn Star Martinis and Broken-Hearted Cake

Emma would be coming home for Easter and, although it seemed an eternity away, I couldn't wait to see her. I'd already planned her favourite dishes and bought her a number of little gifts: a beautiful scented candle that had cost almost a day's pay; a lovely gold notebook; and, of course, several special Easter eggs. The problem with buying any chocolate so soon is that I always eat it, and I had already had to replace some of the Easter eggs. Craig always said I bought Emma too much but, in spite of her parents' break-up, I wanted Emma to take pleasure in coming home for the holidays, not dread it.

Work was much the same, with Mandy suffering from her usual hangovers and filling everyone in on her raucous nights out, and the day after the broken Florentines incident at the deli, she was helping me. I was doing Jan Weston's new 'Kelly Hoppen' look (not an easy ask on someone with straight black hair) and Mandy was free so said she'd pass me the curlers. Jan's husband had just left her and she was going for 'sophisticated older woman, Dragon's Den interior designer chic', in a vain attempt to peel him off the twenty-something blonde he'd abandoned her for.

'Okay, I may or may not have tried to fly-kick people in the street,' was Mandy's comment on her previous evening's drinking session.

'Fly-kicked?' Jan looked horrified.

'Oh, it's a turn of phrase,' I lied, hoping Mandy would get that it wasn't appropriate to say this in front of clients. For God's sake, this woman was in a fragile state and the last thing she needed was to be in fear of a sudden, involuntary fly kick to the head from the resident Beauty Therapist of The Heavenly Spa.

'Dude, after twenty-four Jaeger bombs, even *you'd* start fly-kicking...' she chuckled to herself as she handed me another roller.

'I can assure you I wouldn't,' I smiled at Jan, willing Mandy to stop. I tried to give her a look, but she was back in last night. 'So, we're on the floor, Kat's humpin this dude's leg and Flick's flashin her...'

'Can we leave Jan's hair and check it in ten minutes, please?' I said, desperately trying to manoeuvre her away and lock her in the bloody 'Heavenly Spa' before we arrived at the inevitable.

'Ten mins, yeah, yeah...' But she didn't budge and Jan was turning pale green. 'So, there I am, lyin in the road, when this guy rolls up—and you'll never guess what he says?'

'We must stop meeting like this?' I offered, trying to turn what I knew was going to be disgusting into a U-rated comment.

'Nope. He says, 'Can you catch? Cos you've got two balls comin your way...'

At this, I wrapped a towel very quickly and tightly around Jan's head, in the vain hope she wouldn't hear the X-rated diatribe Mandy was about to issue. No one needed to hear any more. Hadn't poor Jan suffered enough? All she wanted was a little Dragon's Den glamour sprinkled into her dark existence of betrayal and abandon.

I excused myself, leaving an alarmed Jan with her head wrapped tightly in a towel, and manoeuvred Mandy to the wash basins for a private chat, 'Mandy, don't talk in front of the clients about your... night life. But... do you know how dangerous it is to have sex with someone you picked up on the street?'

'Yeah...'

'You can't just say yes to the first person you meet...'

'Oh, we didn't actually have sex on the street... well, not quite. We went back to his.'

'No, Mandy, I don't mean literally *on* the street. It's all wrong on so many levels, love. You're better than that—you're a lovely, attractive girl and you need to believe in yourself,' I sighed, patting her shoulder. I walked away, I always felt somehow responsible for Mandy.

'Okay. I know I shouldn't sleep with strangers,' she called over from the washbasins. 'But I'm not a slag, Faye... I made him buy me a kebab first.'

'You and I will have a talk later,' I smiled. She mistook this for approval and smiled back proudly.

I was 'in recovery' when the shop door tinkled, so held my breath and asked Mandy to keep an eye on Jan while I dealt with the customer. I daren't let her loose on reception—the uninitiated weren't ready for Mandy's weekend activities. Breathless, I landed at reception and looking up and was greeted with the loveliest smile. Dan was there and he was holding what looked like a cake box. It struck me with huge embarrassment that Dan may be under the impression my lunge across the salon had been my attempt to leap at him and it might have looked desperate. 'I wasn't running like that towards you because... I wanted to get *at* you. I don't mean get *at* you... in a weird way, I wasn't jumping on you, I mean. No. I had to get to you before Mandy arrived and talked about sex in the street!' I said, like this made everything clear.

'I'm sorry?' he looked a little crestfallen. Oh, God, I'd done it again. Here he was standing there with what looked like a cake and I have to ruin a beautiful moment.

'Oh... sorry. I don't know what made me say that. You didn't need to hear that. God, I mean, it's just... just Mandy—she talks about sex all the time and... I'm going to stop talking now.'

'I think that might be a good idea,' he smiled down at me like a kind teacher. 'I thought I'd bring you the results of the carnage you caused the other day.' He was holding up the box.

'Oh... I was going to call in but I've been really busy,' I lied, reddening at the memory of scattered olives and smashed Florentines.

'As you were the cause of it, you and your friends should get to taste it,' he smiled, putting the box on the counter top.

'Oh... that's a shame... sharing? Sorry, I don't share cake. As I was the one who broke the Florentines, I assumed the cake would be all mine?' I said, in mock disappointment.

'No, I'm afraid that's your punishment: you have to share this cake with your friends,' he teased, leaning in to whisper to me, 'So where's the one whose husband left... the online dating queen with the Darth Vader lover?'

I giggled, overwhelmed by how good he smelt close up, like sunshine and beaches. 'Sue's in later today—had a bit of a night with a new man... no light sabre but I think he stayed over... that could mean anything.'

'Sounds like she may be in need of some of this broken-hearted Florentine cake.'

I nodded and peered into the box for a more intimate look at the thick, fudgy topping with shards of broken Florentine poking out (artistically) and chunks of glace cherry studded in the icing like little rubies on brown velvet.

I smiled, licking my lips and imagining the crunch of Florentine against the squidgy denseness of chocolate fudge. Dan seemed so keen for me to sample the cake, I ran into the back for a knife and emerged within seconds to cut it.

As I cut into the gooey topping, I wondered briefly if the chocolate icing would work as well as chocolate body paint on the Adonis standing before me.

'What the bloody hell are you two up to?' Dan and I jumped apart as Mandy's dulcet tones pierced the air. 'Hey, you're the guy from the deli... G'day cobber,' she said, nudging his arm like they were old friends. He smiled at her, taking in her long, slim legs, tiny waist and big blue eyes. Her hair was long and shiny black and she tied it loosely, her youth and beauty not reliant on a mane of black hair, merely accentuated by it. He was looking at her quite intently, and I was surprised at the sudden sting in my chest.

'Hey, was it you on that podium at "Hot Latin Nights" last Wednesday... you know, with all that water spray?'

He was amused and caught my eye. 'No... I definitely wasn't on a podium last Wednesday—Thursday perhaps?'

His eyes twinkled, but Mandy was in Mandy-land. 'Ha! Well, I was on the Porn Star Martinis so I don't know what I did or who with... well, you don't know what happens until it happens, do you?' She paused for breath and I saw the surprise on his face. He was assimilating this beautiful young woman who looked like European Royalty with her apparently colourful social life—on the surface the two just didn't compute.

'It was a good night, Bruce... you'd love the Porn Star Martinis—they make you do crazy shit. Hell, you're only young once so go for it, I say.'

'That sounds like a good philosophy for life,' he offered, but her attention was now distracted by the fabulous confection in front of her. Like a little girl, she forgot everything to stand on tippy toes and peer into the opened box, then look to me for an answer.

'Dan brought homemade cake,' I said in my mother voice, cutting into the fudgy icing, cracking the Florentines and wanting to push it all in my mouth with my hands. I handed Mandy several pieces on napkins and she passed it around the salon while I cut myself a small slice (I wanted a huge great wedge of it and hoped he was leaving it with us so I could commune with it in private later). I bit into it and the combination of brittle, sweet nutty Florentine with deep, soft melting icing was truly orgasmic. I tried not to groan with pleasure.

'Did you really make this?' I asked him, seduced by the light sponge, sweet, crunchy nuts and those firm brown arms sprinkled with blond hairs.

'Yes... I did. You were my inspiration.' I looked up and I swore he was looking into my eyes longer than he should.

'So I'm a cake muse...' I said randomly, finding it hard to take my eyes away from his.

'This is sick,' Mandy hissed through crumbs and chocolate.

'What's sick? I'm only forty-two—I can talk to a guy, can't I? For God's sake, Mandy—you and Emma seem to think anyone over forty doesn't have sex,' I huffed. 'I don't mean you, Dan, don't think that... Well, I don't know what you think about me having sex; it's... not something that... I'll stop now.'

He nodded, with a wink and a smile.

'I meant the cake... *sick* means good, Faye. I never said anything about you having sex...'

'God, Mandy, you can't go five minutes without talking about sex... If it's not sex, it's body paint, people putting chocolate over each other and licking it off, and...' I turned slightly pink. My Tourette's had officially taken over. 'Chocolate body fudge icing and...' the joint stimulation of a handsome man and chocolate cake had been too much.

Dan just stood there, taking it all in, no doubt horrified and wondering if he'd walked into a hairdresser's or a lap-dancing bar. Since his arrival I had completely filled the air with sexual references while pushing chocolate cake into my mouth. Forget a lunch date in Pizza Express—this is the last I'll see of him, I thought.

At this point, Sue appeared in the doorway, like an angel. She introduced herself to Dan, eyed up the cake and looked from me to him in that way that implied she knew exactly what was going on between us.

'I'll get off then,' Dan said hesitantly.

'Okay... Thanks for the cake.'

'Hey, you should try my lemon cakes... I use an old recipe of my mum's... I'll make some for you.' He leaned forward and whispered in my ear, 'I don't make lemon cakes for anyone, you know.'

'Really?' I smiled my most sensual smile, while trying to hold my stomach in—multitasking at its finest—he really did smell incredibly good and I just wanted to breathe him in. 'I bet you say that to everyone.'

'No,' he looked genuinely affronted, so I dropped the sensual and went for something a little more 'teasing'.

'Oh, I bet there are lots of pretty young girls just dying to try your lemon cake,' I batted my eyelashes but was aware Sue was watching me and felt very self-conscious.

He leaned towards me and said in a low voice, 'Yeah, but I don't like girls... I like women.' This took my breath away. He was really close, his warm breath in my neck, his hand on my shoulder.

'Is that yours?' he suddenly said, nodding his head towards my copy of *Jane Eyre* on the reception desk.

'Yes, I've just started it.'

'Yeah? I'm reading it too. I thought I should read some decent literature for a change so I made a list of all the books I wanted to read while I was away. I have a couple of Aussie ones on there too... and American. I have spent my life reading crap and I'm finally going to educate myself.'

'Me too. I had to drop out of an English Lit degree and I've always regretted not finishing it,' I explained. 'Anyway, I grabbed a copy of my daughter's book list—she's doing English at Manchester. I thought it would give us something to share and she can help me to understand it... if she gets time.'

'We should swap notes,' he said, picking up the book and reading the blurb on the back.

'Yes, we should.'

'Okay... what about next week? Let's meet up for a beer and discuss *Jane Eyre*.'

I was now aware the salon was quiet and everyone was probably listening, but heard myself say, 'Yeah, that would be great.'

He waved goodbye and smiled, like I was a mate. Perhaps that's what he meant—a beer with a mate? As the door closed behind him, the chatter and dryers started up again behind me. I daren't look round because my face must have been very red, and I was so elated, I had this overwhelming compulsion deep within me to suddenly sing Rihanna's *You Da One* at the top of my voice, which thankfully I resisted. It may have caused concern to the clients and even got me sacked.

I smiled, pretending to be engrossed in the appointment book. I couldn't believe he'd asked me to go for a beer with him. It was one up from lunchtime in Pizza Express... A beer was night-time for a start—but I was new to this and still not too sure in what capacity he'd asked. Was it a date? Was it a beer? He'd said we could swap notes on *Jane Eyre*—oh, God was it a bloody book club? Going out with someone of the opposite sex was different these days, so I told myself not to get too excited. This could just be a beer and friendship based on a mutual love of Charlotte Bronte.

'What was that you were saying before about not saying yes to the first guy who asks you, Faye?' Mandy shouted across the salon with a giggle.

I laughed and pulled out my tongue... just as he walked back in.

'Oh... hi, again,' I tried, pretending I was doing something very important on reception.

'I was just thinking...'

'Yes?'

'If we're going for a beer, we should... swap numbers?'

It was such a long time since anyone had asked for my phone number, I wanted to leap up and kiss him, but had to keep a lid on it or my inner Rihanna might beat me to it and start singing to him.

I gave him my number and he texted me his, then moved back, without a smile, looking directly into my eyes and walking slowly out of the salon. I watched him go and a feeling emerged from the pit of my stomach, flooding my veins like warm, sweet icing. I was addicted to sugar and I'd eaten broken-hearted Florentine cake while on a diet—but that's where it had to stop. I mustn't lose perspective; I was freshly single, very vulnerable and completely unworldly—while he was a major flirt and no doubt knew the effect he had on women like me.

He probably had a million young lovelies throwing themselves in his wake and he was just being nice to me because I appreciated cake in a shameless way no skinny young girl could. I wasn't stupid—Dan was not remotely interested in a hairdresser with ageing knees almost ten years his senior; he just wanted beer and book talk. Didn't he?

❄ ❄ ❄

'My hormones must be playing up again,' I said to Sue at the end of the day as I swept the salon. 'I'm like a bloody teenager lusting after every man I see.'

'Hmm... I saw the way you were looking at that deli guy this afternoon.' She pursed her lips then smiled.

'Oh, it didn't look like that did it? I wasn't lusting after *him*... just his cake,' I sighed. 'And what's the harm in going for a beer?'

'None, love. I think he likes you,' she said this slowly, pretending to be scrubbing at a spot of dye on the chair, but waiting for my reaction.

'Oh, it's just a beer...I'm too old for him.'

'Yeah, I suppose you're right,' she said. 'But he's definitely got a soft spot for you.'

'Do you think him asking me for a beer is a date?'

She stood back, looking at me. 'Yes, of course it is. You should make the most of it—a real date... it's better than bloody speed dating.'

'Christ, I couldn't go through that. My already crushed ego doesn't need to be rejected by multiple men on the same night,' I sighed.

'Same night? Same hour? Last Wednesday they were in and out of there like a rat up a drain; all the skinny young girls got picked and I was left sitting on the gym vault with the losers, metaphysically speaking. Anyway, you did the right thing saying yes to Dan—he's very attractive...'

'Do you think he's too young for me, Sue?'

'Do *you*?'

'No.

'Then stop worrying about what everyone else thinks and just go for it.'

She was right. I carried on cleaning, thinking about what I'd wear if we did meet for a beer. What did people wear these days for a beer anyway? I didn't have anything suitable and would have to wear lots of make-up to cover the wrinkles.

'You'll need a push-up bra if you're going on a date,' she said. 'I bet girls he goes out with are pert and... you're quite well endowed but, let's face it, over thirty-five it all goes south, so if nothing else you'll need to lift them.'

I winced. I was only going for a beer; did my gravity-defying breasts really have to be hoisted up for a night in the pub?

'You'll also need to work on your sexual techniques, buy lingerie, sex toys… a rampant rocket.'

'I don't want a rampant anything Sue—I'm going for a beer, not turning tricks.'

'Oh, everyone's got them these days, love. Men expect a lot in bed too; it's not like when we were teenagers and you could get away with a quick blow job and half a pint of cider. They see it all on the Internet… they think we're all bloody porn stars now. Take it from me that Dan will think there's something wrong with you if you don't have something with a battery in the bedroom. You can buy them online now. I blame the rampant rocket for Ken's first affair… the one with Dawn from next door.'

'Rabbit… you mean a Rampant Rabbit?'

'Yes, at it like rampant rabbits they were. He was jumping over the fence… who'd have thought it? Dawn on the doorstep… all toothy smiles and big boobs and, "Can I have a cup of sugar?" No wonder that fence needed constant creosoting; it was worn down with him slipping over it every afternoon. And there she was with her big bust and her O-level French, turning his head with dirty talk and sex toys… men love sex toys.'

I swallowed hard. This brave new world of women on top and online toys in sparkly pink was scary for a separated forty-something who'd only slept with one man. How was I expected to compete with the likes of Dawn with her huge breasts, dirty French mouth and extensive collection of sex rockets?

'It's a jungle out there,' I sighed, gazing ahead and rubbing up and down hard on a foaming water tap and wondering what I'd let myself in for.

✱ ✱ ✱

A couple of nights later, Dan called me. He suggested we meet in The Bell, the local pub, the following evening. I said that sounded great and made small talk while trying hard not to dwell on Sue's advice about taking along a bag of vibrators and sporting a push-up bra.

I arrived a few minutes after eight so I wouldn't be standing there on my own and was relieved to see him already at the bar.

He smiled as I walked in, and as he embraced me to say hello, I felt sunshine warmth on my face.

'You look lovely,' he said. I was wearing Sue's blue linen dress with wedges, a layer of fake tan and my hair tied up. I'd felt casual and very summery at home, but looking around the pub as he ordered my drink, I suddenly felt overdressed. I glanced over at Dan in jeans and an old T-shirt and realised I would seriously need to learn the art of dressing down if I was going to go out with younger men. It was all so new to me; the only time I'd been on nights out recently was with the girls and then we'd dress up to the nines. This was different—this was casual, it might not even be a date... and he was in his thirties.

He handed me my glass of wine and we went to sit in more comfortable seats in the corner.

'So, Faye, you're a single mum?'

'Well... I suppose so. I'm separated... it's quite recent, although we've been estranged for a long time.'

'Oh... I'm sorry.' He looked surprised. 'Well, I'm not really sorry.' He gave a wicked smile and my heart melted. 'I assumed you were single—I've never seen you wearing a wedding ring.'

'I had to take my wedding band off a few years back as it would get caught up in hair and the chemicals can damage jewellery.' I said this like I believed it, but suddenly I wasn't convinced it was true. I'd actually taken my ring off around the time I'd opened my secret savings account. Along with the pink rucksack of precious things, I reckon I'd been subconsciously planning to run away from home for quite some time before I found the courage to do it.

'So, when will you go back? To Australia... you must miss it... the weather and everything?'

'I'm planning to go back home in the autumn. It'll be our springtime then and the right time... for me. I'd always planned to do Europe this summer...'

I did a quick calculation in my head. 'So you're only here for another four or five months?'

He nodded. 'Yeah. I haven't really decided how long I'll stay in the UK though. A friend of mine has a place in Santorini, said I can stay there if I fancied going... I went there a few years back. I love it there.'

My heart skipped a beat. A Santorini Sunset was on my living list. 'What's it like... Santorini?'

'Great. Amazing place... I was there with an American girl I was seeing. We stayed a few days and my friend was there too. It was good, but they ended up sleeping together.'

'Oh, my God—were you upset?'

'Me? Nah... she wasn't worth losing a friendship for.'

I was surprised at his lack of jealousy; he took everything in his stride.

'So, why now? Why are you doing a gap year at the grand old age of thirty-three?' I asked, keen to find out all about him.

'When everyone else was doing Europe, I was too wrapped up in other stuff,' he said. 'My mum became ill, Huntington's Disease. It damages certain brain cells and affects how you move, feed, live—it changes the person you are and it can take years, but you slowly get worse and worse and then... you die,' he said slowly, looking into his beer.

'Oh, Dan, that must have been awful... I'm so sorry.'

'Yes, it's a long, slow death sentence and it's caused by a faulty gene, usually inherited.'

I stayed silent so he'd continue, but he didn't need to; I'd heard, 'faulty gene' and 'inherited'.

'My bro and I were obviously high risk and were offered a test at eighteen. He went for it, but I was a coward; I... didn't want to know.' He took another sip of his beer. This was obviously hard for him to talk about, and I held my breath as he put down his glass and continued. 'I dropped out of university and went a little crazy for a while... stupid stuff. Drugs, women, drink... you name it, I took it.' He looked at me as if he thought I wouldn't approve. 'I broke some hearts, including my mother's. Do you still want to spend the evening with me?'

I took a breath. 'Yes, I do. I would never judge someone for reacting like that. Dan, you were losing your mother and there was every chance your own life might be cut short. Christ, I would probably have done the same.'

He shrugged. 'I don't even know why I'm telling you all this... but you are so easy to talk to, Faye. I like that about you. But I just feel like I failed everyone—my family, myself...'

He was clearly in pain and I just kept on talking to him to try and help him through it. 'When we're young, we all have these plans about the life we'll lead, the sort of person we'll be, but rarely does it match the reality... life gets in the way. We're not always the people we wanted to be. I understand how you feel.'

'I know you do.' He looked up at me, reached out and squeezed my hand.

I squeezed mine back and looked at him; 'Life gets messy. It has no respect for the plans you made when you were naive and filled with hope... You had such a lot to deal with at a very young age.'

'Yeah, I guess. But it's no excuse for running around town drunk and high while my Mum is dying. Anyway, I tried to turn things around, and on my twenty-eighth birthday, I realised that was how old my mum was when she first became ill, so I decided from that moment to live.'

I nodded, just listening.

'And around that time, I met someone.' He sighed. 'If I was going to live a better, cleaner life with someone else, I had to know what was waiting down the road for me... for us. Mum's agony had been the thought of leaving us all behind, and I didn't want to do that to anyone, least of all myself. So I took the test— but it scared me; I had a tough time waiting for the results, just hanging around to see how long I'd got. I told myself that whatever the outcome, I was going to start to live and do and see all the things I wanted to before it was too late.'

He looked at me. 'The chances of inheriting the gene are fifty-fifty... I tested negative. Guess my bro wasn't so lucky.'

I squeezed his hand again.

'My girlfriend couldn't handle it and she left. I knew if I stayed In Australia, I'd slip back into my old life too. The really terrible thing is that I haven't seen my bro for a while...'

'Why?' I asked, gently.

'Guilt? Fear? We were forced to play Russian roulette and he lost. His symptoms started last year and I can't bear to watch another person I love being eaten away by the disease.'

'Is there a cure?'

He shook his head.

'You are still feeling the guilt about your mum's death, aren't you? About what was going on in your life when she died?'

'Yeah... I guess.'

'You need to work through that before you can begin to face what's happening to your brother. I lost my mum and it's taken me two years not to cry when I think about her, cook a recipe of hers, watch a film she loved... but you were so much younger. You need to allow yourself to grieve.'

'Why should I be allowed that luxury? My mum spent her last few years wondering where I'd gone and my brother was told soon after mum died that he was going the same way... where's *his* comfort?'

'You're both probably going through the same horrors, just different sides of the fence...'

'I just remember how it was with my mum, and at the end I was there for her, when it mattered, but it was too late. I can't... I just can't deal with it.' His head was now in his hands. This wasn't the date night I'd been expecting, but my heart went out to him.

'Is your brother dealing with it?'

'Probably. He's my big brother; he deals with everything. He taught me to ride a bike, drive a car... if there was ever a problem, he dealt with it, like he's dealing with it now. I'm no use to anyone. He's my hero... I can't watch him die.'

I looked into his face and there were tears in his eyes.

'Faye, I'm a coward.'

'No, no, no. Don't say that. You will find the time and space to... to come to terms with it and share the burden with your brother. Perhaps you're just not ready yet?'

'Perhaps I need to grow up first.'

He sat up, lightened his voice; he didn't want to dwell on this. 'God, I didn't want to bring you down—this was supposed to be fun. Let's talk about you.'

'You don't have to pretend it's all okay just to keep things *fun*,' I said. 'If we're going to be friends, I want to know all about you—the good and the bad and the bits in between.'

He leaned his head towards me. 'Do you want to be just friends, Faye?'

I didn't answer him. Of course I wanted more than that with him, but was it too soon? Was I risking just another broken heart further down the line?

'I don't know, Dan. I haven't really had much experience with men,' I announced, stupidly. I'm sure that's on a list of one of the ten things *not* to say on a first date—and if it isn't, it should be.

'You're special and I knew it when I first saw you and then when you cried that time... about missing your daughter. It touched my heart.'

It was lovely to hear, but I felt almost embarrassed; no one had said stuff like this to me before.

'Oh, God, you make me sound wonderful, but really I'm not... I can be silly and childish and mean and... I say stupid things that are completely inappropriate at the wrong time and...'

He put his hand gently over my mouth. I had an urge to lick it. 'And... and the way you can't stop yourself from saying stuff, Faye... it's funny. I love it. You can't help it because you're so honest and you're just saying what you feel.'

I smiled and took a huge gulp of cold wine. It tingled into my chest. I was on a date and the guy was gorgeous, and despite the upsetting nature of our earlier conversation, he'd just made me feel like a million dollars.

'Faye, I reckon us meeting was fate,' he said, looking seriously into my eyes.

'Ah, so you believe in fate?' How romantic, I thought. 'My friend Sue of the online dating disasters believes in fate. She reads her stars every day and makes decisions on what to wear, whether to go and meet someone, what to have for tea based purely on them. I'm a Leo and she's constantly telling me I need glamour and passion... Who doesn't?' I giggled; 'What star sign are you?'

'I'm a Sagittarius, so, ironically, I'm the star sign that doesn't believe in astrology,' he smiled.

'Well, it may be because I'm a Leo with the sun in my seventh heaven or something like that, but I would love to travel around Europe like you. I've said no to a lot of stuff in my life, and what you said before about deciding to *live your life* and really embrace opportunities struck a chord with me.' I continued, 'Since my separation, I've made a promise to myself to say yes to everything from now on.'

'Yeah? Like what?' He leaned his chin on his hand and looked into my eyes, waiting, interested in what I was about to say.

I was a little disconcerted; I wasn't going to share my 'living list' with him yet. I knew he wouldn't laugh at me like Craig would have, but I didn't want him to think I was naive. 'Oh... well, it's early days and a bit scary, but nothing's come up yet for me to say yes *to*... When I say "yes to everything", I don't mean... anything—like I wouldn't say yes to sleeping with someone on a first date or anything... or not... I mean I wouldn't rule it out, it's just...'

'It's okay, Faye,' he chuckled, 'I know what you mean. What you're saying is that life's short and we just have to take it and run with it—whatever it is. Sometimes it's worth saying yes, especially to stuff that scares you.'

I nodded. 'That's it... exactly. And it's what I intend to do from now on.'

Later he walked me home and we embraced on Sue's doorstep like teenagers. There was no kiss—I wanted to, but I think all that talk from me earlier about not saying yes on a first date had made him wary of scaring me off.

'Can we do this again?' he asked.

'Stand on Sue's doorstep in the freezing cold? Yeah, sure,' I joked.

And we both laughed and I leaned into him and he kissed me on the cheek like a friend. Then I heard the lock on Sue's door, so I said I had to go and he said goodnight. I would have liked to stay talking to him a bit longer, but I wasn't ready to have some awkward three-way conversation in Sue's living room sipping tea from her best china. She meant well and I loved her but I would have given anything for some alone time and a little privacy. But just as I closed the front door and started to tiptoe upstairs, she was there. 'Come on, you... the wine's chilled and I want a blow-by-blow account.'

Chapter Nine

Strappy Dresses and Malevolent Blondes

By the beginning of March, the winds were dying down. Daffodils were emerging on side roads along which I walked from the car park to work. I'd been staying with Sue for almost three weeks. So much had changed and it was working well. I was slowly emerging from a marital cocoon where nothing had mattered—and now everything did. Life wasn't predictable and grey anymore; it was in colour. Like a head of mousy hair after a vigorous session with Cruel Plum or Sarcastic Scarlet, life was taking on a new vibrancy, and I loved that.

The mild air held the promise of strappy dresses, blonde highlights and chilled rosé wine after work with Dan or the girls. I was on my way to the salon, imagining a holiday to a sun-drenched beach somewhere in another country. Now it was a real possibility. As much as I loved the autonomy of my new life, it came with responsibilities and I couldn't blame Craig anymore for the things I didn't or couldn't do. It was up to me to do those things now and while I was giving myself time and space to work out what to do next, I was taking deep comfort in the fact my life was now in my own hands.

It had been over a week since I'd been to the pub with Dan. We'd chatted in the deli, exchanged a few texts and he'd suggested we meet up one night after work some time. It was all a bit vague and I was happy with that; I was enjoying my freedom and didn't feel ready to start a full-on relationship. I wasn't going to stop at the deli that morning, but as I passed I was completely bowled over by the window display. Yellow bunting, creamy-coloured cheese wheels, piles of lemons and limes, and in the centre a beautiful pyramid of lemon cupcakes. I sighed at the little gingham triangles strewn across the window framing the lemony sponge with the buttercream icing. It was a work of art and I was imagining a mouthful of lemon cupcake with rich, creamy topping when the bell on the door clanged and it opened. 'Hi, Faye.' Dan was carrying a ladder and looked so pleased to see me, I blushed.

'Hi...' I managed, surprised again at how good-looking he was.

'I thought I'd clean the windows—after all the hard work I've done on the display, I want everyone to see it,' he smiled.

'So you bake, you're well-read and artistic too. Is there no end to your talents? Do you surf? You look like you surf... not that I was looking... or anything...' I said, trying not to lick my lips at the thought of tongue-tingling lemon icing and Dan in trunks on a surfboard, hard thighs covered in sea spittle. He nodded. 'Yeah, I love surfing. Bondi has the waves for that—as high as skyscrapers.' He smiled at the memory as he straightened his ladder against the outside wall. He leaned on the ladder looking suddenly puzzled. 'Why didn't we talk about fun stuff like that the other night when we went for a drink? Sorry; I was on a bit of a downer.'

'Don't be daft. I had a great time.'

'Me too,' he said, holding me with his eyes. After a couple of beautiful seconds, he seemed to remember where he was. 'I'm hoping the window will draw people in,' he said, still leaning on the ladder and nodding towards the display. 'My aunt Jen's a bit worried; the shop's been quiet, like everywhere else on the high street. I want this to work for her... she was so good giving me this job, I really owe her one. You know?'

'Well it looks great; I'm sure it'll bring in the customers. I can't take my eyes from... it,' I said, trying to drag my eyes from him.

'Fancy a coffee?'

I was already late for work and was about to say so, but instead I said, 'Yeah... that sounds good.' My cut-and-blow lady could *hang* a while, as Mandy would say.

I followed him into the shop. Jen was behind the counter. I'd seen her in there before. She said hello, recognising me as a regular no doubt.

'It's great doing freshly ground... we get to smell fresh coffee all day now,' she said, wiping the counter top and tidying the display.

'Hey, we have some new biscuits in and a new kind of olive... Greek, quite bitter but delicious,' he said, excited as always by food.

'Hmm—you throw vague areas like "Greece" at me, but you know I won't buy unless you can tell me exactly where they came from,' I said, in mock seriousness. Jen looked up, a little surprised.

'I can't give you a grid reference exactly but I'm guessing somewhere in the south?' he offered, handing me a paper cup of coffee. 'Probably that olive tree in Crete... you know, near where the old Greek guy lives?'

'Oh, that one... where they tie the goat up? Okay. I'll have a small pot please...'

The last thing I wanted was salty Greek olives at eight thirty on a weekday morning, but it seemed to give him such pleasure to put them in a small polystyrene pot for me, I couldn't say no.

'On the house,' he winked at me. I looked at Jen and she smiled indulgently at him, seemingly quite happy for him to give her stock away.

'That's really kind. Thanks.'

'We never talked about *Jane Eyre*. Have you read it yet?'

'Yes, I have. I loved it. I have a weakness for Mr Rochester, all dark and brooding and masterful.'

'Oh, so that's the type you go for, is it?'

I lowered my voice, 'Yeah, but I have a weakness for light-hearted blonds.' I couldn't believe what I was saying. Wow, this new Faye was quite outrageous. *Go me*, I thought, trying not to blush.

We sat with our coffee on a couple of rickety chairs in the corner of the shop by a display of fancy chutneys and alcohol-laced jams. Looking at the fruit chutney reminded me of my day ahead.

'I've got a "Cruel Plum" this morning and I need to prepare—both mentally and physically,' I smiled, rolling my eyes as we sat down.

He looked puzzled. 'Oh, yes, the Lithuanian situation—you never did explain that to me?'

I quickly filled him in on the whole 'celebrity Hair Colour' farrago.

'I reckon I'm a malevolent blond... what do you think, Jen?' he asked, calling over to her.

'Ooh, I'm probably edging towards 'spiteful scarlet,' she giggled. She was nice, in her late fifties, attractive. He'd told me she was his mum's sister and I could see the family resemblance. We chatted a little longer, finished our coffee and I suddenly remembered the time and really had to leave.

'Oh, God... I've talked too much for too long as usual,' I said. 'I have to go.'

'Wait... one minute,' he held up his index finger and ran into the back. I stood for a minute or so, awkwardly smiling at Jen and wondering if I'd heard him correctly. Had he asked me to wait? Perhaps it was an Aussie thing to say 'one minute,' like saying 'see you later' to someone you knew you'd never see again? I was aware Jen was looking at me and I peered into the glass counter, smiling awkwardly if our eyes met and pretending to study the cheese. Okay, so this new sophisticated brazen Faye came and went a bit, but she'd settle in soon.

Then the shop door opened from outside and someone tapped me on the shoulder. 'Ooh, you dirty old cougar, Faye; you only come in here to have a perv on that Dan's arse, don't you?' Mandy shrieked. I almost died. Jen slipped discreetly to the other side of the shop and started filling shelves... she had so heard. Mandy was obviously on her way to work too and had spied me through the window as she passed.

'Shh! Keep your voice down. I came in for... coffee... and olives.' I lifted the empty polystyrene coffee cup like I needed proof I wasn't 'perving' over Dan.

'Oh, you can't fool me—coffee and olives... since when do *you* eat olives? You would love a grind on that...' she hissed, referring to Dan.

'I eat olives and I do not want to grind on—oh, Dan... I wondered where you'd got to...'

Dan re-emerged, smiling and holding a small box.

'G'day. Bruce,' Mandy piped up.

'G'day. Sheila,' he teased back.

He handed me the box, nodding at Mandy. 'Try these, ladies, and let me know what you think... Aussie sunshine in a box...' his fingers brushed mine as he took his hand away. My insides sparkled. I began stammering but tried to hold it in, and I must have turned scarlet because Mandy said, 'Faye, you've gone all weird. What's wrong with you?'

'Nothing... nothing.' I looked into the transparent top of the box and inside were six of the perfect lemon cupcakes from the window. Swirled with lemon cream and topped with a tiny slice of lemon, they looked delicious and so pretty I couldn't believe this handsome rugged guy had made them.

'Thanks, Dan. I can't wait to get my gob round one of those,' Mandy said, then she nudged me. 'Faye... Faye,' she was speaking under her breath, without moving her lips, 'will you get me a sandwich and I'll pay you back later?'

'We don't really have time...' I said, wanting to get her out of there before she said another word. She looked disappointed, like a little girl, and I was always a sucker for that. 'Oh, okay then. What do you want?' I muttered.

'Two bush oysters on wholemeal. I love those,' she whispered.

I looked up. Jen and Dan were both smiling expectantly.

I was surprised that Mandy even knew about oysters but was happy to encourage her enjoyment of fine foods: 'Oh, and can I have two bush oysters on wholemeal please?' I asked, in my 'foodie' voice, keen to impress.

'Kangaroo?'

'I'm sorry?'

'No, I am, because we don't stock them—but if you really want two kangaroo testicles on wholemeal, Faye, we'll order them,' Dan said, serious face, but his eyes were laughing.

I didn't know what to say.

'Bush oysters are kangaroo testes,' Jen smiled.

'I saw that on *I'm a Celebrity*,' Mandy sniggered.

'Oh, Mandy, you're awful,' I said playfully, feigning a giggle. Mortified, I began walking to the door, in the desperate hope that Mandy would follow. I wanted to leave before things went any more downhill.

'Thank you so much for making me say *kangaroo testicles* to Dan and his auntie,' I hissed as we left the shop.

'Ooh, get you, Faye Dobson... you've gone all shy, I told you... you're dying for a grind on that.'

Mandy had a point (not about the grinding, I hasten to add): I did have a thing for Dan. But I didn't want to make myself too vulnerable. I was surprised and a little horrified to discover it was apparent to others... especially Mandy. Yes, he was cute and I could see me kissing him on the lips, holding hands... but 'grinding?' I wasn't even completely sure what 'grinding' involved, but it certainly wasn't coffee or peppercorns in Mandy's world. Rather than batting their eyelashes, Mandy and her friends would apparently register their interest by wrapping their legs around the love object and 'grinding' up and down. I found it hard to imagine but one thing I was sure of in these uncertain dating days, approaching a stranger and mounting him like a dog on heat wasn't in my repertoire—now or then.

'I reckon he wouldn't mind a go on you, too,' she said as we walked along.

'A go? He'd like a go?' I smiled, playfully slapping her arm, horrified but delighted and intrigued. 'You are outrageous. Anyway, Dan isn't interested in an old lady like me,' I said, trying to sound dismissive but not achieving it, as she stopped and stared at me.

'Hey, I caught him red-handed,' she sniggered, speeding up to catch up with me. 'He was definitely eyeing your arse as we walked out of the shop.' She was giggling and nudging me with her body. 'And don't kid, Faye; you were definitely looking at his...'

'Anyway, stop going on about me looking at men's bums,' I added, keen to push her further on her theory that he liked me... or, as she so delicately put it, might like 'a go' on me.

'Oh, his arse is *okay*, but you should come to Faliraki with me and the girls... you'd love it, Faye. We see some sights...' she started, the previous conversation about Dan now lost forever in a sea of sick and Bacardi.

'My heart wouldn't take it, Mand... in fact just hearing about your exploits in the Med makes me shake,' I laughed, not wanting any further embellishment on Mandy's Greek holiday. It was too early in the morning and I couldn't take the intimate detail or the aftermath of hangovers and STDs.

I wanted a quiet morning alone and a chance to savour a lemon cake. I also wanted to think about him, go over and over what he said, the way he looked, swirl it around my head like a round fruity boiled sweet on my tongue.

As we entered the salon, I took off my coat and went into the back to hang it up, placing the box of cakes on the side. I went to leave, but was drawn back to the box, and as I was alone, carefully opened the lid. The fragrance of lemon filled the air as I carefully took one of the swirly little cupcakes out, holding the citrus sponge on my open palm. It looked delicious and I couldn't resist a second longer and bit into it. The sponge was light, with a lemony echo balanced by a sweetness that melted in the mouth. The buttercream was rich and bittersweet and my jaws ached with the sheer deliciousness. I'd never tasted anything quite like it—lemon, sugar and sunshine. This was indeed 'Aussie lemon cake', and I swear, on that cold March morning in the poky back room of a hairdressing salon somewhere in The Midlands, the Aussie sun was shining.

❋ ❋ ❋

Dan texted the following day and asked if I was free to go out one evening, but as Emma was due home I couldn't. On Friday, though, I popped into the deli during my lunch hour. I was like a teenager again, timing the point I would walk to the shop, excited about seeing him and at the same time a little scared. Breathless and dry-mouthed, I managed to wander in with an air of casualness I found hard to pull off.

'Hi!' I smiled, walking into the deli. The strong, salty smell of cheese and meat laced with the warm tang of freshly ground coffee filled my nostrils. I took deep breaths. He looked up. Oh, those big blue eyes, that blond hair, rough and choppy like the sea, his sleeves rolled up revealing the strong, brown arms, more boyish than big muscle-man... but man all the same.

He smiled when he saw me, his twinkly eyes immediately engaged, amused. Dan was one of those people who had an infectious fun about them that made you want to laugh with him. You didn't know what he was laughing at, but you just had to join in.

'I just wanted to say thanks, for the lemon cakes. They were delicious. I was a bit greedy and ate two,' I lied. 'What do you put in them? They are like catnip to a woman like me.'

'Yeah? It was my mum's recipe; she used to make them for birthdays and special times. She always told me there was a special, secret ingredient... but wouldn't tell me what it was... then one day I guessed.'

'And what was it?' I said.

'Ah... I'm not telling you... *you* have to guess.'

'I'll take a wild stab at it... lemons?'

'No, there are no lemons,' he teased. 'Mum always said to bake was to love, and if you didn't put love in your cakes, they wouldn't taste good,' he smiled at the memory. Then, perhaps feeling a bit silly, 'She was almost as bonkers as you.'

'Ha, she sounds perfectly sane to me.'

'Well, she would.'

'So,' I said in my sultriest voice; 'you squeezed some love in with that lemon juice?'

'Yes, but only because they were for you.'

'Good job it was only me that ate them then,' I confessed.

'What... you ate all six?'

'No... well, yes actually,' I giggled. I don't think he believed I'd eaten all six, but at least I'd told the truth.

'Anyway, I'm not here to talk about cakes. I'm here because there were a few bits and pieces I left intact last time,' I started. 'There's a whole sheet of glass here with cheese behind it... and who knows what havoc I could wreak with low-flying hams? Thought I'd have another go...'

He smiled and leaned forward on the counter just as I reached it. We both put our arms out at the same time and almost touched hands. There were customers about so I quickly moved mine and, though I'd arrived with confidence, suddenly felt it all melt away like lemon drizzle as I began to talk with too much enthusiasm about lemon cakes and what a wonderful baker he was.

'So... what you are trying to say in a roundabout way is... you like cake?' he said finally, when he could squeeze a word in. He was standing there bemused, arms folded across himself in a protective way, smiling, observing.

'Hmm... I came in also to...' (Christ, I hadn't thought this through. Sue said I mustn't be too keen and had to play it a little cool. She had a point; I didn't want him to think I'd gone there just to lust after him, which I had). 'Oh, what was it now... oh, yes, I came in for more of that coffee,' I said, inspired by the sight of the big, Italian coffee machine.

'Okay, just the one?'

'Yes, a latte please, with an extra shot. I like it strong. Like my men... not that I, you know, I'm not saying...' I shut up. He couldn't hear me anyway over the coffee machine. As he made the coffee, I shouted over the frothing noises and loud steaminess, asking if his mum had taught him to bake.

'Yeah, she did. It's one of my earliest memories—licking the spoon, helping her weigh ingredients, me covering the kitchen with flour. You wouldn't think it now... I'm not like most blokes; I tidy up after myself.' He was pulling levers, and I could barely hear him over the hissing steam.

'Wow, you'll make someone a lovely boyfriend... for someone... you're lovely and... hot... and hot coffee,' I stuttered, pointing to the machine like a three-year-old.

'My last girlfriend used to get fed up with my obsession with food and baking.'

'Oh.' I wasn't sure I wanted to hear all about his stable of stunning exes, all probably much younger and thinner than me.

'She used to say I was anal,' he added.

'There's nothing wrong with anal,' I shouted over the still steaming racket. 'Anal is good...' I added, turning to face Janet, our client, as she walked into the shop.

'Hi, Janet,' I gave her a little wave. She'd obviously heard what I said and gave me a rather disapproving look so I felt I should explain.

'Janet, when I just said to Dan that anal was good... I hope you don't think I was talking about that... anal...' I yelled over the noisy coffee machine. 'I meant it as an adjective—you know, like it's a good thing to be... I didn't mean anal like *that*...' I was now using hand gestures, but she just looked more horrified and I really had to stop. I was making it so much worse.

I could see Dan's shoulders shaking behind the coffee machine; he was obviously laughing to himself as he continued to pull levers and pour coffee. I obviously cracked him up—not exactly an ego boost—but at my age I took it where I could and was grateful for any kind of response from someone under forty.

Janet had just been in for her root touch-up with Sue and 'Fuming Flame' was living up to its name.

'I was... just talking to Dan about baking...' I tried.

'Sounds like that's not all you were talking about,' she said tightly, pursing her lips.

'Oh... I think you've got the wrong idea, Janet...'

'Can I help you?' Dan stepped in over me to shut me up. He was flushed with stifled laughter, his eyes twinkling in amusement.

I stood by as Janet bought two focaccia and a jar of olives, leaving behind a whiff of Lithuanian hair chemicals and strong disapproval.

'Oh, God. Janet's such a gossip; she'll tell everyone I was in here talking about anal sex and by this time tomorrow the story will have wings. She'll say she caught me on your counter, spread-eagled, shouting, 'Take me now between your big cheeses, chorizo boy!' God knows where that came from, but clearly my filter was off.

At this he collapsed with laughter. 'Faye,' he was wiping his eyes, 'you don't know when to actually stop saying stuff, do you? And then it just gets ...'

'Embarrassing?' I offered.

'Funnier... and, as I said the other night, more honest.'

'Yes, but I really wasn't talking about anal sex,' I insisted.

'No, I know... Don't start all that again,' he laughed, shaking his head. 'Anyway... who cares what anyone else thinks... free yourself up, Faye. You need a bigger landscape; you're too good for this place.'

I'd never thought of myself in that way before. I liked the idea and glowed at his compliment. He really seemed to like me and find me fun and honest, and I was beginning to like me through his eyes, too.

'So, apart from coming here to buy coffee, your main aim was to provide distracting sex talk?'

'Yes,' I smiled, 'distracting.' Oh, God, no one ever told me I was distracting before... I rather liked that too.

'So, do you have time to drink your coffee here... with chorizo boy?'

'Oh... yes, that would be nice,' I said, blushing and trying not to dwell on the image I'd just conjured of me on his counter demanding to be taken between his continental cheeses.

'If you just take a seat over there, madam, I shall bring it over,' he gestured towards a rickety table with bags of coffee piled on top and brought out a laptop from under the counter.

'While you're here, can I show you some ideas I've done, for Jen? I think she should do event catering from here... I'd love your thoughts.'

'Oh, yes... I'd love to see your ideas. My mum always said, "The best parties are catered, dear," I said in a posh voice, taking a seat.

'Yeah, Jen needs to make some more money. I worry about her, you know? I love this place; it would be a shame to see it close.'

'Oh, I hope it wouldn't come to that,' I said, shocked (how awful if it closed—no deli and no Dan).

'Yeah, well, that's why I came up with these menus... you need to branch out these days; nothing comes to you if you just sit around. You've got to be ready to go.' He grabbed the coffees and sat down opposite me. I couldn't help notice his legs in faded jeans were too long for the chair and stuck out awkwardly. I had a strong urge to reach down and run my fingers gently along his thigh. I wanted to feel the hardness of his legs underneath the faded blue. I wondered if the hairs on his legs were blond like the ones on his arms. I tried to push away the vision of him riding a huge wave to the shore. He was saying something to me and I had to focus and not think about his legs. 'Faye...?' he was saying softly, his head to one side. 'Let me show you my possibilities.'

'Oh, please, yes...oh yes, *yes...*' I smiled, sounding like a bad Meg Ryan.

I was imagining him on that wave, firm brown muscles, taut tummy, ocean spray on hard thighs... hair matted with salt and sun bleach. 'Faye... you okay?' I nodded.

My heart was racing and it was only a matter of time before I was openly discussing his naked thighs, or, worse still, on my knees rubbing them. I could hear Mandy's voice in my head saying something like, 'Don't creep him out.' I was trying very hard not to.

So he talked me through his delicious 'possibilities', as I nodded and licked my lips. He spoke of the saltiness of goats' cheese married to the earthy sweetness of fresh figs, the sublime tang of sun-dried tomatoes with spicy chorizo and the delicate crunch of homemade oat biscuits adorned with Manchego cheese and fresh apricot chutney. His voice wafted over me like a warm Mediterranean breeze as he recalled the first time he'd tasted buffalo cheese in Italy a few years before. He talked softly of al dente pasta with sour, melting parmigiano and salty prosciutto eaten under a Tuscan sun with a perfect Chianti. He shared with me the crisp, salty freshness of beer-battered fish and chips in Sydney Harbour, barbecued pork on the beach and chilled golden beers drunk by dying waves in a molten sunset on Bondi.

'I want to go where you've been... see what you've seen,' I sighed.

'Yeah... my mum never saw the world and I don't want to wait until it's too late.'

'I understand you wanting to travel, live like a free spirit, especially after what happened with your mum, but have you never wanted to settle down? Have a family?' I asked.

'Nah... I don't think I'm cut out for a mortgage and marriage... I've never really wanted kids. Maybe someday—who knows?'

'I think everyone should have kids if they can. Our children are our immortality,' I said.

'Yeah, but then some people live through their kids and don't live their own lives.'

'True, but while I'm worrying about leaving everything in my life too late—I will always be glad I had Emma. And having kids is something you should never leave until it's too late... you'd be a great dad.'

'You reckon?' He smiled at that.

'Absolutely!'

'Well, however we choose to do it, we owe it to ourselves to live the best life we can... kids or no kids. Ha. I sound like some hippy-dippy type don't I? But you have to chase that rainbow, Faye... it doesn't come to you.'

He made me think about my own life and how I now had the freedom to do what I wanted and go to all the places I'd dreamed

about. But did I have the courage to do it? For now I was just enjoying the view, happy watching those waves on Bondi... with him.

He closed the laptop slowly, looking at me. 'Why do I get
the feeling that there are a few un-chased rainbows in your
life, Faye?'

'Oh, I suppose you give up on rainbows when you get married and have kids... Rainbows are for other people.'

'Not necessarily.'

'I always wanted to travel... but that's for your twenties, isn't
it? You can't up sticks and see the world at forty-two. I've got a
daughter in uni and I've split up from my husband—there's too
much stuff to deal with here.'

'Yeah? But, Faye, you're a single woman now, so... give yourself permission to have some fun...'

Then he leaned forward and I looked into his eyes, denim
blue, like the sea. I'd never seen him this close before, but if I'm
honest, I'd been imagining it for weeks. His blond stubble rough
against the smooth, bronzed face; his lips, probably soft yet firm.
I studied those lips, trying not to lick my own. They were so kiss-
able. In the same moment we both leaned in instinctively and
our mouths touched awkwardly, dry lips together, then the wet-
ness of his tongue pushing gently into my mouth. The room was
spinning and I swear the stars came out. I was lost. It was only a
kiss but for me it was everything. I felt the sun on my face, and
in those few moments, I tasted another life and heard the roar of
the waves on Bondi Beach. Then, instead of melting into it and
just going with the waves, he pulled away.

'I'm sorry,' he said. 'It's just... I don't want you to feel like I'm pushing you into anything. You're not going to get back with your husband or anything are you?'

'No. My marriage was over long ago,' I replied, then reached out and pulled him towards me. Surprised at myself, I was kissing him this time, holding his firm, narrow back, my other hand moving up those delicious denim thighs.

We slumped down onto the floor, half-kneeling, both completely absorbed in the kissing, when the doorbell clanged as a customer walked in. We fell apart, he pretended he'd dropped some papers on the floor and I was helping him, both giggling like children caught stealing apples. I had to take refuge on the chair for a few seconds while he served the customer because my legs had turned to jelly.

I hadn't kissed another man for years and this had been like the first time for me. I was in a daze, brought alive by long-forgotten feelings and sensations. There was no turning back now.

He served the customer, then another came in, quickly followed by a couple more, so rather than sit in the shop gazing at him in a trance-like state, I decided to go. I was due back at work anyway and didn't want to be late for my client, so gathered myself together and left, giving him a girly wave at the door. He smiled back and I had to turn away or I may have collapsed in the doorway.

Walking out of the deli felt very different than it had less than half an hour before. I felt delighted and drunk walking down the high street of charity shops and pound emporiums which now appeared to me like the set of a Hollywood musical. I wanted to burst into song again.

That kiss had been so unexpected, like a beautiful firework exploding, reminding me that sometimes lovely things can happen completely out of the blue. For something like that to happen on an ordinary Friday in March—I couldn't help but believe anything was possible. Who knew what Faye Dobson was going to do next?

Chapter Ten

German Sausage and Australian Sunshine

It was almost Easter and Emma was coming home. This would be the first time she'd returned since the split so it would be quite traumatic for all of us. I'd had a few texts from Craig, usually to do with what settings to put the microwave on or when the window cleaner was due, but that was good. At least he wasn't crying on the phone or stalking me.

I had spoken to Emma on the phone and told her I didn't mind where she stayed (which was a lie) but that she was welcome to stay with me at Sue's or with her dad. She said she planned to stay for a week of her holidays with us, and, ever the diplomat, said she'd stay three days with Craig and three with me.

Though there had been texts, I hadn't actually seen Craig since I'd left for Sue's that night but I had to face him when I collected Emma. I went into the house to help her with her bags and he just nodded in acknowledgement like I was the bloody taxi driver. I felt nothing. And neither, it seemed, did he. Funny how you can spend more than half your life with someone and it all leads to zilch. Though I was only there moments, it felt strange to be in our old home with the two of them. I felt like an outsider.

'You know, Mum, I was upset when you first rang me and told me about you and Dad...' Emma said the following day when we went out for one of our special coffees.

'Oh, I'm sorry, Em. It wasn't an easy decision.'

'I know and I told myself it was better for both of you to be apart... but I cried a bit the first couple of weeks. I kept thinking, "I'm from a broken home," which really isn't the same when you're twenty and you've already left home!' She shook her head, stirring her coffee and smiling at the memory. 'Silly, really.'

My heart ached at this. 'Oh, Em, the one person I wanted to protect in all this was you.'

'Oh, it's okay, Mum... I worried about you both, but I knew you'd be okay because you've got Sue and the salon. It was Dad I was really concerned about... but to be honest, he seems okay. He's coping quite well, even talking about finishing the patio.'

'That's good,' I smiled. I felt guilty about Craig and Emma, so this was good news, to know her short homecoming hadn't been spoiled by me not being at the family home.

'At first I resented the fact you'd left him... Dad,' she sighed. 'I worried he'd just get worse without you... even grumpier, more insular. I don't blame you, but he's my dad and I love him... I do feel a bit sorry for him.'

'I do too. I feel guilty about going. I'd been feeling it for years but he didn't seem to have a clue. I think me going was a shock, even though I tried to prepare him for it.'

'I know, and as much as I love him, I do wonder how you put up with him all that time.'

'He wasn't always like he is now, Em,' I said, stirring my coffee. 'I wouldn't have married him,' I replied, wondering if in fact he'd always been moody and uncommunicative, but now my perception had changed. 'He was a lovely dad when you were little, always taking you to the park and teaching you to swim, ride your bike... but life changes you. Work and worry take over and we all turn into what we said we never would.'

We sipped our coffees and gazed around the café. It was raining outside.

'So, are you going to stay with Sue for a while?' she asked.

'A little while, I think. Sue's easy to live with, I pay her a small rent—and if and when we sell the house, I'll work out what to do next.'

'Will you buy a smaller house, Mum?'

'Not yet. I... actually I wanted to talk to you about that. I'd like to travel. I thought I might take some time off work. Sue says she'll keep my job for me and I could just see a bit of the world. What do you think, Em?'

'I think that's a great idea. I always felt sorry for you waving me off on school trips when you'd never been abroad because of Dad not flying.'

'So you wouldn't mind if I went away? New York, Paris and... oh, I don't know, I haven't really planned anything—just travel, you know?'

'Wow... yes. You should so do that, Mum.'

'I'd love to see Australia.' The mention of Australia stuck in my throat a little and as I said it I heard Dan's lovely voice. 'And Greece. I'd also love to go to Italy, too...'

'Be careful of the Italian men if you're going travelling, Mum. I'd worry about you being swept off your feet by some hot-blooded Latin.'

'Sounds great!' I smiled.

'Hey, I'm only just getting used to you not being with Dad—I don't want my mum sleeping around Europe, thank you very much.'

I blushed. Little did she know I'd almost got myself in hot water a little closer to home. I gazed round the coffee shop. It was busy for a Monday and we'd been lucky to find a seat.

'Mum, I need my hair doing,' she said, pointing to dark roots in her lovely blonde hair.

'I'll do it tonight if you like?' I said. 'Sue's on a date so we can have a girls' night in with face masks and I can do your nails too if you like?'

'Oh, thanks Mum, that'd be great, but I booked to go to that new hairdressers' in town, you know the one with the big screens. It's very trendy *and* very expensive but Dad said he'd pay, so I could hardly turn it down,' she replied, smiling.

'No... of course. You must take him up on that,' I smiled, sipping my drink, allowing the dregs of milky sweetness to soothe the spiky bits that had come up in my tummy.

It was perfectly natural that Emma wanted to go to fashionable hairdressers, in the same way she wanted the latest fashions. I smiled, looking at my daughter's tiny waist and beautiful long, blonde hair, remembering when mine was the same. Just because I'm her mum and happen to be a hairdresser, it doesn't mean I'm the only one who can do her hair, does it? I thought, placating myself. Yet I couldn't help but feel it was a fray in the ribbon of our relationship, a slight tear in our bond. This was healthy, I told myself; it was all part of her growing up and moving on. Yet inside I knew it was another reminder of her moving further away, living her own life.

It was also a reminder that Emma wouldn't need me around forever and that I had no more excuses to start living my life.

We were discussing Emma's hair colour when I spotted him through the human mist and coffee steam. It was still raining outside and his hair was wet. He ran his fingers through it, slicking it straight back, and it suited him. He was unshaven, untidy and unsmiling, and he looked like a film star to me. He was wearing outdoor boots with laces and a big overcoat worn loose and open, I wanted to climb inside and hold him to me. He looked so gorgeous it made my heart hurt, and the pang of longing flooded in.

I watched out of the corner of my eye as he stood in the queue ordering coffee. His eyes twinkled at the girl behind the counter, his face momentarily coming alive as he gave her his order, like he was telling her something really special. My heart soared and I let Emma talk without listening. I lost myself, remembering his voice and how it felt to kiss him. I nodded at Emma's detailed description of her hair, imagining my head on his chest, recalling our lips clumsily coming together, his tongue in my mouth.

He was still chatting to the girl behind the counter, laughing with her, and I was burning with irrational jealousy.

The girl was definitely flirting with him. I was trying to see how young and pretty she was. Long, black, shiny hair, dimples when she smiled, in her twenties... at that age you're pretty even if you aren't pretty. He moved further down the queue.

The girl's face was now a full-on beaming smile just for him. I knew how she was feeling; attention from Dan was like sitting in the warm, yellow rays of Australian sunshine. He laughed at something she said and my heart thumped down onto the table and rolled around in cold coffee froth.

'Mum, are you okay?' Emma was waving her hand in my face to get my attention. I had been lost for a few minutes and it took a second or two for me to 'regroup.' God, he had such an effect on me—I hadn't felt like this for a long time; it was just like being eighteen again. Emma looked worried. It wasn't like me to switch off mid-conversation, especially when I was with her. Our time together was precious and she was everything to me... how dare he distract me and interrupt our mother-daughter time with his blue laughing eyes and his damp blond hair.

We continued to chat about hairstyles, moving on to French manicures. And if you'd asked me, at any point during that conversation what was actually said, I couldn't have told you... but I could have told you exactly where he was in the queue, every facial expression and every single movement he made. Meanwhile, I constructed vague phrases about hair and nails, so Emma wouldn't suspect I was elsewhere. I wished I'd learned to lip-read so I knew what he was saying to the coffee girl. Hadn't I read in a magazine that Australians are culturally more promiscuous?

Now he was smiling at something she'd said and it felt like I was having a stroke. My heart was beating quite fast—was it the high caffeine content in the macchiato, or was I simply going mad? Fake nails, Vanilla lattes, lemon cakes, body chocolate ...kissing Dan... Dan... Dan.

As he left the queue with his coffee he spotted me and as our eyes met. I waved, not sure how to do this. What to say? 'Look, Emma, it's Mum's new toy-boy lover' just wasn't going to work.

He was walking towards us, slowly but definitely in my direction... Dan. I felt faint.

'Mum... Mum, are you okay?' Poor Emma was alarmed and grabbed my arm. She didn't need this, not now, not after what she'd been through already. Her brow was furrowed. She thinks I'm having a stroke... *I* think I'm having a stroke... *Am* I having a stroke? I didn't want this. Dan was my fantasy lover, my escape. I didn't want him meeting my daughter yet, it was all too soon. If he was going to come over, please God, let him be discreet, I thought. This is why love and lust should be banned for anyone over thirty-five, because an older body isn't resilient enough to take the stress of it all.

Perhaps I was too old after all to be planning world travel and lusting after free-spirited, taut young men from other hemispheres?

With sweat on my upper lip, and my voice louder than it should have been in such a small space, I informed a puzzled Emma we needed to go. I stood up suddenly, knocking over what was left of my drink and attempting to climb out from behind the table, to the amusement of a table of teenage girls

'Faye—hi?' He looked slightly concerned.

'Hi. Yeah... I'm great,' I muttered. 'I'm here with my daughter—Emma, Dan, you must meet Emma. Hey... it's... Emma...' I said, sounding like some crazed chat-show host, turning and introducing a still rather puzzled Emma. She knew me well and my high-pitched voice and unnecessary repetition of her name was textbook Mum-in-a-panic and bound to set her radar off straight away. Whatever happened, she mustn't guess the truth... that I had fallen madly and inappropriately in lust with a younger man whom I'd already kissed, and wanted to kiss again.

'I've heard a lot about you, Emma,' he said.

'Really?' Again she gave a puzzled look, slightly irritated even.

Through my mists of embarrassment, I was aware that Emma then asked him to join us, which I wasn't ready for.

'Thanks... if that's okay...' He looked at me. I nodded, my macchiato insides now swirling. 'I'm waiting for a friend,' he said, taking a seat.

'So how do you two know each other?' Emma asked. I almost choked.

She was quite charmed by this handsome Aussie, and giving him her full attention, which made me feel uncomfortable on so many levels. What if he fell for her and became my son-in-law? I was going mad... I always had to think ahead, worry about stuff that hadn't and wasn't going to happen. I tried not to analyse or predict the next twenty years and concentrated on the conversation so I could intercept at any time if things got tricky.

I could see by Emma's face she was intrigued; he wasn't the usual type of 'Mum's friend'—he was a younger, cooler, good-looking, male and from another country. I smiled to myself as the conversation moved easily, if superficially, along.

'I see Dan at the deli... when I say *see* him, I mean I... he serves me, we say hello... I buy what I need then I leave, that's all... there's nothing...'

'I work in the deli,' he butted in before I went too far. 'Your mum's one of our best customers.'

I nodded in reluctant agreement, thinking this made me sound like my huge appetite required frequent visits to the deli for 'refuelling'... not quite the image I'd been hoping to cultivate. I'd rather he'd said, 'Your mum's one of our sexiest customers.' Then again, it wouldn't have been appropriate and poor Emma wasn't ready for that.

'She has a weakness for goats' cheese,' he continued, like it was a medical condition and I was some old lady who couldn't speak for herself.

He just kept smiling, and looking at me, genuinely pleased to see me.

'Dan was a chef back in Australia. He knows a lot about food.' I tried to put on my authoritative Mum voice, which I wasn't comfortable with in front of Dan. With him I always felt younger than I was, but with Emma here, it wasn't working. I was her mum, not Dan's potential girlfriend, and it was weird having to be two people at the same time.

'Faye is... I mean, your mum ... has a very good palate.'

'Yes. The other day, Dan wasn't sure what to order and asked me to taste three kinds of German sausage,' I said, trying to show Emma how sophisticated I'd been while she was away, though I'm sure a student of Freud would have had their own theory regarding my subconscious.

She looked at me incredulously. 'German sausage?'

'Yes... It's not a euphemism,' I said.

'I didn't think it was,' she snapped, clearly horrified at the thought. 'It's just that you don't like sausages or anything spicy...'

'I do now. I like spicy sausages... well, any sausages since I tried Dan's...' I stopped myself just in time, but I could sense Dan's amusement from the twinkle in his eyes.

Emma gave me an unfathomable look.

'I thought you had a chicken pasty from Greggs every day for your lunch?' she said, like a bloody pastry detective.

'I reckon she has those too, Emma,' he teased, calming any potential friction that might be emerging over Emma's pasty accusations and my new sausage love. For God's sake, she was as bad as Craig who used to tell me I should have a pasty for lunch instead of fancy ham and tasty chorizo. Why was everyone hellbent on me eating bloody pasties? This was a new improved Faye, and if she wanted a big spicy sausage for lunch she would damn well have it.

His eyes caught mine and rested a while. 'Faye's my favourite customer. She brightens my day,' he smiled like he was saying it to himself almost. I brightened his day. Did he really just say that?

He made me feel attractive, vital, like I had something to say and someone was finally listening. But most of all, he made me want to stand on the table there and then and break out into a gutsy rendition of Beyonce's *Single Ladies*, with all the accompanying dance moves. Fortunately, I couldn't get out from behind the table, which was a blessing if only for the fact the nearby table of teenage girls were still fascinated by me. They were too young to witness the spectacle of a middle-aged woman attempting that vigorous and unforgiving routine on top of a table in a high street coffee shop.

'Everything's changed for me, since I became single—even lunch,' I said, feeling suddenly confident and thinking, *watch your mum go, Emma.*

'Yes, well, stick to the pasties, Ma,' she smiled. I know Emma was joking, but that smarted a little. I acknowledged and respected Emma's maturity and change, and I wished she'd recognise and respect the changes in me. But I suppose it's a bit unnerving to come back from uni and discover your mother's forsaken pasties at lunchtime for spicy German sausage with a younger man.

Dan was staring at us both, smiling. 'You don't look old enough to be Emma's mum,' he said.

I appreciated the gesture, but with Emma there analysing it, I felt too self-conscious to accept his compliment gracefully, so gave him a mock-chastising look.

He laughed. 'As always, this woman sees right through me,' he said slowly wiping his finger along the rim of his cappuccino cup and sucking slowly on the froth. I watched, fascinated... and he watched me back. And Emma was watching him watching me... equally fascinated.

'So, what are you ladies doing for the rest of the day?' he asked, still licking froth but not taking his eyes from mine. I had to look away, aware of a change in temperature as Emma looked at me, then back at him. I guessed the penny was dropping; her brow furrowed and she suddenly became very businesslike. 'We're going shopping. And we need to make a move if we're going to book that hair appointment. Lovely to meet you, Dan.'

'Of course. Yes, we'll get off...' I said, reluctantly, dragging my eyes from his. I wanted to watch his finger run along the cup rim until it was completely devoid of all froth. I then wanted to watch as his finger went slowly into his mouth and came out again. Then I wanted him to put his finger in *my* mouth so I could suck it and roll my tongue around it... and call me psychic, but I knew Emma wasn't ready for that display. So, before I lost all control, I picked up my bag and made to move.

'Oh, here's my mate now.' He started waving across at a younger man in a baseball cap who waved back. He stood up, but before leaving leaned over to me. I felt his breath in my hair. 'Come and see me,' he whispered. 'I'm lonely without you.'

I couldn't speak, because my heart had burst and flooded all over the table like hot coffee. I looked down to check, but it was just the remains of my spilled macchiato dripping through the groin of my white linen trousers. Nice.

When I looked up he'd gone.

'Did he just whisper something to you?' Emma asked under her breath. I could tell she couldn't quite put her finger on what had just happened and was about to quiz me.

'Oh, no. He's always kidding around,' I stammered, emptying the dregs of my already empty cup, and almost choking—my heart was still lodged in my oesophagus.

'Hey, is something going on between you and him?' she said, glancing over to where he was now sitting with his friend.

I nearly collapsed, but wasn't giving the teenage girls on the next table that little feast for the eyes. 'Me and Dan? Give over, Emma. There's nothing going on.'

We left Costa and walked towards the Bullring where Selfridges and a feast of fashionable delights awaited us. He was lonely without me. He said so. It made my legs weak to think of it.

'Mum, I hope you haven't got any ideas where Dan's concerned.'

'Me?'

'Yeah... cos I hate to tell you, but you're barking up the wrong tree there...'

'Oh, I'm not barking up his tree, love... I mean, Dan's a nice guy,' I said, trying to sound matter of fact. 'He's from Australia, you know.'

'Yeah. So I gathered.'

'He's very talented...'

'Look, Mum. I know what you're up to...'

'I'm what? I'm not up to anything... Nothing has happened, honestly...' I had to stop before I said anything I shouldn't, so busied myself pretending to check for messages on my phone, knowing my red face would betray me.

'Mum, what are you doing?' Emma grabbed me and man-handled me down the road.

'I'm fine, Emma—I just don't want you to think anything about Dan...'

'I wasn't, Mother, but you clearly were.'

'I wasn't...'

'You must think I'm stupid not to realise...'

I almost died. She'd found me out. My daughter knew me so well and she'd seen it all for what it was: just weeks after abandoning her father, her newly single mother was making a fool of herself over a younger man.

'It doesn't mean anything... it's nothing,' I insisted.

'Hmm, and as long as I'm away at uni, it will stay as nothing... I know your game.'

'I'm not playing games... I...'

'Yes, you are—and it's not the first time.'

'It is the first time. I've never... and, Emma, I know it might be a big mistake but I can't help it. It's just something about him.'

'Yeah, there is something about him. He's a crusty old hippy and I don't care what you say—I will not go out with him.'

'You won't?'

'No. Jeez, Mum, I can get my own boyfriends you know. And no offence, but they dress better. So please, just stop matchmaking.'

'Oh... okay then,' I gasped with relief as we carried on walking.

'Do you really think he looks like... a crusty hippy?' I asked, once I'd calmed down.

'Yeah... in his old jeans and his long, straggly hair and his old coat... Nice guy, but, God, I wouldn't be seen dead.'

I smiled to myself. Funny how what I perceived to be young, sun-kissed and sexy looked to Emma like a crusty old hippy with straggly hair.

'I reckon you've got your wires crossed with that Dan anyway, Mother.'

'What do you mean?'

'Well, all the time you're sizing him up for me... and I reckon he's got a bit of a thing for you.'

'Me?' I feigned surprise and had to look away to hide the smile on my face and stop my inner Beyonce rising in my throat again. This time she would sing with gusto... and dance wildly, in the middle of Birmingham City Centre... She had to be stopped.

'What makes you think he's got a *thing* for me?' I said 'thing' with an excited catch in my voice so had to turn it into a cough to hide the thrill.

'He kept looking at you... in that way, you know?'

'I can't believe you'd think Dan would be interested in me,' I said, like it had never occurred to me and I didn't care anyway—but my heart was doing a happy dance. I had hoped he liked me, after all, we had kissed, but the old Faye always harboured doubts. It was good to have my hopes confirmed by Emma who had picked up on it from just a few minutes' conversation.

'I don't think you realise how attractive you are, Mum. But you must be careful being single now isn't like it was when you were younger. Some men expect sex very early on in a relationship.'

Oh, I do hope so, I thought.

'Now, hurry up. I *have* to try those shoes on in Selfridges... and I've seen a great handbag too.'

'Oh, it's all about you isn't it?' I smiled, linking her arm. But if it can't be all about you at nineteen, when can it be all about you? Because as you get older it becomes less about you every year. And if you don't make the effort and *make* it about you, then you start to disappear.

Chapter Eleven

Sangas on the Beach and Sex Under the Stars

Later that week, Emma went off to see her friends for a couple of days so, as I was off work and had all day free, I walked into town. I was soon drawn into the deli and those blue eyes. The weather was lovely and Dan looked blonder from the sun; he was all stubble and sunshine and I wanted to run my fingers through his hair. I tried not to think about kissing him and concentrated on sun-dried tomatoes instead.

'It's a beautiful day,' he said, slicing feta onto walnut bread.

I nodded, pretending to be engrossed in spicy sausage, but sneaking a peep at him every now and then.

'Are you enjoying your week off, Faye?' I loved the way he spoke, the way his mouth caressed my name—*Faye?*—the raised inflection made it sound soft and rounded and delicious. I'd never liked my name until Dan said it. When Craig had said 'Faye', it was spiky and short, like a chopping sound, no undulating curves, no gentle upward inflection at the end, no affection.

'Yes, it's been lovely spending time with Emma.'

'You should go out and enjoy the sunshine... get some fresh air.'

'Yeah, I think I will.'

'Jen's in today so I can have a break. I thought I might have my lunch at the park?'

There was the inflection again. Or was it a question? Was I supposed to say I'd like to join him? I was very rusty at this flirting thing and, though I didn't want to misread the signals, I didn't want to ignore them either.

'That sounds nice... the park in the sunshine,' I tried.

'Great—you have to make the most of it; you don't get too many sunny days in the UK.'

He was right and I spent most of my days breathing in hairspray and scandal, so we left the deli together and headed for the park. It felt good to walk with him; I was proud to be seen with a good-looking younger guy. I don't know if it was just my imagination, but it seemed sunnier than it had before. Even the charity shops looked appealing and I lied to myself that it was the sun making everything so much brighter, happier... but I knew the truth really.

When we arrived at the park, I walked towards a bench, but Dan wanted to sit on the grass. 'I want a real picnic,' he said in mock petulance, 'and that means on the grass.'

I giggled. 'Okay then, we'll do it your way.'

'When I was a kid we had picnics every day. It didn't matter where we were; Mum would set up a tablecloth and we'd have sangas on the beach or back garden if we were home... sangas are sandwiches in Australian, by the way.'

'Thanks for translating... I thought all you Aussies ever did was throw a shrimp on the barbie?'

'That too,' he smiled, 'when we're not eating sangas by the sea.' I could almost feel the sea breeze on my face, the way he said it.

'Mum would take us down on the beach with a picnic and we'd run in the sea, and she'd roll up her jeans and wade in with us...' He started to pluck the grass, his head down.

'You still miss her, don't you?'

'Yeah... she was special.' He looked up, his eyes even bluer than I remembered. 'Of course everyone's mum is special, but when she died, it was like a light went out. She was always baking, and when she'd gone, I missed the fragrance of her lemon cake... a constant reminder she wasn't there anymore.'

Like Mandy, here was another motherless child whose life had been blighted. I understood how they felt; I'd never missed my mum as much as I had in the last few months. Leaving Craig and starting afresh was scary and I often wondered what Mum would have thought of it all.

'So... the lemon cake is very special to you...?'

His face changed for a moment. 'Well, that's kinda bittersweet. Mum always made lemon cake for my birthday because it was my favourite. Whenever I smell lemon zest, I'm right back there in our kitchen in Sydney. The sun coming through the window, scrubbed kitchen table, Mum in her apron. I was always excited; it was my birthday and the kitchen was filled the scent of lemons, but sweeter.'

'That's such a lovely memory,' I whispered to him.

He put his hand on mine.

We talked for an hour. He told me about his childhood in Sydney in the suburbs not far from Bondi, in a big house with a big pool. 'It was idyllic,' he said, with a faraway look in his eyes.

He told me his father was alive and well and still living in Sydney, where his brother, wife and two children lived. 'I love my niece and nephew so much,' he smiled. 'And my bro—but as I said, I haven't seen too much of him.'

'It might heal both of you to spend time together. He probably has memories of your childhood that he can share with you. When someone dies, those memories die too,' I said, thinking of my own mother.

'I can't face it yet, but what you said the other night about getting in touch with him made me think... and I called him.'

'That's wonderful, Dan.'

'Yeah... and you were right; it has made everything feel so much better. I told him I'd see him as soon as I get back home. After talking to him I don't feel so guilty, and John said it made him feel really happy that I called.'

I was delighted he'd taken my advice. It was obvious but sometimes we needed others to point these things out to us. He was smiling, but looked almost tearful when he spoke about home and his family.

I opened my feta, tomato and black olive sandwich and took a bite. 'Ooh, the sweetness from the sun-dried tomatoes up against that tangy salt from the feta is delicious,' I said through crumbs.

'Hey, you're starting to sound like me,' he giggled. 'I love combining flavours—though some don't always work... I had a tough time with mint and beetroot earlier in the week,' he smiled, biting into walnut bread with blue cheese and bacon.

I offered him a bite of my sandwich—after all, it was his creation. 'Aren't you just loving the way the smoky olives are playing footsie with that feta, Dan?'

He laughed. 'You bet, babe!'

For a while we stayed silent, just the birds singing, the sound of toddlers playing in the nearby sandpit and a blue, blue sky decorated with a couple of tiny white frothy clouds.

'I hope we have a good summer,' I said eventually, looking at the sky, basking in the gentle spring sunshine warmth on my face.

'Oh, it will be. It's got to be,' he sighed.

I finished my sandwich and lay down on my side, resting my head on my elbow in the grass. He was close, doing the same, facing me... I didn't care how it must look to anyone passing by.

'I always wanted to own my own café,' he continued. 'A trendy little place with a bakery somewhere near Sydney Harbour... serving breakfast muffins, pastries, eggs with everything. I wanted to spend my days baking cakes and my own speciality breads. When I decided to spend the summer here in the UK and my aunt Jen happened to be opening a deli, it seemed like fate... or perhaps she just took pity on me.'

'It's good training for your own place,' I smiled.

He nodded.

'Did you come here with... anyone?' I asked.

'Yes—you.' He looked around, pretending to be confused.

'Ha, funny. I mean is anyone here with you in the UK?'

'I only see you here.'

And I can only see you, I thought.

He looked down, started playing with the remaining lump of crust from his sandwich, then thought better of it and abandoned it to the birds.

'I came to the UK with my girlfriend... She's my ex now.'

'Oh, I'm sorry.'

'No, it's fine... We... we don't want to be tied and... I met someone else.'

'Oh.' I was stunned. It hadn't taken him long to cut a swathe through the Midlands. People today behaved strangely around each other, having sex within hours of meeting then saying goodbye and picking up where they left off somewhere down the line. The world had moved on, but who said we knew any better? They had the right idea, I suppose—no danger of ending up with a mortgage and a man you don't love for twenty-two years like I did.

We talked some more about his home, then we talked about *Jane Eyre* and *Tess of the D'Urbervilles* and wondered if what happened to Tess was her fate and something destined to happen.

'I think she made some pretty crap choices,' I said. 'I'm not sure I believe in fate.' I'd come to realise in recent months that, ultimately, we steer our own ship.

'Yeah, but it isn't always about bad choices... Sometimes life can hit you with a curve ball and take away your choices. My mum had no choices to make; she was just handed her fate—and my brother the same. It made me realise early how no one is totally in control of their life and where it's going.' He gathered the packets and screwed them up tightly. For the first time ever, I recognised something like anger in him.

I didn't say anything.

'Which is why,' he continued, finding a much brighter tone from somewhere and tapping my knee with his screwed up handful of sandwich bag, 'we all need to make the most of what we've got. And if we don't have what we want now... then we should chase it, before that curve ball appears out of the sky.' He had suddenly come alive and returned to the happy-go-lucky Dan I knew.

'My mum always said regret is the most wasted emotion,' I sighed, tearing up at the thought of Mum and how she'd never taken her own advice. She'd allowed regret to define her in the end, when it was too late and I was determined to be different.

'Since I made my decision to live, I've travelled and I've seen some amazing sights,' he said. 'I've tasted wonderful food, slept with great women... and, yeah, realistically I may never achieve everything on my 'to do' list, but I want my regret list to be as short as I can make it.'

I nodded. Dan was from another world to the one I knew. He saw things in a completely different way, yet we shared the same dreams and ideals, and I welcomed his challenging conversations and new perspectives a world away from the salon's baroque mirrors and bad dye jobs.

Perhaps I was just another on his list of 'great women' to sleep with and leave... and what if I was? Did it matter? Our time together would be short because he was leaving in a matter of months.

'So, regrets... do you have any?' he asked.

Again I was touched at his interest in my feelings, my hopes and even disappointments... no one had ever asked me those kinds of questions before. Oh, god, where to begin?

'Tragically, I have a very long regret list,' I sighed, 'and it's getting longer by the day.'

'Why don't you turn it around? Dump your regrets and start a bucket list instead? He said, his fingertips gently reaching mine through the grass.

'I always associate bucket lists with dying... I'd rather think of it as my living list.'

'I like that,' he smiled. 'Yeah... a living list.' He played with the words. They seemed to please him. 'What's on your living list, Faye?'

'Okay... My first is to be on a rooftop in New York, the city beneath me, a good-looking man in front of me, dancing, drinking champagne. I want to see a Santorini sunset, learn to ice skate, lose ten pounds, ride a Vespa through Rome, and make a wish at the Trevi Fountain, swim naked in the ocean—and since I met you, I've even added to my living list.' I smiled at him. 'I want to see your waves on Bondi... that olive tree you talk of in Tuscany; I want sex under the stars and... oh, a million other places.'

'You mean you want to visit a million places or have sex in a million places?' he teased.

I looked at him and the old Faye would have blushed and become tongue-tied, but the new Faye brazened it out. I meant I wanted to visit a million places, but heard myself say, 'Sex—I want to have sex in different places... under every bloody star.'

He looked around like he was surveying the area for a suitable spot and we both started laughing.

'There are a few things on your list I think I could help you with...' He gave a wicked smile.

'Yes, but where to start?'

'I reckon sex under the stars is a good start.' He moved his hand onto mine, very gently. Pins and needles shot up my arm... It was either sexual frisson or I was about to have a lust-induced heart attack.

'Sex in strange places aside—what about your list?' I said, to calm the hot flush that was creeping up my throat and no doubt turning my décolletage an unbecoming rashy red.

'I want that café bakery in Sydney Harbour,' he smiled. 'I reckon I'd have a queue for my lemon cake... Will you come and buy some, Faye?'

'Yes, I will definitely be in that queue,' I replied in a slightly breathy voice. 'The day I tick Bondi off my list, I'll be straight down that coast to your café.'

'I'd like to go back to Santorini too.' He looked at me. 'Only this time I'd want to see the sunset with someone I love.'

He looked down and began plucking at the grass again. 'I wonder if we'll ever get our dreams.'

I was lost. The rash was now rushing up into my face and I wanted nothing else in the world but to be with him in the sunset. I tried to compose myself.

'I hope we can live at least some of them. I am determined to dance on that rooftop in New York, one way or the other...'

'Yeah, but that's the problem when you're a dreamer; you never quite get your shit together to live those dreams.' He looked up at me. His eyes went straight into mine and I melted.

'Following your heart shouldn't mean abandoning your dreams,' I said, tilting my head to meet his eyes, 'because sometimes our heart takes us to places we'd never even dreamed of.'

He looked at me directly and I couldn't think straight. 'Did your heart tell you to come and find me today...?' he asked.

I nodded, and he kissed me, his tongue pushing gently but firmly into my mouth. My stomach exploded with tiny stars, and his hands circled my waist, bringing me closer to him.

I'd never wanted anyone like I wanted him at that moment. I was jelly in his arms. The kiss was like a huge excavation of something from my past, a vague recalled memory of being young, being me. I was fifteen again and being kissed for the first time.

We sat together on the grass, both wanting more, both knowing we couldn't have more... not here on the grass in broad daylight. But we continued to kiss like the rest of the world had gone away. I saw and heard nothing else.

I pulled away from him. 'I don't know what's happening here, Dan.'

He was looking at me, smiling and puzzled at the same time.

'Sorry, I must sound really stupid. It's just I know you probably have lots of women in your life already, but I just want you to know, you're lovely. You make me feel so happy, so different and... I'm talking too much again, aren't I?'

He laughed. 'I love to hear you talk; I've never heard anyone talk like you. I love your accent and the funny things you say... but, yes, you're talking too much,' and he kissed me again.

'Hmm, well, it just comes out that way,' I said, feeling the need to defend myself as we emerged from another incredible kiss.

He leaned back, resting on his elbow. 'So, what makes you think I have lots of women in my life?'

He put his hand gently and discreetly on my arm and was gently moving it up and down in a soothing motion. No one else could see; it was just between us and was the most erotic thing I have ever experienced.

'Oh, you're quite attractive... and you just seem at ease with women. And you had a girlfriend and you finished with her because you were seeing someone else, and...'

'Whoa... hang on. I said I had met someone else; I wasn't *seeing* someone else... That's why Gabby and I ended it. I realised when I met this other woman that it wasn't right... between Gabby and me.'

'So you're not seeing this other woman then?'

'You tell me?'

'How should I know?'

He smiled and leaned towards me again. I wasn't sure my heart could take another kiss; I was likely to explode and leave unset human jelly remains all over the picnic rug. But as I'd already come to realise, my willpower with Dan was like my willpower with food: I knew it was bad for me as it approached my mouth, but I was unable to resist.

So we kissed again, this time holding on to each other while lying slowly back on the grass, our lips never parting, our heads together in the sunshine. His hand was on my thigh and I was on another planet. I was a different Faye Dobson: a world traveller, philosopher, reader of books, in love for the first time ever with Dan, the delicious deli guy, who actually listened to me and cared what I thought.

'Faye, are you free one night next week?' he asked. 'We could tick off something on your list. My stomach did a flip.

'Oh, er, yes...' All I could think about was my underwear, my less than pert breasts, my thighs naked, and whether any of it was up to a night under the stars.

'Okay, I'll pick you up after work... I'll teach you how to skate.'

Up until now, I knew what I'd be doing on any given day in the next thirty years, but looking at him in the sunshine, his eyes twinkling, I thought, 'I don't care about next week, next month; I want to be with you now, for as long as I can.' I was intoxicated by him and, in the spirit of saying 'yes' and not having regrets, I was ready to open up and have my heart broken. I was only just discovering that love wasn't about white lace and promises—sometimes it happened when you least expected it, with someone you never thought possible. And it didn't have to end in marriage, or even a steady relationship. It was two people just being together... He was only here until the autumn... but what fun we could have until then.

Chapter Twelve
A Weekend Lost and Found

Sue was planning to spend a couple of days with her friend in London the next weekend, leaving on the Saturday after work. She wouldn't be home until Monday night and, as Emma had now gone back and Dan was up North visiting long-lost Aussie relatives, I had the weekend to myself. I was looking forward to being alone. I welcomed the time to just relax and think.

I was grateful to Sue but I didn't get much peace at her place—what with her entertaining her dates, and her celebrity yoga on the mat in front of the TV. I'd also gone from Craig's indifference towards me and what I did, to Sue's obsessive checking on me. I appreciated her concern, but if I picked up a book, Sue saw it as a sign of depression and immediately tried to engulf me in wine and chatter: 'We don't want you left thinking on your own too much,' she'd say. But that's exactly what I wanted.

So that weekend, despite missing Dan, I was really looking forward to undisturbed reading, my own music, and my own food—on my own. I was imagining the bliss of all this while waiting for my client to be shampooed and watching Julie Sharples (Wednesday cut and blow, boyfriend into bondage) being transformed into a princess bride.

'Mandy's doing my make up,' Julie nodded enthusiastically. 'She does lovely smoky eye make-up and I'm having a vajazzle too—a Vegas, that's a landing strip with jewels on. Mandy does great ones... Dave can't wait.'

'I bet he can't,' I smiled. Given his penchant for bondage, that would be a wedding night to remember.

Despite her drinking, sexting, swearing and sleeping around, Mandy was very artistic when it came to anything creative and her vajazzles were legendary. Her face make-up was good too, and once she'd asked if she could try out some new products on me, and when she'd finished, no one could believe how different and how much younger I looked.

'Vibrator,' Sue mouthed over Julie's coiling hair.

'What?' I mouthed back.

'Mandy's got her a vibrator for a wedding present,' she hissed. I rolled my eyes as Sue excused herself and trotted over to me, all tight lips and limp hands.

'If you get chance, have a word and tell her not to be waving it about the salon. I've got Gayle Jones coming in this afternoon and she doesn't want Mandy shoving a rampant rocket in her face.'

'From what I hear, Gayle's had worse shoved in her face,' I smiled in response.

'Gayle is classy—she only does it with millionaires and footballers, Faye, I don't want her being offended.'

I nodded. It all made perfect sense in Sue's world, if not mine, and once my lady was finished I popped up to see Mandy and pass on Sue's request. I'd wanted to check on Mandy anyway, as this weekend was the anniversary of her mother's death and she hadn't popped down to see us like she normally would. It was always a tough time for Mandy and I wanted to make sure she was coping.

When I went into the Spa, she was waiting for Julie, the 'gift' wrapped and ribboned on the side. She had her head down, washing her make-up sponges.

'You okay, love?' I asked.

'Yeah. Fine.'

'You know you can talk to me if you want to, Mandy,' I said gently.

'Thanks. You know how it is... it just hits you, on the anniversary and birthdays and Christmases... oh, man, every day really.'

'I know, love. You're not going to be on your own this weekend, are you?'

'Yeah. Flick's going away with her boyfriend and Dad's with Andrea, so I might as well go out, get bladdered and forget about it.'

'That's not the answer, is it?'

'No... but what else is there? No one gives a toss so I might as well get off my face and have a good cry.'

My heart ached for her. I thought about Emma and where she'd be if I wasn't around. There's no one like your mum—I was a grown woman with my own daughter, and I still missed my mum.

'Actually, Mandy, I was going to ask you a big favour,' I started.

She sat up, eager to hear, eager as always to help. She really did have a heart of gold.

'It's just that... Sue's going away to her friend's in London tonight and I'll be all on my own. I hate being on my own, and I wondered if you'd mind coming over to keep me company... at Sue's?'

She flushed with pleasure. 'Faye, you don't even need to ask. I will be there, girlfriend. I'll bring some DVDs. I'll do your nails too if you like?'

'Ah, thanks, Mandy, you've no idea how relieved I am. I was dreading being on my own,' I lied. 'I'll order a takeaway and get a bottle of wine, shall I?'

'Yay!' She jumped up and down clapping her hands like a little kid and my heart melted.

Then she stood up and ran at me, hugging me so hard, I felt tears welling up. Her head was in my neck and she whispered in my ear, 'I'll look after you, Faye. You don't ever have to be on your own. I'm always here.'

I nodded and opened the door to head back downstairs with a lump in my throat.

'I'll come with you and get the bride,' she said, back in her usual loud Mandy voice, linking arms with me down the stairs the same way Emma did.

'Oh, I almost forgot—Sue says don't wave Julie's wedding gift in the face of any VIP customers... Oh, and please don't tease Camilla and have her doing anything with it inadvertently; she won't know what it is and we don't want an incident.'

'Ha... I hadn't thought of that. What if someone told Camilla it was a head massager and she had been chosen to massage all the clients' heads with it? You are a bloody genius, Faye. That would be fucking hilarious.'

'No, Mandy.'

'Aw. It's all right for you, Faye; you don't need a vibrator now you're humping that Aussie,' she virtually yelled.

'I'm not!'

'Oh, admit it Faye... you're giving Deli Dan a good old humping...'

'That is enough!' Sue snapped. 'Can you stop talking about Faye humping the deli man in front of customers please, Mandy.'

'Has Faye been humping that guy from the deli...?' the bride started.

'For God's sake. I just wish everyone would mind their own business. *I AM NOT HUMPING THE GUY FROM THE DELI* I yelled over the dryers... which had just at that moment been turned off, as the guy from the deli walked in.

A wave of deep embarrassment and silent expectation swept through the salon. The only sound was Mandy, sniggering. Dan had clearly heard my outburst and was standing against the counter, defensively clutching *The Great Gatsby* to his chest like a shield. I walked stiffly towards him, everyone watching from under rollers and dye. Sue raised an eyebrow in the mirror at her lady and carried on cutting.

'I just dropped this in... thought it might be on your book list,' he smiled awkwardly.

'Thanks. I... I wasn't talking then... about humping you... if you thought it might be... that?' I said, shaking my head, digging myself in deeper.

'It's okay, Faye... really.'

'Yes, but I would hate you to think that I had talked about... told everyone or even thought about... any part... of you.'

'You should stop talking now,' he whispered, leaning towards me.

'Okay.' I looked down at the book as he passed it to me, and a secret smile passed between us.

The whole salon was watching from under their hair and I wanted to die.

Then he raised his eyebrows, lifted his hand in a saluting gesture and left.

I wandered back into the salon feeling distinctly sick. I'd once enjoyed sharing my life with the girls here, moaning about Craig, worrying about Emma and complaining about the cost of central heating. But now I saw the salon as an intrusion into my life. Dan was special to me; he was the first person I'd cared about for a long time and a stepping stone into a new, more exciting future, whether he stuck around or not. I gazed around the salon, and for the first time I felt like an observer—the Lithuanian hair dye, Sue's incessant search for online love, and Mandy's need for approval were all part of my life, but I wondered if they would soon be part of my past.

These friends had helped me grow and become the woman I was, and their love and support had helped give me the courage to take those first steps and leave my unhappy marriage. Thanks to them I was moving forward, but the sad part was, in order to really embark on this new journey, I had to leave them behind.

❊ ❊ ❊

We finished late that night. Mandy did a great job on Julie and she looked beautiful for her wedding, as did the bridesmaids who'd descended the stairs after their 'session' with Mandy, hair on end and shell-shocked faces. One could only imagine what those innocent young women had been subjected to that afternoon in The Heavenly Spa—one thing was for sure: they would never be the same again.

Later that night as Mandy and I enjoyed a chicken tikka, two family bags of Revels and a bottle of white, she told me about her mum.

'She was lovely, Faye. I remember her chasing me through the garden, and I was laughing so much I couldn't run, and she caught up with me and tickled me. I must have been about five. There are times I can't actually remember her face, but I can still smell her perfume and feel her tickling me.'

We talked about her dad's marriage to her stepmum which, at sixteen, Mandy hadn't taken well: 'I refused to go to the wedding. They said I was having a tantrum and I was a troubled teen. But, Faye, Mum had only been gone a year. I still didn't believe it—and then my dad marries Andrea and she brings her kids along. It was the worst time in my life: I'd lost my mum, then my dad,' she sighed.

No one had ever really listened or talked to Mandy since her Mum had died. She'd lost the person she needed most in the world and had donned a plate of armour so no one could ever hurt her again. She had been labelled 'trouble' simply for grieving for her mother. I wasn't surprised that she slept around for love and drank to forget.

'I was still at school and lived for Saturdays when I could come to the salon to work,' she said. 'I just felt safe there with you and Sue and the ladies. I love going on holiday but I miss the salon and all of you... and sometimes I dread Sundays and Mondays when the salon's closed and I have to be at home. Don't tell Sue but sometimes I even go there at night, when it's shut... I stayed all night in the spa recently after a row with Andrea.'

We shed a few tears then watched *Sex and the City* and marvelled at what life would be like if we lived in New York. I told her about my dream to dance on a rooftop under the stars.

'Oh, Faye, you should so do that, man,' she said, clasping her hands together with excitement. 'I can see you in a long frock, hair down, red lipstick, a bit of liner on your upper lashes dancing under those stars... dead classy.'

I smiled. She actually thought it could happen... me in a big city in a different life. She didn't laugh or see the flaws; she just accepted it because she believed I could do it if I wanted to. Perhaps it wasn't such a stupid dream after all—and if Mandy believed in me, why couldn't I?

'So, Faye, you need to think about your look.'

'Do I?'

'Yeah... you have to start wearing make-up, buying new clothes. You have to stop saying "Don't look at me, I'm married," and say, "Hey boys... come and get it." She was waving her arms in the air and jiggling her breasts.

I giggled at the prospect. 'Not sure I can pull that off like you can, Mand,' I sighed, tearing open the second large bag of Revels. I crammed a handful of chocolates in, vowing I'd starve myself the following day and knowing I wouldn't, but this was the only way to enjoy guilt-free chocolate.

'Faye, you're gorgeous... you could have anyone.'

'Oh, perhaps a few years ago, Mandy, but I got pregnant and married and everything stopped. I know I'm always warning you about drinking too much and having sex with strangers, but at least you have fun. When you're my age, you'll have no regrets and a lot of good memories,' I said, my mouth full of chocolate orange Revels. I hate the orange ones. 'I just wish I'd gone out with more guys when I was younger, lived a bit, you know.'

'Faye, what are you talking about? You are still young.'

I pulled a face.

'Well, youngish. You can still live it up and meet guys. You're going out with Bruce, aren't you, and he's a bit of all right. You see, you're getting your mojo on, Faye... you didn't do it in your twenties 'cos you were saving it for now,' she smiled.

I nodded. I liked that.

'Now that you're single, you could have a vajazzle.'

'Me?' The old Faye rebelled at the idea, but the new Faye said, 'Why not?'

'I've got my vajazzle exam on Monday afternoon but my bloody model's dropped out...'

'Do you need a vajazzle model?' I asked, holding my breath for the response, wondering what I was about to say. 'I could do it?'

'OMG, Faye... Really?

I nodded.

She rummaged around in her beauty kit and offered me an open palm of glittering fake jewels.

'We will cover your lady landscape in priceless jewels.'

'Okay.' I flinched a little at the phrase 'we' when talking about the vajazzling process. 'We' conjured up an image of Mandy, Flick and their friend Big Jess clustered around my 'Lady Landscape' sticking on paste diamonds like it was a bloody arts and crafts play date.

'They're quite pretty, aren't they?' I said, taking one of Mandy's jewels and holding it up to the light.

'You won't regret it, Faye. Men love vajazzles.'

'I'm not having it for a man,' I said, mildly indignant. 'I'm having it for me.'

'Yay... You go, girl. Faye, you are turning into a kick-ass cougar!' she screamed, grabbing the wine bottle and draining it into both our glasses.

'A kiss-ass cougar? Yeah, I guess you're right,' I smiled.

Chapter Thirteen

A Glittery Groin and a Sparkly Future

Monday evening I found myself lying on a beauty bed at the local college where Mandy was taking her Advanced Beauty exam. I wanted a glittering 'Vegas Strip' as opposed to the more demure and undecorated, 'Landing Strip'—if I was going to do it, I might as well do it big. I was quite excited as I lay on the beauty bed while Mandy mixed up lotions and potions before ferreting around my bikini line and shouting; 'Oh, my God! When was the last time you waxed?'

'I only wax for holidays,' I said, embarrassed.

'Well, now you're single, you need to be ever ready,' she said, looking up from my thighs and wagging a finger. The job of being a single woman was more time-consuming than I'd imagined, with regular waxes, fake tans, pedicures for naked toes and cellulite rubs so you didn't scare them when the lights went on. I couldn't imagine when these brave new single girls found time for the obligatory ten minutes with the rampant rabbit.

It was like starting a new school and needing a list of equipment and uniform requirements, and each day was a revelation as more kit was added to the list. I just hoped this vajazzle was low-maintenance and if I did ever have sex with Dan I wouldn't be leaving a jewelled calling card in his twisted sheets.

Mandy told me she'd wax first, and to relax and lie back, but as a vajazzle virgin I didn't know what to expect so was a little tense, especially with a swearing, chortling Mandy between my legs. Her 'bedside manner' left a lot to be desired, and as she applied boiling hot wax and I whimpered slightly, she laughed, 'You think this hurts? Wait till I rip it off... it will hurt like *A BITCH*!'

I can only liken Mandy's Brazilian waxing method to pouring petrol on the vagina, waiting a few seconds, then taking a lit match to it. According to the Beauty Examiner (a fully paid-up member of the Marquis de Sade Olympic team), 'The Brazilian tests the skill of the technician, while providing a blank canvas for the art.'

I couldn't scream or cry or thrash around in pain, because Mandy might fail the exam, so I clutched at the beauty bed and grimaced throughout. I blamed my watering eyes on the chemicals and told the examiner my whimpering was merely humming, but as I pointed out later to Mandy, it was in fact more painful than childbirth.

The next stage was the 'jewel application', which wasn't actually painful, but was psychological torture watching Mandy at my now throbbing groin with a pair of tweezers, medical-grade adhesive and a bag of glitter.

'I'm doing a special picture just for you made of real crystals. OMG, it will be crayzee!' Mandy enthused from my nether regions. I had been quite thrilled at the prospect of a vajazzle, but the pain had taken its toll and I'd never felt more vulnerable as she carefully positioned each jewel, while growling like a tiger.

After a tortuous ninety minutes, which felt like three years, Mandy looked up and announced, 'It's finished!' It certainly felt like the end. Burning agony had now turned to just plain agony but I could see the pattern glinting from where I was and lifted my head, mustering a pained smile and a groggy, 'It's lovely.'

'Nice cup of tea?' Mandy offered. Yes, it was just like childbirth.

Mandy's friend Trish waltzed over and peered down. Her make-up was orange and her eyelashes so long I swear they tickled my flesh as she swept them across my groin.

'Grrr,' she roared, waving her long blue nails like claws, which didn't make any sense—but then much of what Mandy and her friends did made no sense.

The examiner appeared from behind the curtain like something out of a medical drama, inspecting me, tutting and taking notes like I'd just had a big op. I couldn't wait to get out, and as soon as she'd diagnosed 'excellent' and swept back behind the curtain, I was off the vajazzling bed. 'Can we go now, Mand?' I called across to her chatting with a group of girls. I could think only of submerging my crystal-bedecked vagina in a very cold bath.

'Cool your tits, Faye. She can't wait to go home and show her sparkly pussy off, can you?' she giggled to the girls.

'No. Mandy, I'm in pain, actually,' I huffed, trying not to think about my fiery 'lady landscape,' which was emanating more heat than the sun.

'Okay, I just need to pack my gear,' she said, marching back to me, 'then we'll get off. You okay?'

I nodded, while gingerly stepping into my big pants. 'Thanks, Mandy, it looks lovely from what I could see, from upside down.'

Having walked out of the building, we were now striding through the car park and, despite the tenderness and pain, I felt a rush. To look at me, no one would guess that my vagina was covered in crystals—who'd have ever thought Faye Dobson would have a vajazzle? I was surprising myself. I'd never have done this when I was married; Craig wasn't one for anything fancy or different. If I'd had a vajazzle when we were married and he'd seen those crystals, he'd think he was hallucinating.

'So, which lucky man is going to see your vajazzle first, Faye?' Mandy asked as we got in the car.

I was climbing in gingerly: 'Oh, who knows?' I giggled, then groaned as I manoeuvred gently into my seat. 'So many men, so little time.'

I put on my sunglasses, started the car and applied new red lippy in the car mirror. 'You are looking good, girlfriend,' Mandy smiled. 'I reckon you could pass for thirty- five... and your lady garden glitz will just blow his mind. You go, girl!'

❋ ❋ ❋

At work the next day, my crystal vagina was the talk of the salon, and Sue decided it would be good for advertising Mandy's skills to show clients what she had done.

'Go upstairs with Faye and have a look at her crystal fairy,' she said, which made her sound like a Madame and made me feel like a prostitute. I refused of course, but both Sue and Mandy made me feel like I had something to hide, so after much harassment I allowed them to take a photo.

Mandy soon had several 'shots' of my vajazzle and left me in peace, but showed them to anyone who asked. They all gasped in awe and said how clever she was while Sue took several bookings off the back of my 'glittery triangle'.

Later when Mr York, one of the local councillors, came in for his short back and sides, Sue's opening comment was, 'Have you ever seen a vajazzle, Bill?' I knew what was coming next, so before she began flashing the photo around, I left the salon and went for a walk—a line had to be drawn.

I was feeling like an observer again and questioning everything. Where else in the world would one's co-workers take pictures of your vagina and show them to clients? I loved them all, but my groin being the talking point of the salon was just one more reason to run away.

I'd come a long way from quiet Faye who went home every night to a loveless marriage and sausage and mash, to a single woman with a sparkly groin and an even more sparkly future. I smiled secretly and wondered just what that future held for the new Faye Dobson.

Chapter Fourteen
Anything Could Happen!

It was a warm April day, the air fresh and light with the promise of summer, and for the first time in ages I was excited about what it would bring. There was no annual fortnight in Weston-super-Mare, no overheated appliances, no endless Sundays watching Craig heal white goods with the laying on of hands like an evangelist plumber. There were no certainties anymore, and I had fallen in love with those three little words: *Anything could happen.*

For most people, the signs of early summer are new buds, emerging leaves and birdsong, but in Curl up and Dye it was hair removal, sun-kissed highlights, fake tans and shiny pedicures for the beach.

I could barely contain myself I was so excited and nervous about going ice skating with Dan. I smiled and nodded at my clients who chatted away about their kids, their holidays—and I didn't hear a word. I'm ashamed to say I also didn't care who had what on their hair or why. All I could think of was Dan and I Ice dancing to Bolero like Torvill and Dean.

It was on my list because I'd only ever been to the ice rink a few times in my life, and everyone else just seemed to take to the ice gliding effortlessly along while I clung hysterically to the barrier. I was always so scared and stiff that when I eventually plucked up courage to venture out onto the ice, my legs would fly from under me and I'd end up in a crumpled heap. I'd watch my friends, envying their elegance and grace on the slippery ground, but as they chatted and glided, I just body-slammed barriers and jerked across the rink. Consequently, as all my friends were whipping round, ponytails in the air, legs smooth and swaying, I'd be in the first-aid room being strapped up. I wondered at the wisdom of going to this arena with Dan. Did I really want him to see my inelegant lack of co-ordination?

As Dan helped me onto the rink, I clung to him like a limpet, insisting he stay with me and not leave me alone under any circumstances. He was calm and gentle and clearly at ease on skates, but my nerves got the better of me and I stiffened as soon as he moved me away from the barrier. Instead of being impatient or disapproving, he was smiling, both arms guiding me gently across the deadly sheen. 'You'll be fine. Relax into it, Faye, you're too uptight. What's the worst that can happen?'

'Concussion? Leading to brain swelling, deep coma and then... death?' I offered as my legs began to go in different directions. 'Aargh... stop! Get me off!' I screamed, as little kids skated easily past me. I pulled away from Dan and made a lunge for the barrier, almost knocking him out of the way. It was probably the most ungainly display ever seen at that rink, but he was still smiling. After a few seconds' recovery, I looked around to see him waving at me from the other side. I smiled, and tried to wave back, which inadvertently caused me to do the splits and two kids had to get underneath my armpits and heave me back up against the safety of the barrier.

Desperately hoping Dan hadn't witnessed this circus, I spotted him in the distance, through the throng of skaters. He was whizzing around the rink, so fast and strong yet so relaxed, so laid-back. Nothing ever fazes him, I thought as he deliberately turned direction to skate towards oncoming hordes, swerving and bending, just missing the other skaters by a whisper. I had to close my eyes, fully expecting to see a twenty-seven-person pile-up on the ice. I couldn't watch, it was so scary, and when, after several laps of honour, he rolled up at my side panting, his face flushed and cold, I was in quite a state.

'Oh, God, Dan... you just kept going and... how did you do that?'

'I was trying to show you how much fun it is. It's exhilarating. You just have to relax.'

'You are kidding,' I was saying, shaking my head and walking like a robot as he led me... well, *forced* me back onto the ice. He held me firmly around the waist, let me stay near the barrier, but kept talking, telling me it was fine as he guided me slowly round. I was beginning to feel a little calmer after a few minutes, only screaming if someone went past me too fast or bumped into me. We continued for a while slowly, until I could feel us gradually gaining speed.

'I've had enough; I want to get off,' I said stiffly.

But he just said, 'It's fine, it's good fun,' and pushed us on through the cold and the crowds.

'Stop!' I shrieked as I felt my legs taking me faster, his arms holding me tight.

'Faster!' he yelled, laughing as we pushed on past the crowds of skaters then through them as I screamed again. I soon realised screaming wasn't working—it just made him take us faster, so I shut up and clung harder to him. The spiky cold whipped through my hair, stung my face, taking my breath away as he whizzed me along, and I yelped as we hit more speed and reached a point where I seriously thought I was about to crash and die. Then, suddenly, I felt elated, like something was lifting me high above the crowds, above the ice, and my breath slowed down. Inside I felt a delicious thrill run right through me. The chill of the ice, the speed, the fear and holding onto Dan filled me with an exhilaration I had never felt before. Like a little kid on a fairground ride, my heart was in my mouth and I started screaming again... this time to go even faster.

❄ ❄ ❄

Later, as we drank hot chocolate and ate hot dogs in the rink café, I sat close to him, still scared and excited and clingy, but happy. 'I can't believe I just did that,' I said as he painted my name in tomato ketchup on his hotdog.

'You are bonkers,' I smiled, watching him with both my hands around the polystyrene cup for warmth. The bottoms of my jeans were soaked from the ice and my hands red raw.

'I told you, you can do it—you just have to *believe* you can.'

'I wasn't sure for a while back there I would come out alive, but thank you... for helping me tick something off my list,' I said.

'My pleasure,' he smiled. 'Now eat your hot dog—I want to tick another thing off your living list tonight.'

He waved his car keys at me—he'd borrowed his aunt's car to take us to the rink.

'What?'

'You'll see.' He reached his hand out, I took it and we ran giggling like children into the car park. He started driving and after about twenty minutes we were down a country lane and he pulled up near a huge field bright yellow with rapeseed. It was early evening, the light was fading and he wound down his window, leaning his head back. 'So quiet here. I love it, the peace.'

The air was thick with silence, only a few miles from the motorway and busy life yet here we were truly alone in our own cocoon. He lifted his head and slowly, almost hesitantly leaned towards me, one arm sliding down my back, the other on my waist. We kissed slowly, then his hand slid under my T-shirt and I swear he must have been able to feel my heart beating out of my chest. Just like the skating, everything started off slow and gentle but seemed to move faster, suddenly more urgent and passionate. The rest of the world receded as I took to the ice again, becoming breathless, chills sparkling through my whole body. After a little while, when I couldn't take much more, he pulled away and, looking into my eyes, whispered, 'Come on, it's time to tick another thing off your list.'

We got out of the car and he led me over a gate, through a smaller field and into long grass. By now it was dark and a little chilly, and he stopped and lay down in the middle of the grass. 'What?' I giggled.

'Look up there. I can see The Plough,' he sighed. I slowly sat down. The grass was cold but he felt warm as I lay down next to him. I looked up to see the canopy of stars in a very dark sky. 'Wow... I've never seen so many,' I said.

'No light pollution out here. I wanted it to be perfect for you.' He turned to me, and we started to kiss again, slowly, perfectly in sync, his warm hand now under my bra, my breasts filling his hand. His kisses moved down, covering my breasts. 'Just look at those stars,' he whispered huskily and slowly, languorously. We rolled around the cold ground, giggling, kissing, grass tickling my face and my thighs as he slowly pulled down my jeans. Naked from the waist down, I lay in the field, the stars above me, not a soul around, and I felt like I was bathing in the Trevi Fountain. He kissed my breasts, my stomach, slowly going down my body, I was watching the stars and his face was in my groin. I couldn't believe this was happening. I stiffened slightly, like I was back on the rink. I'd never felt anything like it before; a million tiny explosions, as his hands caressed my breasts and... Oh, God, he was licking me gently and I was riding fast across the ice, through Italy on a Vespa at high speed, swimming naked, my whole body submerged in the most intense pleasure. Soon he was inside me, moving fast, effortlessly, and I watched the stars and clung tightly as we sped through the night. When it was over, I lay there, staring

up at the stars and thinking, *Faye Dobson just had sex in a field...
under a million stars.*

We continued to lie in silence, side by side, then I said, 'Thank
you for making two of my wishes come true.'

'It's okay... It was a selfless act.' He turned to me and kissed
my forehead as I snuggled into his arms. 'Hey, you're a dark
horse, Faye Dobson.' He gestured towards my vajazzle, glinting
in the moonlight. 'You're full of surprises, aren't you?'

'Oh, yes... I'm full of surprises these days,' I smiled into the
thick, starry blackness.

Chapter Fifteen

Kick-Ass Cougars on Very Thin Ice

That night I arrived at Sue's in quite a delirious state. I didn't go into too much detail, but she guessed the main bit. 'So you had sex with him?' was her opening gambit as I staggered through the door, still high on lust.

I nodded and she smiled knowingly.

'I saw the way he looked at you when he came into the salon with that book... I knew then it was a matter of time before you two had carnival knowledge,' she sighed. 'Sagittarius, too, which is a perfect fit for Leo. I told you, Faye, you need to read your astrologicals... it's all in there about you meeting a Sagittarian and making big changes.'

'He's wonderful, but it's just a summer fling,' I sighed as she poured us both another drink. 'I just hope I'm a bit more than a one-night stand.' I was getting there slowly, but still the old Faye would pop in occasionally to cast doubts and lower my expectations; she'd been around a long time, she wouldn't disappear overnight.

'You could go back to Australia with him? According to Rory Bland Astronomer to the stars, Leos are going to find their suns rising in the fourth house and you might be spending time in far-flung places... and there are surprises on the horizon.'

'I'm under no illusions, and for once I'm not going to spoil it all by worrying about what happens next. He's almost ten years younger than me—the last thing he needs is an older divorced woman tying him down.'

'You could pass for younger—and you don't realise how attractive you are, Faye. My Ken always used to say you were a bit of all right.'

I smiled. 'Thanks, Sue.' Given the low bar (that Ken would shag anything with a pulse), it wasn't exactly flattering, but I appreciated the sentiment.

'You're right. Whatever happens, just have some fun, love... you deserve it; enjoy every minute while it lasts. Me and Mandy have been worried about you, Faye, but in the last few weeks you've been more like your old self.'

She was right. I felt more like my old (younger) self. Dan had brought me back to life, re-awakening my love of books, inspiring a passion for food and cooking, and now the sex... Oh. My. God. The sex. To quote Mandy, who knew I could be such 'a kick-ass cougar'?

Before going to bed that night, I took the New York Rooftop postcard from my handbag and stared at it for a while, leaning back on the pillows, imagining the sound of that saxophone playing through the dusk. I still wanted to dance on that rooftop, but in the meantime, there was other stuff on my living list to work through. I smiled to myself as I ticked off 'learn to ice skate' and the recently added 'sex under the stars', Two down, many to go... swimming naked, The Trevi Fountain, a Vespa ride through Rome and a Santorini sunset. I finally fell asleep at five a.m. in Sue's spare bedroom, clutching the postcard to my chest and dreaming of a rooftop, high above New York City.

At work the next day all I could think of was Dan, in the darkness, grass underneath my naked thighs, Dan's breath in my face.

I hadn't eaten and only having about an hour's sleep hadn't helped, yet I felt so awake—so alive. About two o'clock I had a break in between clients so went upstairs to make a black coffee and think about the night before.

Mandy appeared in the doorway. 'My body hates me right now...' she said, opening the box of tea bags.

'Oh, really, why?'

'Two words... no, three... oh, a few actually.' She leaned on the worktop to face me while she concentrated on the number of words. 'Free drinks, Kat shitfaced snogging the bloke I fancied— me fly-kicking him up the street.'

'Oh, dear. That sounds like quite a night. You're okay aren't you?' I sighed.

'Yeah, I'll live. Sue says you had a good night?'

'Oh, did she? Well, I really wish she wouldn't discuss my sex life with everyone. Okay, so I had sex in a field... and yes, it was good. It was bloody good. Happy?'

'Whoa... go, Faye! She never said anything about you doing it in a field... she just said you'd had a good night at the ice rink.'

'Oh... yes... skating.' Me and my mouth.

'Anyway, I'm glad you've finally let yourself go. You used to be a bit uptight you know, and Bruce has definitely loosened you up. Anyway, tell Bruce you need a night off from his bush oysters—me and Sue are gonna take you on a girls' night out,' she sang this last bit and waved her finger almost threateningly at me.

A chill went down my spine. I'd been out on these girls' nights with Mandy before and nothing good ever came of them. If you liked wet T-shirt competitions, obscene cocktails and sex games, you would probably enjoy one of Mandy's girls' nights. These were usually rounded off with her face down in a kebab on the pavement—not a euphemism... or perhaps it was?

'You're booked in tomorrow night for *fun* so you can lie in on Sunday morning. And you're gonna need that lie-in 'cos you is gonna be *off your tits,* missy. Me and Sue will make sure of that.'

It was delivered in my face as an ultimatum and, before I could protest, she'd made the tea and gone. It was lovely of them to be so supportive of my single status with a girls' night out, but what happened to girls' nights in? I wanted face packs and chick flicks and big tubs of Ben and Jerry's from the safety of Sue's made-to-order soft furnishings. I didn't want to be hauled round the region's fleshpots while Mandy flashed her breasts and force-fed me alcohol until I didn't know my name.

I smiled to myself. It was my own fault; I kept telling everyone I wanted to have a social life and wouldn't make the same mistake as before and give my life up for a man. Mandy and Sue were keen I retained this new independence and, though the girls were crazy and Mandy thought *The Great Gatsby* was a cocktail, they were always good fun.

That evening as Sue and I waited for Mandy, we shared a bottle of rosé wine in a bar call The Med.

'Sue,' I said, pouring us each a second glass from the first bottle. 'Are you happy? I mean, do you think you ever could be... again?'

'Apart from the divorce and Aeroflot Annie and all my...'

'Soft furnishings? Yes...' I added, moving the conversation along before it dissolved into a thrashing session about stolen cushions and ransacked pelmets.

'I don't aim for 'happy', love. I just try and get through each day without committing suicide or murder. That's what it's all about, isn't it? Life. No one's happy all the time are they?'

'No, but sometimes do you wonder if we've got it right? We spend our lives looking for something and we often don't even know what we're looking for... then we have a laugh at work, a good night out, a curry at the weekend and before we know it we're back on the bloody hamster wheel.'

'What else is there?'

'I don't know... I just admire people who really embrace life on their own terms... chase rainbows, don't just accept the status quo, reject a nine-to-five existence.'

'Do you mean people who work night shifts, love?'

'No, I mean some people don't live and work and wait to grow old in the same place they were born in. They see other countries, different things and meet new people, and if they're unhappy, they leave... free spirits.'

'I don't like the idea of that—you wouldn't know what you were doing or where you were going next.'

'That's the point Sue. We get stuck in a rut. When we're younger we want the safety and security of marriage; we want to be rescued from the nightclubs and the leering men, and live in nice homes with cars and safe husbands. But then you hit forty and it all looks different, like you're missing out on something bigger,' I said, taking a large sip of tingly cold wine.

'I just want my old life back,' said Sue, despondently.

'I can understand that—we all want what we don't have. But time changes you, and I feel so restless. It was different when Emma was growing up, there was always stuff to do, somewhere to be, someone to do it all for. I was swallowed up in her life and her future, but when she left home it all stopped... as suddenly as it had all started. I was on my own and in my forties and I thought—where did my life go?'

'Well, now you and Craig are apart and you're in a new relationship, you can start again.'

'Yeah... but I feel like I've met myself twenty years later and I don't know who I am anymore... like I lost myself along the way.'

'I reckon I lost myself around about 1996,' she sighed. 'I suppose Ken and the salon have been my 'Emma'. You put so much of yourself into other things, other people, you've nothing left for yourself at the end of it all.' She was holding the globe of her wine glass and looking into the clear liquid like it was a crystal ball.

'The midlife crisis has a lot to answer for,' I sighed and glugged more wine. It occurred to me that it would be wise to stop drinking now. I was missing Dan in that way you do when you've had one too many and you're in the early stages of a relationship. It was all so new and fragile and so exciting, I didn't need alcohol to give me a high, but Sue was ordering another and swaying in her seat, her voice raised—she was well on the way.

Around the bar, the photos of Mediterranean scenes, turquoise oceans, and pale, sandy beaches seemed to beckon. I wanted to dive into that turquoise water and the sunsets... oh, the sunsets. Listening to Dan talk about life in Sydney and travelling through Europe had opened up a mental brochure I was now constantly flicking through in my head. I told myself to leave it... stop imagining us both by those pools, infinity blue eyes staring into me. Since that first kiss, I'd dumped Kevin Bacon and Brad Pitt; even Ryan Gosling was on the sub's bench—they just couldn't compete. Everywhere I looked, all I could see was Dan.

Sue was watching me, sipping her wine, but saying nothing.

'What?' I said.

'Just the way you've been recently. You're happier but sometimes you're miles away. You're in love, aren't you?'

'I don't think so...' I lied.

'Well, whatever—but bloody hell, I'm proud of you—you aren't letting the grass grow under your feet,' she said through giggles. 'You've kept that deli in business, popping in for a bit of sausage every day...'

At that we both fell about laughing. Sue fell to the floor. The rosé wine had now officially taken over.

I immediately stood up to help her onto her feet. Sue always drank on an empty stomach. She told me once that she had to stay slim for when Ken came back; he hated weight on a woman and she didn't want it to come between them. What a shit he is, I thought, lunging towards her in my drunken state.

'Come on, Sue, I can't manage you on your own,' I said, but couldn't get her onto her feet; she was too floppy and far heavier than she looked. I began dragging her along the floor in an attempt to get her to the front door and outside for a breath of fresh air.

Having arrived at the open doorway, I leaned through it, trying to help her out into the night for a breath of air. It was still quite early, but as it looked like Mandy had stood us up, I was keen to get a taxi back so I could lie in bed and think about Dan.

'O.M.G, WTF?' came a string of letters in an alarmed voice. I looked up to see Mandy and 'her girls' dancing towards us in skimpy shorts, orange tans and eyebrows that were so big and independent I reckoned they had their own Facebook page.

'Hey, have you two started the party without me?' she yelled in mock outrage. Never had I been so pleased to see her. 'Mandy, give us a hand. Sue has just gone—I can't get her up. I'm going to have to take her home,' I called, as if it needed an explanation as I dragged her along the floor like a rolled up carpet. Mandy and her posse headed towards us, not before engaging several passersby with flashes of their breasts as if it were an ancient tribal greeting.

They landed at our sides and, no doubt having had to deal with this level of comatose drunkenness on a nightly basis, those girls stepped to it. They soon had Sue in a fireman's lift, Mandy shrieking and linking arms with her friend, with Sue slumped between them like a rag doll. I averted my eyes for a second time, unable to watch as my oldest dearest friend was being bounced along the road to the tune of Rihanna's *Rude Boy*.

'I'll call Terry the taxi and get him to pick us up,' Toyah yelled over Mandy's chorus. 'We can't carry her all the way,' she added with surprising sense and lucidity for someone whose drunken multitasking I could only watch in awe. She was holding Sue up, dialling a taxi and flashing a group of young men her thonged backside—all at the same time. Respect, I thought, wondering if any of this would be required of me if I re-entered the singles' world.

So, after much shouting and raucous laughter on the pavement from Mandy and co, 'Terry the taxi' pulled up and we all piled in. His opening line was to ask politely that we didn't 'vomit' or 'fight' in his cab—a request I've never received from a taxi driver before or since.

'Scruples!' yelled Mandy from underneath a very sleepy Sue. 'Yeah!' agreed Toyah and the other girl with over-bleached hair and no bra, who I think must have been the infamous Flick (nose piercing, lipstick tattoo, weakness for blow-up willies).

'*NO!*' I shouted. 'Sue and I are not going. Sorry, Mand but we have had it.' I was a bit annoyed because now we had to go all around the town to drop them off at 'Scruples' night club before heading home ourselves.

Journeying through the outskirts of the town in the back of
Terry's taxi, we were treated to all kinds of nocturnal activities.
Girls weren't just falling out of night clubs; they were hurling
themselves onto pavements one after another like loud, glittery
lemmings. I looked away as young lads dropped their trousers
and others collapsed in drunken heaps... two girls were jaywalk-
ing, clinging to each other and staggering though the night. I
watched them anxiously, always a mother, and worried for their
safety. I was thinking about Emma and hoping she didn't pull
stunts like that in the middle of the road. I doubted it.

Then I saw him through the crowds, clear as anything: Dan,
standing outside a wine bar. I recognised the blond hair, the way
he was leaning... I knew that stance so well, the slightly slumped
shoulders, the tilt of the head. My heart was in my mouth and
I was seriously contemplating leaping out of the moving taxi or
at least winding down the window to wave to him. He'd said
he was meeting friends for drinks and suddenly I wanted him
to see I was young and vital and out on a Saturday night too.
Then... someone moved and my heart almost stopped. Through
the crowded pavement, I saw her... a pretty young woman. Dan's
arms were around her shoulders, his chin resting on her head,
their bodies close. I caught my heart in my throat as the taxi sped
through the night. And then they were gone—in one thunder-
clap moment everything had changed.

My heart felt like a balloon, swollen with water that someone
had just burst with a pin. How could I be so stupid? I felt faint,
and once we'd passed them, I slowly wound down the window

for air and space. I had to deal with this. One night we'd had sex under the stars and tonight he was with someone else. It was clearly all just a game to him; another night, another conquest. It was my own fault; I'd wanted this new life and all the joy and agony that came with it... Well, here comes the agony, I thought, like a great big Bondi Beach wave. Of course he saw other girls— neither of us had said we were exclusive—where on earth did I get that idea? He was cute and affectionate and fond of me... but when did we ever have a conversation about exclusivity? He'd said he liked me, but I now realised I was probably 'a' girlfriend, not 'his' girlfriend. That's how people are nowadays—no commitment, no tomorrow. It was all meaningless and I'd been naive and stupid. He was a good-looking, bright thirty-something in a different country, where women were probably throwing themselves at him. Sleeping with him had been a huge moment for me... but that didn't mean it was for him. Dan was a nice guy, and in my highly vulnerable, hormonal state I'd got it all wrong and assumed it meant more.

How ridiculous; I was behaving like a teenager. I couldn't stop thinking about them both, and as painful as it was, I had to force myself to accept how 'right' they looked together... how I didn't fit in his world. I went over and over it all in my head, feeling the keenness of the pain. Even though it was only a fleeting glimpse, my mind had photographed the scene and it kept flashing through my head. Like a black-and-white photo you'd see in a magazine advert for designer perfume, their heights were perfectly matched, their bodies both lithe, both sun-kissed... both now Instagrammed in my head forever. The only consolation to my agony was that I'd been dead inside for so long that this was a sign I was alive—and almost better than feeling *nothing*, as I had for years now.

❊ ❊ ❊

I woke the following morning with a terrible hangover and a splattered heart. I went to work and spent the day just going through the motions. Dan texted to ask, 'Are u free tonight?' and I had to stop myself texting back to ask, 'Why—is ur gfriend busy?'

At six p.m. I wandered out onto the still sunlit pavement and strolled slowly past the deli. It closed at five so I didn't expect to see him, but thought I heard his voice calling me. My finger ends tingled. I hadn't indulged in a fantasy cocktail with Kevin, Ryan or Brad for weeks, but perhaps all the recent emotional turmoil had affected me more than I'd realised. Christ, the fantasies had taken over reality—instead of Hollywood A-listers I could hear Dan's voice in my head. I was in real trouble now. But there it was again, unmistakable, with the Australian enunciation, so different... or, as Sue had remarked after she'd met him at the salon, 'very extinguished'.

I turned to see him running after me from the direction of the deli.

'Hi, I was just locking up when I saw you. Did you get my text?' he smiled, out of breath but apparently happy to see me.

I nodded, unsure what to say. I wanted to ask him who he was with last night but it felt like a cliché and I'd sound like a bunny boiler.

Seeing him with the girl had changed everything for me, but his smile and easy manner suggested nothing had changed for him. I looked away from his eyes at the teatime traffic slowly moving down the road. I couldn't smile; I could barely speak. He was waiting for my embrace, my gushing hello, but I just felt closed off, my arms folded in an attempt at self-preservation. We'd been lovers, which meant everything to silly middle-aged me—but what did that mean in his world?

We walked along slowly, side by side. I couldn't breathe and he asked me if my muscles ached after skating—a double meaning; he was talking about the sex too.

I shook my head. 'No, I'm fine.' I was monotone, refusing to acknowledge the double entendre, the intimacy of our shared secret. We arrived at the park gates and I walked through, assuming he was heading the same way and would walk in with me but he stopped.

'Faye? Are you okay?'

'Yes... I'm fine. I'm going for a stroll in the park,' I offered, trying to sound unfazed and casual, not something I carried off well.

'I texted to see if you were free tonight. I want to cook for you. I know it's short notice, but Jen's not home.'

'I don't know, Dan...'

'Oh... It's okay if you're not... I mean... if...' he looked puzzled.

I shrugged. I didn't know what to say.

'Is it something to do with the other night? Me and you... was it too soon?'

'No.'

'Then what's the matter?'

'I'm not like you,' I blurted. 'I can't sleep with someone and then be with someone else. I thought I knew what I wanted, but I don't. I don't know myself and I don't know you and I've given you the wrong impression. I know I said I don't care about tomorrow and I only want "now" but for me that doesn't mean I'm okay with sleeping around. I don't want multiple partners.'

'You don't have to have multiple partners,' he half-laughed, waiting for me to join in.

'I'm not talking about me!' I snapped. 'I'm talking about the conveyor belt of women you seem to have on tap.'

'What are you talking about?' He touched my arm, genuinely concerned, he seemed genuinely confused.

'I saw you... last night in town, with a girl, hugging a girl... a young... girl.' I was determined not to cry, but was finding it hard. I had changed, hadn't I? Here was the new Faye who called the shots; she was sexy and in control... I mustn't lose her now.

He was looking at me like I was crazy. 'Girl? I was with a... oh... last night. That was Gabby—you must have seen me with Gabby.'

'I don't know who it was, but you had your arms around her, you were leaning on each other... which is absolutely fine. It's a free world, you can do what... who you like... but I... I was surprised how it made me feel. I couldn't believe it—you both stood hugging and...'

'Yeah, I suppose we were... I can see how it might have looked. She was upset, a little drunk; a guy had dumped her and... me and Gabby go back a long way. She's just a friend, Faye.'

'She's just a friend? Do you always hug your friends like that? It looked like more than friends to me, Dan...'

'Yeah. She's my ex but that doesn't mean we can't be just friends now I told you, we broke up once we got here. It's tough to let go. We came here together... we're kind of stuck with each other.'

That made sense, sort of. 'Look, you can kiss and hug and sleep with who you want... but I can't deal with that if we're together.'

'Faye, you've got it all wrong, totally—yes, I probably had my arms round her, it's what we do. We were friends before we were lovers and now we're friends again.'

'It all seems so... loose, like untied shoelaces—lovers one minute, friends the next. How can you make such big changes?'

'I suppose because... I was never in love.'

'You can say that now, but seeing you last night with your arms around her...'

'So why didn't you come over and yell at me? If you had, you'd have realised I was comforting her. She knows the score. I told you, we broke up after we got here...'

'Yes, because you met someone else. You seem to do a lot of loving and leaving. But I can't do it. That isn't what I signed up for...' I started to cry. 'I'm forty-two and I can't compete with younger, hotter women. My breasts have gone south and... I can't give you children... not that we are going to have children... I mean...'

'Oh, dear. I usually ask for a woman's gynaecological report *before* I go out on a date, and on this occasion I took it as read that you were fertile and able to breed as and when, so you can imagine my disappointment.' He was trying to make a joke but, like the first time with the panda hat, I cried even more.

'I'm almost ten years older than you. What are you... doing with me?'

'Stop! Faye, I thought you understood? I explained to you that day at the park that I'd ended things with Gabby because I met someone else. Didn't you get it? That someone else was *you*.'

Oh, God. When I'd asked if he was 'seeing' the woman he left Gabby for, he'd said, 'You tell me,' which seemed rather odd at the time. I'd dismissed it, and the kiss that had followed pretty much obliterated everything else.

'Faye, I don't care how old you are and I don't set out to hurt people. I finished with Gabby after going for that beer with you. It might have been just a beer, but after that night I knew it was more than that. I thought about you, missed you, one of your hairs was caught on my jacket and I kept it... weird, I know, and even slightly creepy,' he smiled, 'but my point is, I've never done that with anyone else's hair.'

'It's probably as well—you're right, that's creepy,' I said, with half a smile.

'The way you listened to me and the way I felt I could open up to you about my family, my life, I've never done that before. Younger, "hotter" women, as you put it, don't want to know about my family gene, my mother's death, my brotherly guilt... there aren't a whole lotta laughs in there... But you listened, you cared.'

I realised in that moment I had completely misread what I saw on the street, and I was surprised to see how desperate he was to prove there was nothing. I opened my arms and we embraced. 'I'm sorry. I'm sorry; I really thought you... I've had the worst twenty-four hours of my life, just thinking you didn't care... that I was a notch on your bedpost.'

'I'm sorry you went through that, but I have friends who are girls... pretty girls, some I've been out with. I won't lie; in the past I probably would have slept with one or two women at the same time and called it 'an overlap', kidding myself it was okay. But not with you, Faye. Not anymore.'

I pulled away and, holding him slightly at arm's length, I looked directly into his eyes. 'I know you have lots of female friends, but I'm from a different world. I was married until a few months ago and I don't have male friends, so it takes a little getting used to. I don't want to clip your wings, Dan... but if we're going to continue to have sex, it has to be exclusive, even if it's only for a week."

'I want that too. I can't bear to think of you with anyone else. I've never felt that before either.' He reached out for my hand and I let his fingers curl tentatively around mine.

'Okay... no overlaps?' I said.

He nodded and we kissed, there in the bright evening sunshine with people walking past. It felt tantalisingly bad and wholly inappropriate—which made it even better.

'So. Are we okay... you and me?' he asked.

'Yeah... I think so. But just so I understand, where is Gabby now?'

'She's away in Scotland, then she's off to Europe. We have some other mates who are travelling and she's going with them. I've decided to stay here.'

'Really?'

'Yeah. I told you... I kinda met someone,' he laughed, grabbing me around the waist and kissing my neck.

I was torn between feeling very relieved and very stupid. I'd given Glenn Close a good run for her money in the world's biggest bunny boiler award but it had also made me realise how vulnerable I was. It never ceased to amaze me how being with Dan awoke feelings long forgotten. Jealousy, lust, learning to love and trust someone again were all feelings that had been lost, buried in years of marriage and motherhood. I was now rediscovering little bits of me, piece by piece, uncovering the sands of time and obligation and duty and guilt—and believing in myself all over again.

'So you'll come over, tonight?' he breathed into my hair.

'Yeah,' I breathed back, hearing my own voice husky with desire.

We said goodbye and I walked home alone, wanting to skip and wave my arms in the air, but realising that would look rather strange. There were some things I probably still couldn't do. Shouldn't do. I took out the postcard from my handbag and looked into that picture and wondered who would be with me when I finally got to that rooftop in the city that never sleeps? Could I dare to even hope it might be Dan?

❊ ❊ ❊

Sue was as excited as me when she came home from work and I was trying on clothes.

'Oh, it's all working out for you, love,' she smiled, watching like a proud mum as I painted my nails a lovely nude shade. I hadn't painted my nails since the previous summer, partly because as a hairdresser it was pointless—the varnish came off with all the hair washing—and also because no one noticed, least of all me.

Over the past few weeks, I'd ticked another thing off my living list without really trying, and that was to lose ten pounds. Sue said it was 'the divorce diet' and she'd done the same when she and Ken split. I reckoned it was down to love and life chaos too, but whatever it was, I could now squeeze into Emma's old jeans, and I'd recently bought a new pale blue T-shirt, which Sue and Mandy said made me look 'less frumpy'.

I'd been surprised when they'd said that. 'Do I usually look frumpy?' I'd asked. They'd both nodded; 'But you've made a start—leaving Craig has taken ten years off you, love.'

'That's the only trouble with having a younger man,' Sue said as she did my hair that evening. 'You need to be on your toes, love—casual, flirty fashion... but no mutton.'

'That's the last thing I want. Oh, I wish I'd met him when I was ten years younger,' I sighed.

'Yeah, but he'd have been twenty-three, love, and that's too young even for you... cradle snatcher.' We laughed at that but it did sting a little. Where was I going with this guy? He was heading home in a couple of months and it was thousands of miles away, even if we considered a future together, the age difference would matter. I know he joked about it when I said I couldn't give him a child, but he was so young! One day he might want that; he might want a family, a young wife and all that went with it.

I decided not to dwell on that side of things. It wasn't going to be an issue because we'd both have to go our separate ways soon. I decided to put all negative thoughts to the back of my mind, pack it in the suitcase with the old photos, the living list and the scarlet silk dress.

Sue had put my hair up in a soft, messy 'updo' and lent me a string of blue glass beads to go with the T-shirt.

'Do I look okay? Or like a frumpy forty-something?'

'Stop putting yourself down; I've told you, you're gorgeous,' she squealed, squirting half her bottle of 'Flower Bomb' all over me. I couldn't sneeze for laughing or laugh for sneezing, which wrecked my mascara and added even more 'messy updo' to my lovely hair style.

I didn't care. It was ten to eight and I wasn't going to waste any more precious time messing with my hair when I had so much life to live. I didn't feel the need to dress up or play games with Dan; we were friends first—and, besides, he seemed to like me for being me... messy hair, life in limbo and filter permanently off.

Pulling up at the large, Victorian terraced house on the tree-lined street, I was surprised I'd never been down here before as it was only half a mile away from my house... or what had been my old house. It was a lovely summer evening; the birds were singing in the trees and I felt an incredible sense of freedom, my head and heart full of promise as I skipped up the step, a smile on my face and a bottle of Ken's good wine under my arm.

Dan opened the door, his face lighting up as he saw me. The smell of warm tomatoes and garlic wafted down the hall, adding to the warm welcome. It was perfect—a beautiful moment of expectation and infinite possibilities that I would keep forever. I often think about that night; like a pebble in my pocket I secretly caress the smoothness, reliving the memory through my fingertips.

The house was lovely. High ceilings, deep skirting boards, big airy windows, trendy artwork, bulging book cases and a big, fluffy cat in the middle of a squashy sofa scattered with eclectic cushions of every shade and shape (Sue would not have approved—nothing matched). Dan gestured for me to go into the kitchen. 'Come and observe the artist at work,' he said, his hand in the small of my back, his breath on my neck. It was early in the evening, but I was already faint with desire and could barely concentrate on his menu for looking at his beautiful, stubbly face. He talked about tomatoes on the vine, free-range chicken and Italian herbs, but I just wanted to kiss every crevice of his face—and move down.

I put my bottle of wine on the side and he took it, smiling and studying the label.

'Oh I didn't know you were a wine buff?'

'Oh, it's just some I had in,' I smiled. 'Mmm, that smells good... there's something sweet too?' I said, sniffing the air like a truffle pig.

'Yeah, I was nostalgic for home so I've baked my mum's lemon cakes.'

My heart melted.

'I don't suppose your supermodel girlfriends eat cake when you invite them over for dinner.'

'No, they just have a stick of celery then sex on the table—so predictable.' He pulled a disapproving face.

I smiled. 'You are joking, right?'

He laughed and nodded.

'Oh, God, that stuff earlier... I came over all possessive, didn't I? I don't want you to think I'm... I'm not some stalker. I mean, if you had sex on the table, I wouldn't mind. I don't mean I wouldn't... I don't mean I wouldn't have sex on the table, I would... I just meant...'

'Faye. Enough,' he smiled. 'Eat some of this bread and stop talking about sex all the time—you're obsessed,' he rolled his eyes in mock annoyance and I giggled.

We sat at one end of the big wooden kitchen table and ate homemade walnut bread with olive oil and balsamic vinegar. The bread was warm and nutty and the kitchen was filled with pots and pans and jars of herbs and spices, and I wanted to stay there forever. Terracotta tiles covered the walls and the air smelled of the Mediterranean: sharp, sweet lemons, the savoury perfume of herbs and earthy garlic. The wine was red and deep, and I sipped it as he laid platters of salad and rice and fragrant chicken on the table.

'This is delicious. You are so clever,' I said, taking large mouthfuls of food. My emotions were all over the place and, having felt lightheaded and giddy all day, I was now feeling a sudden surge of hunger. It was so healing, being with him, and the more I ate the more we talked, and the tension in my shoulders seemed to recede along with my tiredness. I could never feel tired around Dan.

'I'm glad you enjoy my food. It's like when you create a great hairstyle or a new colour, like any artist—we want people to enjoy our work however big or small,' he said, reaching out his hand across the table, touching mine.

Watching him eat and talk, it occurred to me in that second that the thing Dan showed me more than anything was respect. He thought I was a good mum and considered me to be wise, funny, and even showed respect for my job. He wasn't belittling me or putting down my career, he was likening what I did to that of an artist and I'd never thought of it in those terms before. He was right; I was creative and worked hard to achieve the right colour effect, the perfect cut that would suit my client. It might have been the wine, but my inner Beyonce was on the move and I had that urge to dance on the table again. Why was I only just experiencing this euphoria? Why had it taken me so long to realise that life could be like this and that it is never too late to unearth the very core of who you are, what you've been looking for... and what you can still become?

After we'd eaten, Dan produced a batch of perfect lemon cakes and lovingly placed them one by one on a tiered cake platter. They looked so pretty and I was so touched he'd made them just for me, I didn't want to spoil the display. 'I'll eat one later,' I promised.

'Don't put the moment off, Faye... if you do, it may never come round again. Go on... take one while you can,' he said, plucking a lemon cake from the pyramid, breaking a lemony lump off and leaning across the table. He gently offered the squidgy, fragrant lemon morsel to my lips and I slowly opened my mouth to let it in, my tongue tingling with lemon and sugar, my whole body buzzing with him. He watched me, licking his lips, his mouth almost moving with mine as he broke off some more, again gently pushing it between my lips. I licked his palm and my mouth glittered with sugar.

He smiled. Standing up and taking my hand, he helped me up, clearing the plates across the table with one arm to make a clearing. Then he put his hands around my waist and lifted me onto the table, kissing me, gently forcing his body between my knees. 'Should we be doing this? I mean, your aunt... when will she be home?'

'I don't know... and I don't care,' he whispered, his hands under my T-shirt, caressing my breasts as my hand moved towards the zip of his jeans, grazing the bulging denim.

'She has lodgers too.' He kissed my breasts. 'Any of them could walk in at any time—it's... very... very dangerous. And... very, very exciting.'

I felt like a sixteen-year-old again, worried about being caught on the sofa by our parents. I slowly lay back on the table, taking a deep breath. The air was infused with lemon zest and sugar and he was gently pulling down my jeans. 'You're so beautiful...' he sighed.

I held on to his strong, slim back. His firm thighs were now between my legs; I was unable to resist and within seconds we were having sex on the kitchen table. Oh my God, I thought, I am like a porn star; I'm just doing it anywhere and everywhere these days—is this really me? The lemon cake feeding foreplay had excited us both, and just moments later he exploded as I groaned in ecstasy.

We both lay on the table, entwined in each other's limbs, I was amazed at how he made me feel. It had never been like this for me before. The old Faye Dobson wouldn't have had sex on her *own* kitchen table, let alone anyone else's.

'I forgot about your tiger...' I heard him say. I opened my eyes and slowly came to; 'Oh... what?' He was gesturing towards my vajazzle. I'd forgotten about it too. In fact, during sex I'd also forgotten about my unleashed breasts, ageing thighs and baggy baby tummy. He made me feel young and beautiful again.

'I couldn't see it properly in the dark the other night, but it's quite good, really detailed,' he said, his fingers caressing the jewels. Then he looked at me; 'Why a tiger?'

'A tiger? What do you mean?' I'd only looked at the vajazzle from above; as I hated my body, I tried to avoid looking at myself naked in a full-length mirror. I sat up, and from my rather uncomfortable vantage point tried to make out the shape from upside down—then realised Mandy's little joke: it wasn't a tiger, it was a cougar.

'I wondered why everyone growled when they saw it...' I said.

''Everyone?' Everyone?' How many people have you shown it to, Faye?' he asked.

'Loads... Mandy took a photo.'

'Jesus, you Pommy girls are out there, aren't you?' He was teasing again.

'No... it was for her portfolio. Don't say anything else or I'll keep talking,' I giggled. 'It's a long story... and I don't want you to stop to listen to... me... going on about my... vajazz...'

He was gently pushing me back down and moving up my body to kiss my mouth, and then we were having sex again, only this time on the kitchen floor. We writhed around and I wondered why I'd never had sex on a kitchen floor with a younger guy before—because it was *so very good*. And the old Faye was telling the new Faye that Dan's Auntie Jen may walk in on them anytime—and the new Faye was panting, 'I know, but that's what makes it so very... very dangerous and... very... very... exciting.'

❉ ❉ ❉

We lay on the floor for a while, but I reckoned we were now tempting fate and the prospect of being caught while having sex tended to lose its potency in the afterglow. I really didn't want 'Auntie Jen' to walk in on her nephew naked on the floor with the local hairdresser who'd just left her husband.

'I've never had sex on a kitchen table,' I said as we sat up and gathered our clothes together.

'You haven't lived,' he kissed me.

I smiled and moved from his arms, gathering my clothes around me, and we wandered through into the living room and sat cuddled together on a sofa.

'I've never had sex with anyone but Craig,' I whispered.

His arm was round me and he stroked my hair.

'Was your break-up difficult?' he asked.

'He's the father of my child. We have a shared history. I loved him once... in my way, but it wasn't earth-shattering, soul mate love. I was pregnant and we wanted the baby... but we should never have married.'

'That's sad.'

'Yeah, it is, but I can't regret it because that would be like regretting my daughter —and she's my best achievement, the love of my life and the thing I'm most proud of.

'You are lovely, Faye... you gave up a lot. College, all your dreams of travelling, living abroad... that rooftop in New York.'

'Yeah, and that Santorini sunset...'

I was still in his arms and he cuddled me to him, kissing my forehead.

'Is that next on your list?' he asked. 'To see a sunset on Santorini?'

'One day... but next I'd like to see another lemon cake,' I said. My time with Dan was borrowed. I wasn't going anywhere while he was still in the UK; I wanted to be with him until the very last second when he got on that flight back to Australia.

He left the room and I slowly got dressed, glad of the opportunity to squeeze into Emma's jeans without being observed. As I hopped on one leg and wobbled up and down pouring myself into the blue denim, I was grateful Dan wasn't around to see it.

He wandered back in with a cupcake on a plate, just as I'd zipped myself up.

'Ooh, a post-coital cupcake,' I said, taking the plate from him and crossing my legs on the sofa.

He stood watching me, smiling.

'What?' I said, attacking the moist, fragrant lemon cake with all my concentration and pushing a wedge of citrusy deliciousness into my mouth.

He wandered towards me on the sofa and opened his mouth. I shook my head, 'This is too good to share.' I turned my back on him and he tried to grab me, or the cake, but I fought him off.

'But I thought, as we'd just shared our bodies... we might share a cake?' he said, trying to rugby tackle me on the sofa.

'You are kidding. Sex is one thing... but cake is a very different matter,' I said, laughing through citrus crumbs as he tickled me. I continued with the delicious, lemony confection, the bitter-sweetness making my jaws ache, the moist sponge light and crumbly. I fought him off to finish the last crumb off the plate, and Dan feigned surprise.

'Oh... you weren't joking... about eating it all yourself?'

'Joking? Dan, if we're going to be seeing more of each other, I just need to lay down some ground rules. I love beautiful, crafted dishes, continental cheeses, Italian leaves and rustic artisanal breads, and anything your deli has to offer. But if we're going to have a good time this summer, I want us to begin with total honesty. Yes, I love fine food, but I also love junk food, and when I am desperate for a fix, I've been known to go to the corner shop and stock up with white bread, crisps, chocolate and cake. So, along with my "no sharing" policy, be prepared for me to sometimes behave like a slut in the kitchen.'

'Oh, yeah...? I already saw that, just now.'

I punched him in the arm. "I always knew Australians were coarse,' I teased, and we began to play-fight with Auntie Jen's cushions, which led to more kissing. I couldn't believe how confident I was with him; I wanted him all the time and, despite the lateness of the hour and the fact his auntie could appear at any time, I wanted him again. Who knew Faye Dobson was like this? I didn't.

I ran my fingers down his arm and he sat up so he could see me.

'I remember when I first saw you, I thought you were like no one I'd ever known. You are so different with your tan and your blond hair and your lovely accent.'

He looked into my eyes, caressing my cheek as he spoke. 'I thought you were something special too. You're gorgeous—but I've since realised you're quite impatient and hungry. I mean, you have a big appetite for life... okay, and cake.' He sat up properly, facing me on the sofa, his legs crossed, an arm on each of my shoulders, more serious now. 'Most of all, I love your honesty... you don't play games; what you see is what you get—I love that. We're probably being stupid starting something we both know will have to end... but I don't care I just want to be with you.'

'I'm a big girl... I know you have to go home one day, but let's not talk about that. Let's make the most of our time together, even if it's tinged with the fact that we both know it will end. It's bittersweet, like lemon cake.'

'You're an infuriating optimist who likes to gloss over the bad bits and pretend everything's great, aren't you?'

I nodded.

'Well that's good, because so am I.'

He reached down and kissed me a million times. And all I could taste was love and lemon cake.

Chapter Sixteen

You Hear The Music and You Just Gotta Dance!

'I fancy Cuba,' I said one afternoon about a week after sex on Jen's table. We were lying together on Sue's sofa. She'd gone on a dog-walking date and though I'd hoped it would be a success, the signs weren't good—not least of all because she didn't actually have a dog.

'Yeah, Cuba's lovely,' Dan sighed. 'Daiquiris, beautiful women, laid-back sounds... I loved Cuba.'

'Is there anywhere you haven't been?' I asked.

'Oh, probably—I just never like to be in one place for too long.'

'I've been in the same place doing the same thing for too long,' I said, lying back into his arms, stroking his thigh. We'd just had wild sex on the sofa and I was feeling a little sleepy but as Dan had taken the day off specially to be with me, I felt we should make the most of it.

'Let's do something exciting!' I said, sitting up.

'We just did.'

'No—I want to do something totally inappropriate for a woman my age.'

'You just did.'

'Okay. Stop it. Think of something.'

'I don't know... fly to Cuba, get your nipple pierced, have my name tattooed across your chest?'

'Hmm...not sure about your name across my chest, but I've always wanted a tattoo,' I said, feeling a sparkle in the pit of my stomach.

'Okay, let's go then.' He stood up and threw his T-shirt on.

'Now?'

'Why not?'

'Because it's not something you do on a Monday afternoon. You have to think about these things. I can't just go and get tattooed.'

He flopped back down. 'Of course you can. I told you, stop putting everything off. No one "thinks" about a tattoo—it's like you hear the music and you just gotta dance... you know?'

'Do you?'

'Yeah. I got mine on a whim; just fancied it when I was drunk one night in Thailand. I just did it. If you don't do it now, you never will.'

'What would Emma think of me getting drunk and going for a tattoo on my day off?' I said.

'She'd think, "My mum's the coolest chick I know.' He stood up. 'Come on—let's do it. You have to stop worrying what everyone else thinks. Do what's right for *you*, not Emma, or Sue... or even me. Do what *Faye* wants... and stop judging her.'

'Do I judge myself?'

'Yeah, big time. Stop beating yourself up, Faye. If you want to do something, trust your instincts, feel good about doing what's right for *you* and just do it.'

He was right and I did want this. It would be a symbol of my newfound freedom, my new approach to life. A tattoo would be fun and young and make me feel good about myself. I had to stop judging myself and worrying about how my choices impacted on everything else. I was going to do it—and get down to that tattoo parlour before I changed my mind.

'Okay, then. Let's go,' I said, jumping up and grabbing my handbag.

An hour later I was in a bar high on pain, drinking neat whisky. I was also the proud owner of a small, cute, lemon cupcake tattoo on my left shoulder; 'I feel... kick-ass crazy,' I said, pulling a face as the stinging whisky hit my gullet.

'Yep, you're one crazy bitch,' Dan laughed, and ordered us another.

'And I haven't finished yet,' I said, admiring my beautiful but rather sore shoulder tattoo. 'Dan, I just feel *soooo* good. It's like I've been asleep forever, and I've just woken up. Why have I never done these things before? Why did I wait so long? I should have done all this when I was eighteen!'

'Perhaps you weren't ready then, but you want it now, girl, and you sure as hell are getting it... and who cares how old you are when you get it? It's all about the stars colliding... and I reckon you had a stellar collision.'

I reckoned he was right.

'So, what's next on your agenda?' he asked.

'Oh, I don't know. What's left on my list? There's swimming naked... I want to go away, see some stuff... but I don't want to leave you, not when our time is so limited.'

He was a dreamer just like me. I'd always suppressed this part of me with Craig; he'd always laughed at my plans and my silly ideas so I'd learned to hide them from him. But Dan and I took each other's foolishness seriously because we both understood what it was like to want everything—now. There were no rules with Dan. We had sex outside, stayed up all night and got drunk in the middle of the afternoon... It was pure hedonism, anything was possible and I loved it. In Australia he used to cliff dive and I reckon he was always looking for the next cliff, the best high— and I was now right behind him in the queue.

✳ ✳ ✳

Later we drank coffee in Sue's back garden watching the stars, a blanket round us both to keep out the evening chill.

'What about you and me seeing that Santorini sunset together?'

I looked at him.

'Thing is, a few of my mates just went out there for a few weeks. I was going to go with them but wanted to stay here with you... a bit longer.'

My heart filled up like a balloon and I slipped my hand in his—I had no idea he'd forsaken a visit to Santorini to be with me. He placed his other hand on top of mine. It felt so good.

'It's my mate Ben's dad's place—a huge apartment with loads of rooms and they're really up for anyone staying there. What do you think?'

I smiled uncertainly—I wasn't sure about 'the mates'. I'd envisaged a holiday together as just me and Dan alone. I wasn't into communal living and a shared fridge like at Emma's student house. Then again, I didn't want to seem old and scared of something new. This is the new Faye, and she's cool, I reminded myself.

'Sounds wonderful,' I said, after all the accommodation was free, neither of us had a lot of money and it was all about being together in a beautiful place.

'Okay, let's do it.' He texted Ben straight away and when he quickly received a text back he smiled triumphantly. 'He says we've got to go out there,' he turned to look at me, 'because it's a really romantic place.'

I melted.

His phone pinged again, he picked it up and a big smile spread across his face. 'Ben just checked and Santorini flights leave on a Wednesday.'

I took out my mobile. 'What dates did you have in mind?' I asked, looking into the screen.

'Wednesday.'

'Yes, but which Wednesday?'

'The day after tomorrow Wednesday.'

'No... I can't do that,'

'Why not?'

'I can't just go to Santorini in two days, I have a job and there's Emma and work and... stuff to do.'

'Like what? Sue will let you have a few weeks off and Emma's an adult with her own life. She'll be fine. The summer's slipping away...'

'I can't just go off for a fortnight and not...'

'A fortnight? No use going all that way for a fortnight... I was thinking a month, maybe six weeks? Ben and the guys are planning to go back to Oz from Greece and I could do the same. We could spend the rest of the summer together in Santorini, Faye. Just think how gorgeous that would be—you and me and the sunset. Then I could kidnap you and take you back home with me,' he joked excitedly.

'Dan, there's nothing I'd love more than spending the summer with you somewhere hot and beautiful and away from it all... I dream of it, but...'

'Faye. Don't say "no" again. You say you made excuses all your life not to do something? Well, here's your chance—and you can tick another two off your list...'

'Two?'

'The sunset and... having sex in the ocean?'

'It was swimming naked in the ocean.'

'I just supersized it.'

I smiled. He was so funny and silly and impulsive. I nodded; 'Yeah. Okay, let me work on it.'

He suddenly put his arms around me. 'I'm happy with you,' he whispered into my hair, moving his hands up my arms. He looked into my eyes and pressed his forehead against mine. 'And I think I'm falling a little bit in love with you.'

New Faye had fallen a little bit in love too, but wasn't quite ready to tell him because the old Faye was nagging her about flight times and what to pack and how to break it to Sue that she would be taking at least a month off. Then she brought up the more urgent matter of a holiday wardrobe and the desperate need to buy a month's supply of new pants.

❊ ❊ ❊

'Sue, of all the fifty things to do before you die, I haven't done one,' I said the following day as I began my request for several weeks off. 'I've never spent New Year's Eve in Times Square, walked The Inca Trail, felt the spray from Niagara Falls, or watched fireworks explode over Sydney Opera House. I've spent my time cutting hair, gossiping, dreaming, sitting in front of the TV and blaming Craig, when all the time it was up to me—my fault I never did it, no one else. So, Sue, I'm going to Santorini on Wednesday and I don't know when I'm coming back.'

She was surprised, and once she'd got over the shock and realised Camilla could cover for me, she was delighted. 'I've got a Greek phrase book from when Ken and I went to Corfu,' she said. 'You'll need it because the Greeks have a different word for everything.'

Once I'd told Sue, there was no turning back.

I called Emma and told her about my emergency departure in my coffee break. She took it in her stride; 'You go, Mum,' she said, and I just wished she was there so I could hug her. I explained about Dan, telling her we were great friends and who knew what would happen next, but she was ten jumps ahead.

'Mum, I know it's more than that. I told you, I saw the way he was looking at you. To be honest, I feel better that you're going with a guy and not on your own. At least I know he'll look after you.'

Emma seemed happier than ever. She had a job in the wine bar near uni when she wasn't studying, and she told me all about the mad customers and how she'd made friends with others who worked there. Dan was right—she would be fine if I went away for a while. She was getting on with her life and I was a big part of it but I now had to take a back seat and get on with my own.

'Are you okay, really?' I asked, guilt still seeping into every conversation we had. 'About me going away, I mean, after me and your dad...'

'Yeah, I'm fine, Mum... just have a great time.'

'I know Dan's probably not what you had in mind for me, but I really like him Em. It's funny, you have all these dreams about your ideal man and who would be right for you, then someone comes along who you never imagined yourself with. You can't help it. It isn't always the right man at the right time, or even in the right place,' I sighed, 'but it just feels... right.'

'I know what you mean, Mum. It's about what makes you happy,' she continued, brightening. 'Talking of which, I've met someone too,' the words bubbled up, her excitement tangible.

'Oh, that's wonderful, darling, who is he?' Emma's happiness was more important than mine and if all was going well for her, it would enhance my own joy.

'It's a guy at the wine bar. His name's Phil. Mum, he's wonderful—so different from the other boys.'

'I'm so happy for you, Em... so tell me all about him. What's he studying?' I asked, delighted at the news.

'He's... not at uni, Mum. He's the manager of the wine bar where I'm working...'

'Oh?' I couldn't help myself; I was disappointed. 'I thought he was like you, working part-time while he...'

'He's really good-looking and so wise and funny and... he's thirty.'

'Thirty?' I didn't know what else to say.

'And I don't want you being all weird, but he's got a child, a son... with an ex-girlfriend.'

Whoa. My heart sank. 'Oh, Emma, he's nine years older than you. And has a child...?'

'Yes... a lovely little boy. Don't spoil this, Mum.'

'I'm not... I just always hoped you'd meet someone your own age, someone at uni... who you could share stuff with... travel and books and...'

'Well, like you just said, Mum, the person you fall for isn't always the picture-perfect man who fits all the criteria at just the right time. Sometimes it's just right... isn't it? Phil isn't who I thought I'd fall in love with, any more than you thought you'd fall for hippy surfer Dan. And just because I'm twenty-one doesn't make it any less intense or any easier to resist... or any less "right".'

She had me there. Who was I to question her choices? And if it worked out and they were happy, then great. If it didn't work

out, then it was all part of life's rich tapestry, as my mum used
to say. Emma would have to do what we all do and find her own
way... like when she was a little girl and wanted to 'tightrope'
walk along a wall, I'd let her do it, knowing I'd always be there
to catch her.

'You told me once you shouldn't have married Dad, and you
were unhappy, but you must have been happy once. When I talked to Dad he said you'd both just changed... that the person you
need at twenty isn't always the person you need at forty.'

I was taken aback by this. A new, live and unplugged Craig
appeared before me... sensitive, empathetic, philosophising about
life. I was sure Emma must be adding her own spin.

'I never saw that side to your father.'

'Perhaps you just weren't looking, Mum.'

She was right; I'd stopped looking and listening, stopped
caring, and once that happened, I was never going to see the
other side of Craig, only the one I expected to see. Craig was
right—he had been 'the one' for twenty-something me. He'd
provided the safety and security I needed with my new baby.
But forty-something me needed something more exciting and
unexpected.

'Oh, Emma, life is so bloody complicated... If only we had
a crystal ball or Sue's "astronomical" predictions were more reli-
able,' I sighed.

Emma laughed. 'Poor Sue. Is she still logging on every morning to find out what kind of man the day will bring? Wouldn't it
be great to know, or at least have a clue?'

'Yes,' I giggled, 'and I envy Sue's blind faith, but it wouldn't do to know what the future held. It might stop us doing things...'

I thought about how we are always making choices in our lives and how sometimes they're right and sometimes they're not. Sometimes it's just about choosing a different sandwich for lunch... and sometimes it's so much bigger and we have to take a giant leap into the dark to find out if it's for us. And I didn't worry about where things were going anymore because I knew now, the joy was in finding out.

Chapter Seventeen
The Non-Lithuanian Baywatch Blonde

The night before we flew to Santorini, I looked online at the beautiful people wafting around the island, and worried about what to wear. I desperately wanted to look the part and fit into Dan's world. His friends would be there and might have girlfriends and I just knew they'd be young and skinny and gorgeous. I'd packed some T-shirts and a couple of pairs of shorts but my clothes were all old and boring and even a little big for me.

Financing my escape wasn't a problem; for years I'd been squirreling a little away each month and my 'running away' money was waiting in my savings account. I had always told myself the money could be put towards Emma's wedding, but it was as though somewhere deep inside I'd always known I would need it to leave one day. I'd kept the account card in my rucksack along with my other precious things—the postcard, Filofax and the red silk dress. I was taking it all with me, along with the photos of Emma and my mum.

On the surface I was happy, but remnants of the old Faye sometimes bubbled underneath and there were moments when I wasn't sure who I was anymore. Even now, with the prospect of ticking off a Santorini sunset with the most wonderful man I'd ever met, a tingle of fear bloomed in my chest. The old Faye wondered if her new sandals were too frumpy? She was worried about what would happen at the end of the holiday and what Dan's friends would think about her. Would they see her as one of them or as an older out-of-touch woman, invading their thirty-something existence? But the most pressing question of all: did she have enough pants? I smiled to myself; I was about to fly to one of the most romantic places in the world with the man I loved and all the old Faye could think about was pants.

We had to be at the airport for seven a.m. the following morning and, despite her fear and hatred of red-haired air stewardesses, Sue had offered to drop us off.

Dan had just called to make final arrangements and I was just about to go to bed to try and get some sleep when the front doorbell rang. I looked at Sue. 'That'll be Mandy and Camilla,' she said, opening the door. I was puzzled; I'd said my goodbyes to them earlier and didn't realise we were expecting them.

Sue let them in and they marched into the living room. Mandy was carrying a huge black plastic bin liner over her shoulder, and as she hurled it to the floor like a dead body she announced, 'The makeover team are now in the building.'

'And looks like we haven't arrived a minute too soon,' Camilla added from behind her with a ladylike giggle.

Apparently a Faye makeover night was about to take place and Mandy was threatening to make me look 'really sick' for my maiden flight to Greece.

'What's in the bin liner?' I was worried she was also providing me with sex toys for my trip. She and Sue had been so keen to give me bedroom advice, I wouldn't have been surprised at a grab bag of rampant rabbits and love eggs. 'Apart from the fact I'm not ready to surprise Dan with a colourful array of bedroom equipment, it would take my baggage allowance way over the limit,' I said with concern.

'No, it's not sex toys,' Mandy sighed, 'but I could kick myself because Ann Summers had a sale and we could have got you all kinds of stuff for your hols. No, this is a bag full of summery clothes.' She began emptying it out onto the sofa. 'They're your Emma's. She Facebooked me, said you would need some holiday stuff as you'd never been abroad and she had loads. She thought you might not want to go back to the house so me and Camilla went round to your old place and Craig said, "Take what you want."'

'Aw, thanks Mandy and Camilla.' I was touched and called Emma to thank her.

'You will call me, Em, won't you, if you need anything at all, or if you want me to come back—I will be on the next plane.'

'Mum, stop. I'll be fine. Just have a brilliant time and… make sure he looks after you.'

I smiled. 'I'm big enough to look after myself, Em.'

'Hmm… And don't go round calling everyone "girlfriend" and saying OMG—even as a joke, okay?'

'No, Emma, I won't.'

'And I don't know what "mad" Mandy's taken from my room, but if she's got them, please *DO NOT* let her talk you into wearing the gold hotpants.'

'Okay,' I giggled at the thought.

'Oh, and Mum...?'

'Yes?'

'You go, girl!'

I put down the phone, promising to text when we arrived. Camilla and Mandy were now fighting with the tanning tent and Sue was mixing a non-Lithuanian potion for my hair. They were chattering and giggling and, though I was so ready to move on, I would miss them too. 'Wine?' said Sue, tripping back into the room holding four glasses by their stems and a bottle under her arm

Mandy was now rifling through the black bin liner to help me choose the right clothes for my trip. Emma had so many clothes, I didn't recognise some of them—she'd probably never worn a lot of it as she was so fashion conscious she wouldn't be seen dead in anything twice. As Sue dabbed bleach on my hair, Mandy sorted through the bin bag, shouting, 'Summery dresses, T-shirts, jeans, white cropped trousers and...*OH. MY. GOD*! Faye, you are gonna *love* these bad boys!' She was beaming and holding up the pair of tiny gold hotpants.

❉ ❉ ❉

The girls worked hard, lightening my hair, manicuring, pedicuring and fake-tanning. When they'd finished, I was amazed at the transformation and admired myself in the mirror. 'You look like someone out of *Bay Watch*,' Sue said, titivating my long blonde hair like the mother of a Pageant Queen.

That night I went to bed happy. I had turned the juggernaut of my life around and had achieved so much in the past few months. But I hadn't done it all on my own; I had wonderful supportive friends, a daughter who understood and a new man in my life who listened and cared. I felt very lucky.

The following morning, I woke and finished packing. My hair was much blonder and the spray tan quite deep, and what had looked like a sun-kissed makeover the night before through the mists of wine and electric light looked quite different the following morning. My pillows were orange and so was my face. I looked like an overcooked Barbie doll, and even after three showers was still sporting the Tango'd look.

Downstairs, Sue had made me scrambled eggs and orange juice, and despite my tummy being all over the place with excitement and fear, I thanked her and sat down. 'That tan will fade and you'll like the highlights once they've settled,' she said vaguely, placing a glass of orange juice in front of me. 'You eat up, love. That orange juice is a bit Hasidic, but who knows when you'll get a meal? It took me and Ken almost a week before we found somewhere that did egg and chips in Corfu... it's all talamalamata and humis.'

We collected Dan and, as amazed as *he* was to see my new Technicolor appearance, *I* was amazed to see he was only carrying a large rucksack and wearing the jeans and T-shirt he'd had on a couple of days before. I had a huge new suitcase, and of course my pink rucksack containing my precious things, 'I thought you were planning to go straight back to Oz from Greece?' I said, a glimmer of hope forming in my heart (perhaps he was coming back with me to the UK first?)

'Yeah... I am going straight home, but I travel light,' he smiled.

His casual, laid-back approach to everything was rubbing off on me. I didn't worry so much about the future, what might or might not happen; I was really living in the moment at last—but I hadn't reached 'Dan' point yet. I'd packed far too much for just a few weeks, yet he had travelled halfway round the world with one bag and would travel back the same way. I smiled to myself; he'd clearly never been away with a child or had the same issues around pant quantity that I did.

At the airport I hugged Sue, knowing she was the best friend I had and grateful to have her in my life. She'd seen me through some difficult times and I would always be grateful to her. We both shed a little tear when I said I'd see her again, I just wasn't sure how long it would be. Anything longer than a fortnight felt incredibly long to me and Sue in our small salon world. Dan hugged her and thanked her, then began walking slowly to the departures area, leaving us to have a few words alone.

'Make the most of it and embrace it all. Don't say no like I always do,' she hissed. 'You go for it, Faye... and get whatever it is you want, girl.'

I pulled a sad face, like I understood, and blew her a kiss.

'You do it for both of us, love,' she called. Sue was such a good friend, such a genuinely good person. She deserved more. I hoped she'd find it.

I caught up with Dan who put his arm around me as we walked; 'Babe, I can't wait to get you alone on a beach under those stars,' he smiled and we jumped on the moving escalator, blindly heading towards our next adventure.

Chapter Eighteen

Taxi for Fate

Arriving on Santorini, the first thing to hit me as we got off the plane was the incredible heat shimmering on the tarmac. The sun was searing, bouncing off walls. The deep blue skies offered no cloud shelter and the parched land no shade.

Though Dan had suggested we get a bus from the airport at Fira to Oia as it was only six or seven miles, Sue had insisted on pre-booking and paying for a taxi as her gift, to take us straight from the airport. 'You're gonna look like shit when you get off that plane and hit terracotta,' she'd warned. 'You'll be like the Good Year Blimp—and the last thing you'll need is a bus journey on top of that, my love.' I hadn't even thought about the effects of cabin pressure on my ageing flesh, and almost wished she hadn't informed me of this metamorphosis taking place midair. But coming through customs, I could have hugged her for her prediction. I was tired, my ankles had swollen as predicted, and my face was slightly puffy despite lots of rampant spritzing, which had alarmed both Dan and the gentleman to my left on the plane.

At Fira Airport I had never been more pleased to see someone and wanted to kiss George from Ella Taxis who stood holding a card with my name on... Well, what it actually said was 'Taxi for Fate', and it made me feel a little weird, reminding me how big this trip was in terms of my life, and just how far I'd come.

It was almost an hour's journey from the airport to Oia and the ride was as breathtaking as the views in more ways than one. Dan and I sat together in the back, holding hands and pointing out the beautiful scenery to each other through the car windows. The mountainous journey was along rough, narrow roads cut high into the Caldera, with no barriers, just a sheer drop, and despite the spectacular beauty, that drop was never far from my thoughts. The taxi was fast and swerving and I was genuinely scared for my life, but Dan loved it. He whooped loudly, leaning out of the window, waving his arms and shouting at the endless blue sky.

By the time we arrived in Oia, it was a searing summer afternoon. The sun was high in a cloudless sky, and just like the postcards, the white, blue-domed buildings created a perfect Greek skyline, framed by brilliant blue.

The taxi drove off and we both stood in awe, heat on our faces and bags at our feet. 'Santorini is a volcanic crater called a caldera,' Dan said. 'Oia is built on the slope of the Caldera; that's why it's so steep. Look how high we are... God, I love this place.' I gazed at him under the perfect sky as he turned slowly round, taking everything in. He knew so much and I loved listening to him, and even here the blue skies and spectacular scenery were no competition; I still had to tear my eyes away from his as he spoke.

Standing on the sloping ground, it all seemed so fragile and fairy-tale-like, the bougainvillea-smothered buildings precariously perched on rocky terrain, overlooking the staggering blue of the sea. Moving uphill, I grabbed his hand, my legs wobbly on the uneven ground. I peered through the buildings for a glimpse of the cobalt sea and we stopped for a few seconds to watch a tiny speedboat foaming white in the distance. I will never forget that first moment, gazing beyond land at the endless Aegean, calm, unmoving, unmoveable—yet, in complete contrast, everything on land here seemed so fragile. One gust of wind and I was sure all the sparkly icing-sugar buildings and churches would tumble down the caldera, taking us with them—white powder, blue domes and smashed hearts.

Dan took out the directions from his rucksack while I wheeled my huge case along the cobbles. There was no sign of wind today; everything was still and quiet on the outskirts of the tiny town. The only sound was my heart beating.

Turning into the first narrow street, it was suddenly busy with tourists all turning up for that evening's sunset. They wandered in and out of tiny shops selling everything from high-end jewellery to local honey, and we wandered amongst them, gazing at taverna menus and planning our next meal. We promised ourselves we'd visit the rooftop bars protected from the sun by stylish white yacht sales, decorated with modern sculptures, water features and beautiful people with expensive blonde highlights and huge designer sunglasses.

We stopped for a few minutes to check directions and get our breath back, and the steepness and the heat made me dizzy.

I leaned on Dan, feeling his energy, his lust for life as his arms enveloped me protectively, like he sensed my spark of fear being in this new, strange territory. His eyes were always near mine, his arms always there, and as we stood in our own private huddle, I thought about how present he was, in an emotional and physical way. Dan was the calm, blue sea to my sometimes fragile, topsy-turvy land.

As we walked on, he took my hand, leading me through the heat and the steep pavements, stopping every now and then to admire something in a shop window or share a view of the sea through a gap in the brilliant white buildings. We followed the directions, turning left along the little cobbled backstreets, eventually arriving at several whitewashed apartments propped against and on top of each other like a giant white game of Jenga. We walked on a little further and eventually found a bright-blue door.

'This is it,' he said, knocking hard. The pounding heat on my back, anticipation of what this new experience would bring and the nearness of him made my heart beat faster. We waited. No one came so he knocked again, my exhilaration slowly morphing into floppy disappointment at each knock. After a few more minutes, we decided to walk a little further down the lane to see if we could spot any other villa with a similar description, but as we turned away, we heard the sound of a bolt being moved inside. Relieved, I quickly spun back to see Dan's full, beaming smile. I looked to where his smile landed and couldn't believe who was standing in the doorway. Blonde, tanned, beautiful Gabby.

She was looking straight at him as I gathered myself together, trying not to let the shock register on my face. I glanced at Dan, waiting for introductions, but he just threw down his bag and hugged her. I felt for a moment like he'd forgotten me.

'Gabby, I didn't know you'd be here,' he said. 'Great to see you, mate.' She was smiling and hugging him, beckoning him inside, then she saw me and her face dropped.

'Oh... oh, yeah, I forgot, you two haven't met. This is Faye,' he said, ushering me in front of him to where she stood at the door.

I smiled and said hello and she nodded, a half-smile playing on her lips; 'Hi... Faye.' Then she turned back to Dan, almost with her back to me. 'Ben's gone into town for beer but Nick's here, asleep as usual,' she rolled her eyes and slowly turned to go back into the house, gesturing for us to follow.

Had Dan known she'd be here? He seemed genuinely surprised to see her. He'd said she was somewhere in Europe, but she'd obviously decided this was the place to be. I didn't blame her; it was so beautiful—but surely it was going to make things awkward now, with me here too? I wasn't on home ground, I wasn't used to travel and I certainly wasn't used to the tangled relationships between Aussie backpackers.

Christ, I hoped this wasn't some elaborate plan for a threesome—and I was the last to know. If that were the case, Sue would be telling the story for years to come in the salon and Mandy would add her own fictitious caveats involving landing strips and intimate piercings. I could almost see the shock on Sue's face when I told her who greeted us.

Gabby was holding the door open for me, Dan had gone on ahead and I felt so uncomfortable struggling past her with my case. I definitely got the feeling she wasn't pleased to see me, and I didn't relish the thought of sleeping under the same roof as her. Who knew what she'd do to me in the dead of night while I slept unawares in my new M&S pyjamas? Judging by the way she'd greeted me, I reckoned she'd be hiding in my room with a bloody kitchen knife before the first week was out.

'Leave your luggage here in the hall,' she said, unsmiling. I put my new case down reluctantly. It seemed big and stupid and formal next to Dan's bag, and I worried that if I left it anywhere near her she may open it up and shred the contents.

Walking on ahead on long brown legs in tiny denim shorts, Gabby showed us into a large, airy room. She was clinging to Dan, guiding him through (and away from me?) to the living room, ruffling his hair, giggling and just delighted to see him. I walked behind, feeling so out of it, like I'd been sent there for a job interview.

I stood in the doorway of the sitting room as she talked to Dan about Ben and Nick, ending each sentence with, 'You know what he's like?' Her references were exclusive; she meant to keep me out and I couldn't have joined in the conversation if I'd tried. Was I overreacting though? I had been a little much where Dan was concerned and I needed to chill out a bit; Dan was so delighted to be there, so I decided to ignore my concerns and embrace it. He was just beaming to be with one of his 'mates', both talking in the same Aussie accents, both looking like they'd turned up on a beach after a life in the sun. Not for the first time

I wished I was ten years younger without an orange tan and an unwieldy suitcase bought with Tesco Clubcard points.

As they talked, I gazed round, observing the big squashy sofas and the strewn beer cans. A white muslin curtain wafted the sea breeze through a doorway that led to what I assumed was a balcony. I drank in the cool air, grateful for the respite from the searing heat and light. I leaned against Dan, tired from my flight but also feeling a little threatened and staking my claim. Gazing ahead, I suddenly jumped and let out a little yelp as one of the sofas appeared to move; 'What was that?'

My finger ends tingled as I watched in horror, realising there were other humans, namely a couple of guys, strewn across the sofa fast asleep. Gabby and Dan laughed at my shock, but she laughed the loudest and longest. It wasn't that funny.

'Oh, Faye... what a fuss,' she sighed, shaking her head like I was the biggest joke. 'I think he's called Jim... we picked him up last night—he had nowhere to stay. And you know what Nick's like—he takes in anyone.' Another smile and nod of recognition between them. I wanted to say, 'No, I don't know what fucking Nick's like, but I do know that even cocky Australian women may be at risk with a bloody vagrant in their holiday home.' Christ, I hoped there was a lock on our bedroom—'Jim' could take all my credit cards, murder us in our beds and be on the next boat to Athens.

I must have looked horrified, so Gabby used my gaucheness to do a little extra bohemian bonding with Dan. 'Hey, don't sweat it, Faye,' she said to me, while looking at Dan. 'Jim's a pussycat.'

She wandered over, stroking his head and giggling. Dan just smiled, completely unfazed and unwittingly providing her with another exclusively shared moment.

I watched her stroke the sleeping stranger with the back of her hand but with her eyes only on Dan. I wasn't paranoid after all; she was still interested in Dan, and she was making me feel like an intruder. Gabby was the first person I'd met from Dan's world, and the first time I really questioned my presence there with him. I felt old, unfashionable, unworldly and foolish. I was beginning to wonder what I'd let myself in for, and if Dan's love would last and be enough to sustain us in this foreign place.

I stood with my back flat against the cooling wall, wondering what to do next. Gabby went into the kitchen and Dan winked at me and followed her. I stayed where I was, unable to move. I heard them talking a little and when they returned, he was carrying two bottles of cold beer. He looked sleepy and more delicious than ever. He handed me a bottle and reached his arm around my shoulder in a comforting gesture which meant a lot to me. Any doubts I had began to melt as I buried my head in his chest, inhaling his sweet, faded sweat while my heart beat so loudly I wondered if they could hear.

I put my arm around him, glad to have him back by me, wishing she would tell us where we were sleeping so we could go and lock ourselves in, be alone. Standing against the doorway with her beer, she was observing us. I felt Dan's lips on my head, felt the cool breeze dance the wafting curtain. I was looking at Jim the sleeping drifter... and Gabby was looking at me.

After a while, Dan took his arm away and, grabbing my hand, said, 'Let's look at the view... is it through here, Gabby?' She half-nodded, letting go for now and wandering lethargically into the kitchen, taking her cold beer and frosty atmosphere with her.

We pulled back the curtain, leaving her behind, and I held my breath at the view—an almost navy-blue sea stitched into the hem of a deep, endless sky.

We stood together for some time, holding each other and drinking it all in. When one of us finally spoke, it was Dan. 'I dreamed it would be like this... you and me, on a balcony,' he sighed.

'Me too...' I hesitated. I wanted to address the elephant in the room, but wasn't sure where to start. 'I didn't expect Gabby to be here,' I said, pulling an 'awkward' face.

'Yeah, I thought she was going to stay in Scotland and go back home from there, but... you're okay with it, aren't you? I mean she was so pleased to see us...'

'Pleased to see you.'

'Oh, she doesn't know you yet. I think you two will get along great. She can be good fun, she's easy-going, you know?'

I nodded, doubtfully.

'Do you still have feelings for her?' The shallow side of me couldn't believe that he could possibly prefer me to someone who looked like Gabby. She was slim and young and beautiful and I was under no illusions she would win hands down in the looks department.

'I'm fond of her... She's just Gabby and I'm like a brother to her. She wears her heart on her sleeve.'

She wears her vagina on her sleeve, I thought, desperately willing myself not to say it out loud.

'Anyway, we have time to relax first, before we see the sunset,' he said, picking up my case and beckoning me to follow.

I wheeled my case along the corridor as Dan opened the bedroom door, 'I think this is ours,' he said, guiding me inside. It was fresh and cool, painted white, with a bleached wooden floor and a large window overlooking the sea. A huge iron bed stood in the middle of the room and I walked over to it, running my hand along the pure white linen. It was perfect, and I was overcome with a wave of happiness, determined no one was going to spoil this for either of us.

I took his hand and pulled him towards me and we kissed, falling onto the bed, unable to resist each other for a second longer. Within seconds my T-shirt was over my head, his bristly chin rubbed against my face, my breasts as he pulled at my clothes and me at his. I lay back and he moved gently on top of me, still kissing, both moaning with pent-up passion, relief that we'd finally made it to this place. I wrapped my legs around his firm, narrow back, feeling him inside me so quickly, but I was ready... I'd been ready all my life for this. I never wanted it to stop... we had finally found each other here in this magical place and it felt so right. It was so wonderful I cried.

Afterwards, he held me in his arms while we slept and woke and made love again and stayed together on the pure white cotton sheets.

'Shall we stay here forever?' I asked.

'That would be nice... but it wouldn't be long enough.'

I didn't want to know how long we had; I just wanted to savour the days and nights we spent together.

'Hey... the sun's going down.' He leaped from the bed like an excited little boy and stood at the window looking up at the sky like he was waiting for bonfire night.

I wandered to the window feeling like someone else.

'You look lovely,' he smiled, standing behind me, enclosing me in his arms. Everything was perfect and we stood for a while just watching the sky.

He suddenly sighed. 'Do you think I might be able to convince you to come with me... to Sydney?'

'Who knows? I reckon The Sydney Opera House could definitely be added to my living list,' I smiled. I was struck by the shock of freedom; like a shot in the arm it almost took my breath away. Yes... I could go to Sydney if I wanted to, if Dan wanted me to. I could say 'yes'; I could go anywhere, do anything, I thought, looking at the beautiful man standing next to me in this perfect, whitewashed room by the sea. This was going to be my summer of firsts... and I wasn't ruling anything out.

We went back to bed, where we watched the melting pinks and deep oranges smeared across the Santorini sky, only leaving to stand before the window for the sun's final denouement.

'Our own private show tonight... I arranged it just for you,' he said, hugging me close.

The sea was on fire and the sky flooded with liquid gold, and we stood together for a long time, like many lovers had before us, watching the Santorini sunset before we die.

❄ ❄ ❄

The next few days were a blur of sunshine and happiness. Dan's friends, including Gabby, would smile or say hi if we bumped into them in the hall or the kitchen, but for the most part everyone left us alone. We wandered hand in hand down little cobbled streets, drank coffee in little cafes on pavements, sipped wine as we watched the sunset and made love wherever and whenever we wanted to. We never tired of each other or the spectacular daily sunsets, sinking into the golden warmth together each evening; the sun seemed emotionally charged, like nature was in tune with our feelings.

I abandoned my sensible sandals, painted my toe nails aqua and bought white Birkenstocks. My orange tan was replaced by real gold and my hair became even more 'Baywatch Blonde', which had never seemed right in the UK but here it was perfect. My appearance was changing to fit in with the environment— white linen shirts, T-shirts, faded cut-off jeans, and a coloured braid plaited in my beach-blonde hair.

Our days were spent by pools, on beaches, in bars and our evenings clapping the sunset like kids at a magic show. I had never felt such freedom, such happiness—golden days in every sense of the word.

One night we climbed onto a rooftop with other tourists. 'I want to see it from close range, get even closer to it,' Dan joked. He was laughing and clambering up higher but I was scared and wanted him to stop.

'Don't, Dan...'

He either didn't hear me or didn't want to and kept going higher, holding on with one hand and waving with the other. He was calling me and laughing but I couldn't look. I felt physically sick and just wanted him to stop.

Here on the island I was seeing the free, wild side of Dan even more. Here was the exciting, dangerous guy who hung out of taxi windows on treacherous roads and swung precariously over rooftops. Later, as we lay together in bed, I told him how much he'd scared me.

'Faye... I was fine up there. The view was amazing. I wish you would do stuff like that with me.'

I shook my head. 'I know I've changed in the past few months, and I've learned a lot about myself that's surprised me, but... I'm someone's mother and mothers don't take risks.'

'You are someone's mother...' He nodded slowly, thinking about what he was going to say next. 'But... you're also *you*, Faye Dobson; you're also no one's wife, no one's mother—just *you*. Don't forget that.'

✳ ✳ ✳

Nick or Ben would bring girls back occasionally, always young, always pretty, always different girls. They'd hang around in thongs and tiny T-shirts complaining of the heat oiling their perfect bodies and planning the night ahead.

'Those girls are a constant reminder to me of my age and how it's okay for a thirty-something man to sleep with a twenty-something woman, but not the other way round,' I sighed.

'Why not? We sleep together,' he said. 'You're almost ten years older than me and it's the best relationship I've ever had.'

I was touched.

'I've told you, Faye—stop with the comparisons... no one is judging you but yourself.'

He was right.

'I just think those thongs are a bit much in polite company,' I said to Dan one day, sounding like my mother as we sat on the balcony. The girls were wandering around with their bottoms on view and the old Faye wasn't impressed. 'I would hate to think Emma was walking around like that.'

'What's wrong with thongs?' he said, looking up from his book. 'You should get some...'

'No... I couldn't. I mean I just don't have the bottom for them.'

'Really? Does that matter?'

'Well, yes. I mean they show off your bum, don't they?'

'Do they... I'd never really thought about it.' He smiled and went back to his book and I rolled my eyes in disbelief.

It wasn't until a few days later it became hilariously apparent that thongs to Aussies are what flip flops are to the rest of the world. It had been lost in translation—another reminder that Dan and I were from different worlds, and though we didn't always need words, sometimes we needed a phrase book.

The only thing I wasn't relaxed about was Gabby, who had started to pop her head round our bedroom door to say hi and even sometimes wandered in for 'a chat' with Dan. He took this in his stride, once discussing some bloody book they'd both read while sitting bare-chested with only a towel around him. This gave me mixed feelings because I felt invaded and, yes, I'll admit, territorial, yet as she was in 'my room', I hoped she might acknowledge me. I wanted us to be friends; she was clearly the lynchpin here and Dan was close to her, and it would make life so much easier for me if she included me in her conversations now and then.

Gabby shopped for food, bought beer and told the loudest jokes and was clearly comfortable in men's company. I envied her ease and natural confidence as she floated round the apartment in a tiny bikini, her childlike hips swaying, her eyes giving everyone the come on. I tried to be mature, but couldn't help resenting the way she used her relationship with the guys in the house to make me feel out in the cold. I couldn't tell if it was deliberate or just insensitive, but her behaviour around me always caused a twist of hurt.

Whenever we were all together, Gabby would suddenly recall 'a day at the beach' they'd all shared as teenagers, or a mutual friend from 'back home'. I was interested in Dan's past; it was part of him, and though I wasn't part of the story, I listened with interest and would try to join in, but she didn't acknowledge me. It wasn't overt, which is what made it harder to handle, and I told myself I was being stupid, but I felt she was deliberately excluding me, almost goading me to cause a scene. Gabby was a man's woman and whether or not it was about Dan, or about me, the facts were she didn't want another princess in her tower.

❄ ❄ ❄

One evening we joined the others for drinks. I had consistently made an effort to get to know them all, but it was hard to penetrate the group, and after a few half-hearted questions I decided to just relax and enjoy their company. No one asked anything of me so I just smiled and joined in when required. The guys were drinking shots and singing, and even if the old Faye couldn't help but think it bordered on silliness, the new one appreciated their energy and the fact they were young, and happy with no worries. I got the feeling Ben had a thing for Gabby and she knew it; he looked at her a lot and laughed at everything she said (and trust me, she wasn't funny). She, meanwhile, would smile awkwardly at me now and then and, after a couple of glasses of wine, I sensed a slight thawing. So when she went to the toilets, I went too. I was hoping to chat and perhaps even get her on side a little.

'I love your lipstick,' I said, hearing myself and cringing. I sounded like a ten-year-old—why was I even bothering with this girl? It was a tiny bathroom and I was definitely crowding her.

I was giving her a last chance before I gave up completely and declared indifference, or war. We were squashed so close at the minute sink and mirror, she had no choice but to respond, we were almost touching.

'It's a lovely shade of red,' I tried again, determined to make her acknowledge me.

'I bought it in Italy earlier this year. Dan told me I had to buy it because it looked so hot on me,' she sighed, unsmiling.

She continued to apply it slowly, widening her lips to fill with colour... I wondered how many times he'd kissed those lips and if he would again. Her arms were bare, beautifully bronzed and slightly muscular—she obviously worked out—and with those tiny hips I doubted she'd ever had her chops round Dan's lemon cakes.

'You and Dan were... together weren't you, when you left Oz?'

'Yeah,' she said, 'very much so. Would you like some?'

'Oh...?'

I wasn't quite sure what she was referring to—then I saw she was proffering the lipstick, which wasn't my colour at all, but I felt it might help the bonding process so I thanked her and applied it to my own lips while watching her discreetly. She was about eight years older than Emma and the mother in me wanted to cajole and bring her round, but the woman wanted to tell her to keep off my man.

I applied the lipstick. 'It's red on me... very red,' I said, pouting uncertainly.

'Hot young starlet,' she sighed.

'Oh, I wouldn't say I look that good...'

'I'm not... It's the name of the lipstick.'

'Oh. It's a bit tarty, isn't it? On me, I mean... it isn't tarty on you... at all. I always think red lipstick demands perfect features... you have to be a supermodel to wear red. Not that I'm saying you're not attractive... well, you're not technically a super... model, but that's not to say... I mean...'

I jammed the lipstick to my mouth to stop myself talking I could only imagine the insults my subconscious would unleash under that kind of stress. Putting the lipstick on in the mirror and seeing the two of us, side by side, the comparison was cruel. Her face was small and smooth, her hair golden and silky, while my face next to hers was big and pasty, my hair wasn't sun-kissed as I'd thought; it was beach-wrecked. Meanwhile, the red lipstick was less 'hot young starlet' and more 'cold old tartlet'.

I stared at us both in the mirror and so did she, and we were probably thinking the same thing—that my face looked like the Fun House mirror version of hers. I thought again about Dan kissing her perfect lips, which made me feel even more anxious.

'He's a lovely guy, Dan,' I said, handing the tube back to her. 'I know it's not forever... I mean, he and I are together now, but I know we can't be... together forever. Well, we won't, I mean...' I don't know why I felt the need to explain myself to her, but I wanted to gauge her reaction.

She put her head down. Ah so I was right; she was in love with him.

'Whatever.' She snapped her bag closed. 'It would never last in the real world. It's just a weird summer fling... I mean, you're so much older...'

I was taken aback. She was looking at me waiting for a response, trying to measure the pain she'd just inflicted and we both let it hang there for a few seconds.

At that moment, two drunken girls fell into the toilets and as it was so small we were forced to leave or join them on the floor. I truly wanted to push her head into the door and kick her hard on those long, bronze legs, but I resisted and stood back for her to walk on. She nodded, without smiling, and we walked back into the bar with fresh scarlet smiles plastered across our faces. I would let her have that one—but she'd just declared war in that toilet. Yes, I was older—and that's where I had the advantage, because in my longer life I'd met her kind a million times and she wouldn't get the better of me.

As the evening wore on and the drink flowed, I felt easier in their company and tried not to think about what she'd said. She was a mean girl and I wasn't going to let her ruin any more time on the island by allowing her to torture me.

Throughout the evening, Dan held my hand, or rested it on my thigh, a sign we were together, not just a fling—a real couple in the real world. I appreciated the way Nick and Ben had finally begun to acknowledge I was part of Dan's life and, though it was recent, we had our own, short history. 'Faye, you must have heard about the time Dan almost drowned when his surfboard shot up in the air over the waves without him and knocked him out—he was in intensive care for weeks?' And 'Faye, don't you think Dan's jokes are corny?'

I felt like I was meeting a brand new Dan all over again. This wasn't Dan from the deli who discussed over-ripe cheeses, fine wines and Jane Eyre; this one was less guarded, more animated. With his friends he spoke passionately of riding waves, chasing girls, and playing in bands, and it seemed their lives had been spent on beaches and in bars, drinking, laughing and basting in the Aussie sun.

I squeezed Dan's hand. I was having a wonderful time and didn't want the night to end.

We left the others around midnight and walked back slowly down the cobbled streets to the villa, arm in arm, stopping every now and then for a drunken kiss. I sighed, gazing at the shop windows, the faded hippy blankets and scarves hanging from doorways like a throwback from the sixties. I wondered how many people, over the hundreds of years, had walked those streets above the turquoise Aegean... imagining where their life and love might take them.

We turned into the road of our villa. It was quieter here and no one was around. Dan leaned towards me and we began to kiss, him gently pushing me against a whitewashed wall. It was cool on my back and I wanted him to make love to me.

'Dan... let's go swimming,' I heard myself say.

He laughed and nodded, grabbing my hand. We were suddenly running down through the town. It was late but the bars were still open, people still wandering arm in arm through the streets. I had known he wouldn't turn me down. Sue had said Sagittarians were instinctive, they acted on impulse and Dan definitely did. There was no question about lateness or safety or how we would reach the sea. He'd just taken my hand and set off.

After a short run, I demanded we walk the rest of the way to the sea and after about ten minutes we arrived in Goulas, a small fishing village close to Oia.

'How far is it now?' I asked, already tired from the walk and the lateness and wondering at the wisdom of my impulsive idea.

'Only another 200 steps,' he laughed, guiding me down into the darkness towards the beach.

We landed on the beach, which was more 'public' than I'd envisaged, with several little tavernas nearby. He began to strip but I got cold feet.

'We can't—people might see us,' I said, still a bit tipsy and giggling nervously.

'That's the point,' he laughed. 'Come on—even if you don't take your clothes off, you're going in.' He hugged me, gently wrestling me to the ground and reaching under my T-shirt, discreetly caressing my breast. He slowly pulled off my T-shirt, then jeans and underwear, and though there were one or two people on the beach, we ran hand in hand into the ocean, naked.

I felt so alive, so bad; I'd never done anything like that—and though it was on my living list, it was more of a dare than a dream. Under the stars, in the blackness of the night sea, we swam together, moving close, holding each other, then apart, swirling around like a dance. Unable to resist, the next time we came together, I wrapped my legs around his waist and there in the sea after midnight, in full view of the tavernas, we made love. It was dark and warm and exciting. And it was just our secret.

✳ ✳ ✳

The following day, the others announced they were leaving Santorini to go island hopping and then head back home to Australia from whatever island they were on when they felt like it. I was delighted, especially as Dan shared my feelings, saying he was glad for us to be able to have alone time at the apartment before we eventually said our goodbyes.

The evening before they left, we all played poker on the balcony together. I didn't know how to play so just sat next to Dan, rubbing his back and urging him on blindly, but Gabby was a card shark; she knew all the moves and took great delight in beating everyone. The other guys were impressed and showed it with high fives and admiring glances, but Dan took it in his stride, shaking his head as he shuffled the cards. At one point Gabby smiled triumphantly and stared straight at Dan. For a moment I wondered what she would say, but she didn't say anything, just lifted his beer bottle, never taking her eyes from his, and took a long swig. I felt a little chill go through me and, as she slammed down the bottle and put both arms around Ben, she shot me a look.

I turned away. She was a child demanding attention and I was a grown-up who knew how to treat mean, naughty little girls. The old Faye would have felt insecure and allowed her to walk all over me; I'd have handed Dan to her on a plate, scared of conflict and confrontation. But the new Faye could see through a girl like Gabby. I wasn't playing silly games, I was too old and my time here with him was too short for that.

She continued to be loud and boisterous for the rest of the evening and later, when Dan had gone to the kitchen for more beers, she wandered over and sat next to me. She was quite tipsy and, though I still didn't like her, I thought she may be offering the olive branch and smiled as she sat down.

'I'll move when he comes back,' she said, slurring slightly. 'I know how you like to have him next to you.'

I ignored this.

Then she leaned in and said in a very low voice, 'I'm not being funny... but you're not his usual type. He always goes for young blondes...'

'Well, perhaps he's changed his mind since he met me and realised he needs a real woman,' I said, without smiling.

She looked at me, angry I hadn't shown pain or weakness, and she was now planning what to say next. She'd been hurt by Dan and she wanted to hurt me, but I was stronger than I'd ever been in my life. I wasn't filled with self-doubt about my life, my looks and my age anymore, knowing what I was truly capable of and that Dan found me sexy and fun.

'It won't last, you know... you're too old for him,' she spat quietly, under her breath. 'He loves sex, you'll never keep up, he couldn't get enough when we were together, couldn't keep his hands off me,' a look of hatred and sheer defiance now on her face. She was waiting for my response. I didn't say anything for a few seconds, just sipped my drink, put it down on the table, leaned towards her and whispered in her ear.

'Babe. I'm forty-two. I don't have a problem with it, but for some reason you do. And what you need to know is that in those forty-two years, I've learned a lot. Now, one of the most important lessons I learned is how to look after my man. And, girlfriend, as you brought the subject up, I have to tell you, the hot bedroom action Dan's getting with me is... he says the best *EVER*... did you get that? *EVER!*'

I sipped my drink like nothing had happened and gazed around, an easy smile on my face. She was stunned. She never expected that from me. Her face gave little away but the fact she got up quietly and walked over to sit on Ben's knee said it all.

Later, when we were in bed, Dan said, 'Hey I saw you and Gabby chatting tonight. Shame it happened the night before she goes, but I knew she'd love you once she got to know you—everyone does.'

'Yeah, I think she understands me now.' I smiled in the darkness.

Chapter Nineteen

Film Stars and Rooftops and Santorini's Heart

The others left early the next morning and Dan and I waved goodbye and went straight back to bed. I was so relieved we now had the apartment to ourselves for as long as we wanted it. We could wander around half-dressed and wouldn't have to suppress any sounds of ecstasy when we made love anymore.

'Hey, wanna tick something off *my* living list today?' Dan said as we lay entwined in post-coital sheets.

I sat up, leaning my head on my elbow, intrigued.

'You have to do it too, though,' he warned, rolling out of bed.

'I need to know what it is before I agree to do it,' I said, slightly nervous. 'It might be extreme sex in a public place—and I don't care if it's on your list, I couldn't do that. I just don't have the lingerie,' I smiled.

'Who said we'll be wearing anything?' he smiled, pulling a sun-faded T-shirt over his brown chest. I watched him, wishing he'd take it off again.

'Come back to bed,' I urged. 'Let's stay here and sleep to celebrate the fact we are finally alone together.'

'Plenty of time for sleep... Come on, Faye, get up. Your life awaits,' he pulled the covers off me in one dramatic sweep. I screamed, delighting in the freedom to make as much noise as I wanted now everyone was gone.

Eventually we wandered out into the white-hot day and headed into Oia where we hired a motorbike. I was a little dubious—I'd never ridden one before, and when Dan climbed on and told me I would be perching on the back, I was horrified. 'I'll fall off. I can't just cling to you on the back of that bike—I've seen those mountain roads!' I gasped.

'I've helped you with your living list—now it's time to do mine,' he smiled, handing me a helmet. I strapped the helmet on and tried to retain as much dignity as possible while mounting the hot, metal beast. I may have come a long way, but co-ordination and balance had never been my strong point and all I could see was me being hurled across the road in front of an oncoming goat truck or, worse still, down the side of the Caldera, dashed on the rocks. Don't get me wrong; I could see the appeal—high mountain roads, the wind through your hair and spectacular windowless views—it just didn't appeal to *me*.

Once we'd mounted the bike, I closed my eyes and rested my head on his back, desperately trying to blot out what was happening. 'Well, if it's on your list,' I said, clutching him tightly round the waist, 'let's get going.'

He fired it up. 'Oh, this isn't on my list—this bike's going to take us to what we're going to do on my list.'

'Now I'm worried!' I yelled in his ear over the noise of the bike, which suddenly took off at what felt like a hundred miles an hour, leaving my legs behind. I was terrified. But he'd been so supportive, I had to go along with this. He loved riding the bike, whooping and yelling, as I screamed along extremely narrow, high mountain roads. My screams weren't exhilaration; they were screams of bloodcurdling fear as I shook on the back of the bike. My arms were tightly wound around him—there was no way I was letting go—and when he threw both his arms up, my shriek accompanying his whoops of joy must have made quite a racket on those high, dusty roads. My only consolation throughout the tortuous ride was whatever it was on his list couldn't be any worse than a fast bike ride through hell on mountain roads with no barriers.

I was wrong.

※ ※ ※

We finally arrived at our destination, Amoudi Bay, and I was surprised to see we were actually back in Oia, just around the bay from where we were staying.

'I know, I know,' he said, seeing the realisation on my face. 'We didn't need to take the bike, but I love it and just wanted to warm us up first.'

I was too shell-shocked to answer. I just wanted to get this whole thing over. I climbed off the bike, but the insides of my legs ached and I staggered around on terra firma trying to get the feeling back in my face and thighs. Looking down, my knees were red from the sun and my forehead stung. Oh yes, I was going to look ravishing by the end of today.

'Come on,' he beckoned, parking up the bike in some gravel and heading off down five million steps to the beach. I followed, slowly regaining my composure and the feeling in my inner thighs. He was as excited as I was scared and I was desperately trying to gather a little courage for whatever was about to come next. But as we walked further down the steps, I heard shouts and bodies landing in the swirling water. Looking up I could see a high ledge in a cliff about twenty feet up and someone standing, waiting to leap. 'No. No. Absolutely *no*,' I said, staggering down the steps behind him.

'You are kidding me? I can't do that. Absolutely no way,' I said, shaking my head vigorously to emphasise this. People were passing us to go down onto the beach and I made to go back up the steps to safety, tears in my eyes, my chin trembling with emotion.

He stopped on the step and turned to me, gently holding me around the waist, looking into my eyes. 'You told me that if you'd known a year ago all the things you were going to do, you would have said, 'I can't do that.' But Faye… you did it.'

'It's not the same.'

'Yes, it is. You've done far bigger things. This is just about having the confidence to do it—*believe* in yourself, Faye. You're fit, you can climb the rocks, and you can swim… just jump. I'll be right behind you.'

'I can't and you sound like a bloody life coach from Channel 4,' I said, angry that he'd brought me here, put me in this awful situation. 'I've got a fear of heights and—surprise, surprise—a fear of death!'

He just looked at me with laughter in his eyes. I wanted to be sick. My feet dragged down the steps and I suddenly wanted to be anywhere but here. But reluctantly I let him take my hand and guide me down.

We finally reached the beach and stripped to our bathing costumes. I offered to just stay on the beach and sunbathe and watch him dive. 'I'll support you,' I tried, 'but I don't have to actually do it.'

'Yes, you do,' he smiled. 'I did stuff on your list *with* you. I skated, had sex under the stars, watched the Santorini sunset, swam naked... it was tough but I forced myself to do it all,' he joked.

I rolled my eyes. 'It's not quite the same as hurling oneself into jagged rocks from a great height before drowning in the sea.' I was trying to be light-hearted and funny, but it wasn't easy to do while in the queue for my inevitable doom. 'Anyway... mine was fun stuff... this is torture.'

'I disagree. This is fun stuff too,' he said, taking my hand gently, and, just like the night we swam naked, we ran together into the sea, only this time we swam around the bay, stopping every now and then for a word, a cuddle, an 'are you okay?' from him to me. I was fine with the swimming; in fact I am quite a strong swimmer—but had no intention of doing anything else. Just watching those bodies hurl themselves from the sky, arms flailing, much yelping and whooping followed by a splash was making me feel dizzy... and absolutely petrified.

'It must be a twenty-foot drop,' I said, sheltering by the rocks once we'd landed at the foot of the cliff in a quiet, secluded little cove.

'It is... but that's nothing, Faye. It's for beginners—which is why I brought you. I dived 136 feet in Acapulco, straight into the Pacific. The waves were crashing... it was the most amazing...'

'Stop. You're making me feel quite nauseous,' I said, watching a young, athletic-looking guy scramble up the cliff side and make his way to the ledge.

I agreed to swim a little further and climb the treacherous rocks and rubble, and after much frenzied discussion from me and soothing talk from him, Dan agreed that if I didn't want to, I didn't have to leap. I just had to climb up and face the drop.

He stayed behind me all the way as my bare feet picked their way through the damp rocks, the sun beating down on my back and my heart beating even harder in my chest. What was I doing here? Had I gone mad? Once at the top he held my hand, guiding me all the way to the ledge, where we stood together in the heat and the blue, looking out onto the endless ocean. He kept telling me it was all fine, and I eventually found the courage to look down at the gently swirling foam. I'd always been scared of heights and looking down made my legs go hollow and I almost lost my balance and went over anyway, but Dan was there, holding my hand.

'I believe you can do it—all you have to do is believe it too.'

There was no way I could even contemplate the jump; there were jutting rocks all the way down and that water was too swirly and evil-looking for me.

I moved back from the edge; 'I can't, Dan... I just can't...'

'You *can*, Faye.'

'You don't understand; it's not me... I can't do this.'

'It's not the Faye who *used* to be scared of doing anything in life, I agree, but that's not you now. The Faye I've fallen in love with can do anything she wants to do. She just has to believe she can.' I heard my mother's voice saying, 'Anything's possible, Faye. The only thing stopping you is yourself.'

I took a few steps closer, peered over the edge, still holding his hand, still close to him.

'Are you ready?'

I turned to him. 'Not really.'

Before I knew it, he'd counted us down from three and, holding hands, we leaped together, flying through the air, an exhilarating, thrilling ride through the endless sky into the foam. I hit the water mid-scream and emerged from the watery depths choking and laughing and crying and feeling like I'd just conquered Everest.

'I'm so proud of you,' he was saying, hugging me, kissing my face and bashing me on the back to stop me inhaling any more salty water. 'Me too!' I yelled between coughs.

Eventually, when I had my breath back, we swam to the main beach and lay together in the sun. I had done something that afternoon I had never imagined I could do, and now I really did believe that anything was possible and the only thing stopping me all my life had been myself.

'Thank you...' I murmured, remembering what he'd said on the ledge, 'Dan, just before we jumped, did I hear you say you'd fallen in love with me?'

He was lying in the sun, his eyes closed, a smile playing on his lips. 'Maybe.'

I lay back down, smiling to myself, and fell asleep on the beach, dreaming of that rooftop in New York. I was waiting at the table, holding a glass of champagne, the city below, the stars above, and when the man appeared from the shadows to join me, it wasn't Kevin Bacon or Ryan Gosling... it was Dan.

It's a cliché, but I felt like we were soul mates; he was everything I'd been looking for all my life and I was finding it hard to imagine a future without him. He seemed to feel the same way, and as our time on Santorini continued, I wondered seriously about the possibility of going back with him to Sydney for a while.

I missed Emma dreadfully, but was able to call her and text her regularly which helped us to stay involved in each other's lives. She seemed very happy with her new boyfriend and, although I'd selfishly hoped it might have fizzled out, her relationship seemed stronger than ever. And if she was happy, that's what really mattered.

Meanwhile, Dan and I began to live a kind of life on the island. In August we celebrated my birthday; he baked a lemon cake and gave me a silver necklace made of stars. By September, the crowds thinned out and it felt like the island belonged to us, our very own paradise. We'd shop and cook together, drink retsina and eat fresh seafood in tavernas and watch the sky raging sunset. We'd wander through the narrow stone streets of pastel-coloured buildings, stopping every now and then, holding each other and just *being*. We'd sit on café pavements drinking Greek coffee and eating warm cinnamon pastries, watching other people go about their lives in the bright sunshine. I'd see Emma in the young women with long hair and brown legs, lives before them, voices filled with excitement about what was to come. We'd smile at the other couples walking hand in hand, the sun kissing their shoulders as they kissed each other, the air seemed permanently filled with lust and expectation.

The evenings were infused with anticipation, like the buzz in a theatre foyer just before the performance. Early evening and the star (the sunset) was still dressing, waiting in the wings for her moment as the audience took their seats. I always found it so exciting, it never palled, and each evening I would wait for the heart-stopping moment and the applause at the sun's final act.

There was so much to do, yet so little; we had endless free time and yet our daily lives were full and busy and happy. We'd stroll to the Atlantis Bookshop, where among the densely packed shelves we found all kinds of literary treasures, sharing snatches of poems and beautiful paragraphs with each other. We'd wander through the shops, drink in the bars and considered ourselves natives, often rising early to enjoy the village before the crowds arrived. We'd sip cold frappes under bougainvillea, sharing our pasts, our futures but ultimately enjoying the moment, something I had never done before.

One day we hired a motorbike again and this time I revelled in the high, narrow mountain roads, the breathtaking near-misses. I still had a fear of heights, but it was somehow more thrilling and I welcomed the fear, like one would welcome icy water in the face on a boiling hot day. We travelled the length of the island, staying a while on the black beach in Parissa, then took a small boat to Kamari, where we wandered through the shops and bars. On the way back that evening we ate fresh fish in a seaside taverna and Dan told me again that he loved me.

Later we watched the sunset from the road, just sitting together, holding hands, talking as the night fell over us in a warm, dark blanket. We sat high on a cliff edge in the darkness, the black sea edged by twinkly lights scattered through the landscape like clusters of stars.

'I feel all poetic... like Santorini is offering us her heart,' I said, gesturing towards the view of the caldera opening out before us.

'That's beautiful, babe,' he smiled. 'But I only want your heart,' he was looking straight ahead at the view. I turned to him. 'You have it.'

I'd never imagined in all my previous fantasies about film stars and rooftops and Vespas through Rome and pools in LA that real life could be even better. In that moment, I felt lucky to be alive; it was all so wonderful, yet at the same time so tenuous.

'If I hadn't had goodbye sex with Craig all those years ago, I wouldn't be here with you now,' I smiled. 'Then, years later, I found my rucksack with my living list in and it set me thinking. Then I went into the deli for a sandwich and you set me thinking even more and... on and on,' I sighed.

'Yeah, the butterfly effect,' he said. 'The idea that something as small as the flutter of a butterfly's wing can ultimately cause a typhoon halfway around the world... it's called chaos theory.'

We sat for ages in a comfortable silence and I thought about all the little things in my life that had happened...all those butterflies wings... all leading up to now.

Chapter Twenty

Castles in the Sky

Dan would cook most evenings for the two of us and I was learning so much from him. He fried white aubergines in olive oil, garlic and lemon juice—'The Greeks call it the apple of love,' he said, feeding me hot, sweet, juicy forkfuls in bed. He showed me how to make Santorini's feta and honey pies, salty and sweet, wrapped in the lightest, crispiest filo pastry. I had never tasted anything so delicious. We ate them on the balcony, warm, with chilled retsina during a golden dusk.

By the end of September, the climate had cooled slightly, but the water was still warm for swimming, and most days we'd visit a little cove or hire a bike and spend time on a beach, exploring Oia's little idiosyncrasies. We took great delight in discovering her beautiful flaws, her real life beneath the showbiz sunset, sparkly white buildings and blue domes.

One night Dan received a phone call from his father. 'It's bad news. My brother's symptoms are getting worse.'

I felt numb. I suppose deep down I'd always known it would happen, I just hoped it might be after the summer was over, this felt too soon.

'What are you going to do?' I said, knowing what his answer would be.

'I don't have any choice; I can't let them struggle on...I need to be present in a way I couldn't be for mum. I was younger then, I couldn't deal with it, but I'm a grown-up now.'

Neither of us wanted to contemplate parting, and we'd talked vaguely about staying on through October until our money ran out, but this would speed up the end for us.

That night we sat outside under the stars talking about a time in the future when Dan would be free and we could go to Italy, see the Trevi Fountain and ride that Vespa through the streets. I said it had to be pistachio-green and he said no problem and that we also had to visit Tuscany and a medieval walled town in Siena called San Gimignano.

'I went there a few years back; it has an amazing piazza... gothic architecture and a castle with really high towers. From a distance it looks like a castle in the sky.' He was excited.

'Castles in the sky,' I sighed. 'Is that what we're building here, Dan?' I smiled.

'No... it's real. We will do these things one day.'

'Dan, I realise you will have to go back home sooner rather than later... From what you've told me about the disease, John will need physical support as well as emotional...'

'Yeah, you're right. It's time I stepped up to the plate.'

I nodded. 'Absolutely. You have to... We both desperately want to do all the things we talked about, see all those wonderful places, but it's not just about us is it?'

He shook his head. 'No... I always believed that being happy was just about being free, that it didn't matter about how my freedom affected anyone else; it was about chasing my own happiness. But being with you has made me realise it's not just about me... us.' he sighed.

The end of our time together suddenly seemed so sudden, so final.

'Faye... this doesn't have to mean the end for you and me. Come back to Oz with me?' 'We could start a new life together there, open that little café together. You're a great cook, we'd be an awesome team. And Emma could come for holidays...'

It was all very seductive, the idea of eternal sunshine and Dan. He'd even included Emma in the scenario, which made it even more appealing. I flirted with the idea, rolled it around my head a little and felt that new high that came with knowing I could do anything if I wanted to.

'Yeah...we could, couldn't we?' I said, warming to the idea.

We talked over the next few days about the possibility of me going to Sydney with him and the more we talked the more real it became. I started to imagine a life out there, and as he talked about the sun and the beaches and the life, I could see myself starting again out there with him. Then, one morning I had a text from Emma. Dan and I were eating Greek yogurt and honey in the kitchen as I read the text. 'Oh poor Em, she and Phil have finished, she must be so upset,' I sighed. It was another white-hot day and we were planning a walk and a swim in one of the beautiful blue coves, but now I just wanted to talk to Emma and comfort her.

I looked at Dan. 'She really cared about Phil. It will hurt her now, but in the long run I have to say it's probably for the best. You don't realise when you're young how important it is to be with someone who shares your... passions. I don't mean sex... I mean like you and me; we love books and food and we could fill our whole lives with it. From what Emma said, they didn't have much in common.'

I tried to call her but couldn't get through, so went into town to try and get a signal. When I finally got through, she wasn't picking up and I had to leave a message and I worried for the next few hours that she was upset and I wasn't there for her to talk to. I kept telling myself she was a grown woman now and could deal with this break-up without cuddles from Mum... but I felt bad I was in another country when she needed me and wasn't even on the end of the phone for her. At the same time I kept telling myself I had finally shaken myself free from guilt and obligation and, as much as I adored Emma, I had to make the most of these last few days in Santorini. I was also seriously considering my next move, and if Emma was okay with it, I was going with Dan and ticking Sydney Opera House by night off my list—he said he'd provide the fireworks.

He was aware that I hadn't been present that day, worrying about Emma, but, being sensitive, he hadn't pushed me. 'You okay sweetie?' he asked. It was mid afternoon, and after Emma's text I hadn't felt like doing anything until I could speak to her, so Dan had gone into town and bought some food and wine. He was pouring me a glass and rubbing my back as I sat on the balcony checking for a signal.

'I'm fine, thanks. I have to remember that you kids have tragedies of Greek proportions, which breaks your heart and worries you to death, and within twenty-four hours it's all over and it's, "Mum, stop nagging" again.'

He smiled. 'You are a very wise woman. That's why I love you.'

It was a couple of hours later when I finally got through to Emma. It was such a relief to hear her voice—despite my hard talk, I couldn't be happy if she wasn't, and it was my job now to make her feel better. I just wished I could hug her and make her hot chocolate with mallows and let her talk and talk... As it was, I could only soothe her with my words.

'Mum, I don't want you to worry,' was her opening line.

'Why does that make me feel worried?' I asked, trying to keep it light. She didn't answer.

'Emma, what happened?'

'He said he just didn't love me... he thought he did, but he doesn't.'

'Oh, darling.' I was looking out at the sea from the balcony, feeling helpless just thinking how far away she was.

'He says he thinks I'm a great person... and he's there for me, but he doesn't want to be tied down". She started crying and my own heart broke with hers.

'Oh, darling... I know you must be feeling awful right now and I don't want to just blurt out a load of clichés, but it will get better—trust me.'

'He said we'd get married... so what happened? What have I done to make it all go wrong?'

'It's not you, Emma. He just changed his mind... didn't know what he wanted. Please don't even think it's something you did or the way you are... It's not...'

'It's too late, Mum...'

'It's not too late, Emma. Yes, I know, you loved him, but you're young; you've got your life ahead of you and this time next year you'll have a degree another boyfriend and I promise you will barely remember him...'

'I can't ever forget him. Mum, you don't understand...'

'I do, sweetie. It feels so intense now, like you'll never forget this... him... but in time...'

'I'm pregnant.'

Chapter Twenty-one

A Red Dress, A Sunset and No Goodbyes

We'd both cried over the phone. I'd gone from telling Emma she was stupid to have made the same mistakes I had and had thrown away her life, to assuring her that everything would be all right. 'It will all be okay, Em. We can do this. I just need some time to think it through and I want you to get some sleep, too. I'll call you in the morning. I'm coming home.' I put down the phone. I'd been sitting on the balcony watching the sunset and now Dan joined me and was looking at me.

'What is it?' he asked, looking worried.

In between my tears I told him everything and he knelt down, putting his head in my lap, arms round my waist. We talked for a long time that night—watching the sun go down and come up again.

"I can't come to Sydney with you now Dan."

He looked up at me.

'We could... we could spend our time between your home and mine?' he offered half-heartedly, knowing it would be financially and practically impossible.

'I'm a mum... I can't turn it on and off and skip around the world in between, even if I could afford it. She needs me there.'

The next day Emma and I talked for a long time on the phone and I told her if she wanted to she must finish her degree, perhaps moving to a course nearer home. I couldn't believe she'd done the same as I had and become pregnant halfway through a university course—but as far as I was concerned, that's where the similarities ended.

I couldn't let her do what I'd done and give it all up just for one moment of madness, one moment of lust. I wanted her to have it all and, as the baby's father had clearly stepped out of the picture, the only person who could help her achieve everything she wanted and needed was me.

I was giving up the freedom and possibilities of my new life, the one I'd fought for, but as much as I loved it and as much as I loved Dan my daughter came first.

I had to go home and suddenly couldn't wait to see Emma, to make sure she was okay and to look after her. Despite my doubts and fears for her future, I was excited about the baby and all the possibilities this new life would bring. I wasn't going back to my old life—that would be impossible. I was a different woman now and this time life would be on my terms.

❊ ❊ ❊

On our last day in Santorini, while the rest of the island siesta'd, Dan showed me how to make a Greek Mezze with hummus, tsatziki, taramasalata and stuffed vine leaves. Then we made lamb kleftiko by stuffing a leg of lamb with feta, fresh oregano, onions and garlic. We were having a last supper, both wanting our last night together to be perfect. Typical Dan—he wasn't going to even let our parting cast a shadow and we laughed as much on the last day together as we had on the first.

'Kleftiko means *stolen* in Greek,' he said, chopping onions. 'People used to steal lambs to make this dish—which is where the name comes from. 'We're going to slow-cook it in this big pot; it will be juicy and tender and real sweet... The air will be filled with the fragrance of lamb and Mediterranean herbs while the sun goes down.'

'You are so clever,' I smiled, reflecting on how much I'd learned from him. 'It reminds me of when we first met and you gave me the history of Serrano ham.'

'Yeah, you love it when I talk deli.' He stopped chopping and looked at me. 'It was such a short time ago that we met... kind of blows me away; I feel like I've known you forever. Wow... how someone can come into your life and just... change it...'

'Yeah, I'm a different woman to the one you met in the deli in February,' I sighed. 'You've had quite an effect on me.'

'You've changed me too. I feel more grounded, don't feel like running away from stuff I can't change. You've helped me deal with the guilt I was carrying about my mum's death. I can now face all this stuff with my brother—I need to do it for him... and for me too. Yet... I can't imagine how I'm going to exist without you. Nothing has any colour when you're not there.' He wiped his hands on a tea towel and put both arms around me. 'It's gonna break my heart to say goodbye.'

'And mine too,' I sighed, leading him into the bedroom, leaving the lamb to slow-cook and become tender and juicy and fragrant.

❋ ❋ ❋

Later, I packed my case and, rediscovering the red silk dress in that old rucksack, I put it on for our final dinner together.

We sat together on the balcony that night to watch our final sunset; 'You look beautiful,' he said. 'I will always remember you here, like this in your lovely red dress.'

In the night, I woke up and put my arm out to touch him. He wasn't there and my heart jolted at the realisation that I might never lie with him again. I opened my eyes to see him at the window in the cold blue moonlight and I thought about how much he'd given to me. I wasn't the self-conscious, unhappy woman in the panda hat, too scared to say boo to a goose or jump on a plane anymore. I was a red-dress-wearing woman with a grip on life and the confidence to follow her heart, trust her instincts and enjoy all that life had to offer. Even the decision to go back home was born out of my own desire; it was something I wanted to do. I was excited about the future, about a new life and the opportunity to support Emma and show her that having a baby is the beginning, not the end. She wouldn't make the same mistakes I had, because I would be there to guide her and show her that it's possible to be a good mum, without losing sight of yourself along the way.

I'd lost me for a while, buried under work and worry and guilt, but with Dan's help I'd uncovered the Faye Dobson I'd been looking for all these years. He'd firmly but gently pushed me out of my comfort zone, forcing me to face my fears and realise it was possible to be a stronger, better, happier me. In Dan's world, life had to be grabbed by the balls and it was never too late to do or achieve anything.

I am Faye Dobson. I am forty-three and I have a tattoo. I have sex under the stars, ride pillion on fast mountain bike rides and cliff dive into the sea. But now I am ready to go home, to my daughter who needs me.

I stood up and walked over to him at the window. Slipping my arms gently round his waist, I rested my face on his warm, damp, naked back.

His head tilted slightly and he turned to embrace me. I held on to him tightly, my head on his chest as he bent down and gently lifted me back onto the bed, and I realised that this was everything in this moment. I couldn't allow myself to think or care about the future—I loved him now while we were together, and that was all that mattered. And when I looked into his eyes, he was crying.

We lay together for the last time, both awake, both silent, both knowing this was it.

'I wish things had turned out differently, Dan... I wish we were flying away together—but you warned me about the curve ball, and it landed for both of us. Just know I love you and there will always be a lemon-cake-sized piece of my heart with you in it, wherever I am.'

'We'll meet up maybe...?'

'Maybe, but we both have our real lives to deal with, and perhaps when you've settled back home you'll meet some tanned young Aussie girl with a taut tummy and firm thighs and...'

'No.'

'I think if we'd stayed together, I would have always wondered if I was denying you your chance to be a father.'

'You wouldn't... I told you... I don't want kids.'

'Not now, but children are the most wonderful thing in life and if you stayed with me, it wouldn't have been possible. Now you can decide what you really want.'

'I know what I want.'

I ruffled his hair. 'Okay until we can live on the same continent, why don't you start up that bakery breakfast café you've talked about? Who knows, one day a lady and a baby might just fly over from the UK and join that long queue for lemon cake?'

He squeezed my hand and we lay in silence for a while. I couldn't sleep and neither could he.

'Dan, let me leave in the morning. Don't wake up—let's just remember the good times here together, not the goodbyes.' I couldn't see his face, but reached up with my hand to feel him slowly nodding.

In the morning I woke up, kissed him on the mouth as he slept and silently walked away. Perhaps Sue was right, it's all in the stars, we have no say in what ultimately happens in our lives and Dan and I were never meant to be forever. My heart was broken as I climbed into the waiting taxi under a brilliant blue sky, but I had no regrets as we set off. I gazed through the window at the last of Santorini knowing I'd always have the wonderful memories. And I'd never forget how a gorgeous Australian helped me turn my life around over a long hot summer of love, lies and lemon cake.

EPILOGUE

Stars are emerging slowly through the dusky evening. Sounds of the city drift up through the night air and I'm sitting at a table for two, champagne on ice, two glasses.

I check my watch and call Emma. 'Mum... is it everything you thought it would be?'

'Yes, it's wonderful. I can't believe I'm finally here, Em! I can see the Empire State. I wish you and Rosie were with me.'

'Yeah, me too but she's just too young for the flight, she's been a bit cranky today; I reckon she's missing her grandma.'

'Not as much as I'm missing her,' I smile, thinking of my perfect, pink, chubby little granddaughter.

'Anyway, Rosie says happy birthday, Grandma. She's making a cake for when you get back... Well, I'm baking it—she will supervise from her bouncy chair,' she giggles.

My heart melts. 'I'll look forward to it.'

'Mum... I know you wanted to do this trip, but I hate the idea of you being alone on your birthday. Are you really ok?'

'I'm fine. Ryan Gosling's on his way he never misses my birthday... but joking aside, hey, this is perfect. Who gets to actually achieve their dream? I'm so lucky, Emma.'

We talk for a few minutes about Rosie's sleeping patterns, Emma's exams and our new house, bought with my half of the money from the old one. I tell Emma about the Warhol exhibition I've seen and how delicious the Magnolia Bakery cupcakes were that I ate this afternoon in Central Park in the sunshine.

'A perfect birthday,' she sighs. 'And there's me stuck inside revising for my finals.'

'All worth it, Em. You will have a degree, a career and a beautiful daughter, all at once. Anything's possible. We can both do whatever we want to—and between us, Rosie will be fine. Give her a kiss, tell her I love her and I'll see you both in three days.'

I put down the phone and pour myself a glass of champagne. It's stinging cold and I sit back, thinking of little Rosie, three months old and already the soon-to-be recipient of several New York designer outfits, souvenirs from her over-indulgent grandma. I glance around at the other hotel guests sitting under the stars and wonder about their lives, their loves. I like my life, I like the way I look and I like the way I feel; I'm confident, in control, and to others I probably seem like a sophisticated older woman in New York on business... *my* business.

This is a woman who a couple of years ago would have thought twice about getting a train on her own, had never flown, never stayed alone in a hotel and wouldn't dream of ordering a bottle of champagne just for herself. And yet, here I am, in my red silk dress, drinking champagne on *that* rooftop.

I take out the postcard. Not bad—almost a match; even the waiter had mistakenly brought two glasses, which fit the picture better than one. Two glasses—how ironic. I smile, finally content, happy, free.

The night has quickly swallowed the golden dusk and I look up at the stars.

'Is this seat taken? I believe it has the best view?'

For a second I think the waiter must be Australian, but I know that voice, the raised inflection after every sentence, filled with Aussie sunshine... and my heart almost stops. I look up and there he is, beach-blond hair, tanned, leathery face, beaten-up old rucksack. Dan. As delicious as ever.

I yelp and jump up, hugging him, losing myself in his arms.

'I thought you were in Oz?' is all I can say through happy tears.

'I wanted to surprise you,' he smiles, dropping his rucksack and taking a seat without letting go of my hand.

'When you said in your email last week what you were planning, I just had to share it with you. I emailed Emma; she said it was a great idea, told me where you were staying and here I am. We thought you'd be okay with it... you are, aren't you?'

'I am *very* okay with it,' I beam.

Unable to take my eyes away from his, I pour him a glass of champagne. He hands me an envelope.

'Happy Birthday, Babe,' he smiles, raising his glass.

I open it and gasp, looking at him across the table. 'A plane ticket to Rome?'

'Yeah... all booked for next month. We meet at Rome Airport and take the pistachio-green Vespa from there. Em said the date fits in with your degree course—you don't start until October?'

'That's right. I'm so excited about it and... now you and... this.' I am clutching the ticket, still looking into his eyes, just drinking him in.

'I'm finding life tough without you Faye and I figure if we can't be together all the time, we should meet up once or twice a year in a special place... Let's add to our living lists and tick them off one by one,' he says, his blue eyes twinkling.

'Yes, yes, what a brilliant idea,' I nod, and in the distance the sound of a lonely saxophone drifts through the night, meandering along the chords of 'Happy Birthday'. A waiter appears from across the pool and, as he gets closer, I see he's carrying a cake, sparkles shooting from the top, lighting up our faces as it arrives at the table. Dan is smiling. 'I knew the picture wouldn't be complete without that sax,' he smiles.

'It wouldn't be complete without *you*,' I say, inhaling the zest of birthday lemon cake.

I blow out my candles, making a secret wish.

'Shall we?' He holds out his hand, I take it and there among the stardust and candlelight we dance under the stars on a rooftop in New York.

A note from Sue

A quick hello to all those 'Fayes' out there!

Thank you so much for reading 'Love, Lies and Lemon Cake,' I hope you enjoyed Faye's journey and it's inspired you to start a Living List of your own, however long, short or crazy it may be.

I reckon there's a little bit of that 'cliff diving girl' in all of us, and since writing this have an uncontrollable urge to visit every deli I pass, just in case Dan's in there. He'll be slicing ham with those firm arms, and as I walk in he'll smile with those eyes and ... I have to stop now or I will go all hot.

Anyway, if you enjoyed the book I would love it if you have a minute or so (in between deli stake-outs and cliff-diving) to write a quick review and tell your friends – it would mean such a lot to me – and Faye!

I'm now writing my next book and missing Faye, Dan and the salon girls already, but if you'd like to know when my next book is released you can sign up for email updates at:

www.suewatsonbooks.com/email.

I promise I won't share your email address with anyone, and I'll only send you a message when I have a new book out.

I would love for you to follow me on Facebook and please join me for a chat on Twitter... I'd really love to know what's on your Living List and we can celebrate with cyber cake as you tick them all off one by one.

In the meantime, thanks again for reading, and... if you happen to bump into a gorgeous blond Australian guy in a deli anywhere, would you please give him my number?

For research purposes only of course....

Sue
@suewatsonwriter